Praise for

DARKER THAN THE SKY

"Simply written, touching, and engaging. Matt Tracy's first novel is a winner!"

"The plot kept me wanting to know what happened next, but I slowed down to enjoy the wisdom and camaraderie that flowed among the action."

"*Darker Than the Sky* takes us from a cabin in the redwoods to the forests of Northern California to the Rocky Mountains to a cornfield in Iowa, then back to the dry golden hills and oak trees of Big Sur. Van's story gains new depth and meaning in each location. So well done."

"It's rare that I feel such mixed emotions about characters in a book. I rooted for Van, but also worried for his sanity. Russ was so likable and managed to scare me at the same time."

"The stories around the campfire were my favorite part. Men being manly, but also talking about real worries and regrets and aspirations."

"What a satisfying read. A tale of loss and rebuilding, regrets and redemption, missteps and new chances."

"As enjoyable and wise a novel as you're likely to find this year."

DARKER THAN THE SKY

DARKER
THAN
THE SKY

Matt Tracy

CHILOÉ PRESS

Published in the United States by Chiloé Press

DARKER THAN THE SKY
Copyright © 2024 Matt Tracy
All rights reserved. Printed in the United States of America.

www.matttracyauthor.com

Library of Congress Cataloging-in-Publication Data
Name: Tracy, Matt, author
Title: Darker Than the Sky / Matt Tracy
Description: First Edition. | California: Chiloé Press, [2024]
Paperback ISBN: 978-1-7366459-7-0
eBook ISBN: 978-1-7366459-8-7
Classification: Fiction

First Edition: October 2024

10 9 8 7 6 5 4 3 2 1

Developmental and Copy Editing by Bridget A. Lyons
Cover and Interior Design by Danna Mathias Steele

To Della,
For being unfailingly optimistic and supportive

Chapter One

BLOOD

Every blessing brings the possibility of loss, and my thoughts that hot August morning in 1977 were of what had been taken from me. Sorrow and regret ran through my mind like the words of a song whose melancholy melody was familiar and calming. Sadness enveloped and protected me. Shielded me from the whims of fate. Comforted me. Jenny could think what she wanted; my strategy was working for me.

My son Josh and I loaded a bale of alfalfa into the bucket of the orange Kubota tractor from the stack near the barn. The hay was still wet from the morning dew, and it smelled of green tea. He drove the tractor, and I walked uphill beside him. Halfway to the horses' stalls, he stopped and turned off the motor. A line of baby quail followed their parents, first pecking at seeds, then scurrying to hide in a pile of branches we had left for them in the fall. Their *hu-hee-hu* call felt like home to me. We watched for a couple of moments, then Josh started the tractor again and drove up to the horses. We broke pistachio-colored flakes of hay off the bale and tossed them into the feed troughs in the front of the horse paddocks.

I took off my hat and wiped beads of sweat off my forehead and upper lip with my shirtsleeve. The first rays of light had just reached the area where we worked, but already the sun flared like a fire burning between the steep walls of Zaca Canyon to the east. Most summer evenings in our valley above the Pacific, in the hills east of Carmel, the fog from the ocean filled the far side of the mountains and climbed the ridge. It slithered over the top through the trees in the evening gray, like thick slow smoke moving down the slopes below. Most evenings, it brought with it a satisfying coolness that continued into the morning. That week, the heat had lingered through the night, building each day and waning only slightly in the darkness.

Josh and I drifted among the stalls, taking time to scratch each horse behind the ears or under the jawline, saying its name and touching the softness of its muzzle. Josh and his brother Nate usually fed the horses, but Nate had rolled his ankle playing pickup basketball the day before, so he got to stay in bed. I volunteered to help while he was laid up. I thought that by working together, Josh and I might get back to how we were. It seemed like I couldn't say anything right this past week.

On Sunday evening, Josh had gathered Jenny, Nate, and me into the kitchen. "I have something important to tell you all." When we were seated around the table, he stood up, looked at each of us solemnly, and said, "Mom, Dad, Nate. I've been thinking a lot lately, and I'm pretty sure that I'm more attracted to men than women." Then he looked at us to gauge our reactions.

I thought I responded well. "What makes you think that?"

He didn't agree. "I just said it's what I feel. Are you saying that maybe I'm not?"

"No. No, I'm not saying that." I thought for a moment. "I'm actually not that surprised. I've known you for a long time, after all."

Nate punched him and said, "No, man. Me neither. You can't talk to girls, and I saw you looking at the lifeguard at the pool last time we went swimming. I thought you were trying to figure out how much more weights you would have to lift to look like him."

Then I stuck my foot in it. "But have you thought about it? It would make a lot of things harder in your life." Like I thought it was something he could just decide not to be. Of course, I had just said I sort of knew from when he was a kid, so I knew it wasn't, but that didn't stop stupid words from coming out of my mouth.

Josh's face got red. "Dad! You're such a caveman! You should just quit talking."

That was how the rest of the week went. I couldn't say anything right. The truth was, it was taking me a bit to get used to. I had imagined him getting married and having kids and Jenny and me taking care of the grandkids. All those futures had to be reframed in my mind. I was okay with the whole idea in general, but I found that when it applied to my son and my daughter-in-law and grandkids who I had to erase from my vision of the future, it took a while. He had no patience for that. He expected me to be all-in from the first moment he told me.

I kept trying to say something supportive as I worked through my feelings, and he kept getting mad at me. He didn't understand that though he had been considering the possibilities for a long time, I had just heard of them. As I said, I sort of knew since he was a kid, but that didn't stop me from having pictures in my mind of what would come, and those pictures had to be adjusted. He was already speeding toward his future, and every time I tried to jump on board from a standing start, I just got run over.

I thought back to my mom and dad. All it took was my dad's parents not accepting my mom for my parents to move out to California where they could feel normal. I knew I wasn't as bad as my grandparents had been. That trip to Chicago to meet them had been a disaster. And I thought Josh and I would work it out. But what if I kept saying the wrong thing? The more I blew it, the fewer chances I would have to get it right. I didn't want to be like them.

When we finished with the feeding, we started back around to muck out the stalls. It's not too hard if it's done every day. Horse manure smells sweet and hay-like. It's almost pleasant, not like cow plops, which are foul, especially in the spring after they've been feasting on the new green clover. I drove the tractor, and Josh tossed piles of manure over the wooden bars of the stalls into the bucket in front.

Josh sang as he worked, changing the words to a popular song from "loving you" to "shoveling poo." He knew it bugged me, especially when he broke into falsetto and started singing the "la-la-la" part. That made me feel better about how we were doing. If he was trying to get to me, he might not be that mad at me.

I heard the drone of an airplane coming up the valley toward us. Josh and I stopped working and looked up. He found it first and pointed to it, and I could see it traveling low against the cloudless sky. It was a small single-engine plane, white with red stripes on the wings, the wheels on triangle struts below.

Planes almost never flew in this direction. The mountains rose quickly behind our place, and the plane would have to gain altitude in a hurry to make it over the ridge. As the plane climbed, the engine didn't sound right. It stumbled, then coughed. We watched it for a moment, then went back to work.

When it was closer and about to pass overhead, we looked up at it again. As we watched, its engine faltered, caught, started again, then quit altogether. Josh glanced at me and raised his eyebrows. We looked back up. The plane stopped gaining altitude. Its wings wavered as if the pilot were trying to decide what to do, then he chose and dove, gliding at a steep angle toward the mountains behind us. I inhaled sharply, feeling the buzz of adrenaline in my chest.

Here we go again. Here we effing go again.

I knew what came after a plane crash, and I wasn't ready for it. If Josh looked at me again, he would be confused by the anger and fear on my face. He was just a kid the last time; he wouldn't remember. I pulled myself together and said to him, "The plane might make the upper meadow. Let's get back to the house and grab the truck." I turned the key on the Kubota and drove over to the side of the paddock to dump the manure. Josh stepped onto the running board, holding on to the back of the seat and leaning against the fender. We drove through the open gates of the training corral and through the fruit orchard.

As I drove, I thought about my fight with Jenny the night before. I decided to act on what I had thought about before I fell asleep. I was done hiding. The plane had gone down, which meant I hadn't camouflaged my happiness well enough. From that moment on, I would make fate do my bidding. From then on, I was going to fight with every scrap of strength I had to keep what I cared about. I almost raised my hand to flip off fate, but I needed two hands to drive the tractor over the rough ground. I flipped off fate in my mind. I bared my teeth and told it to stay away from my family.

When we got to the house, Josh leaped up the stairs ahead of me two at a time. I followed, slower. The front door opened before he reached it, and he stopped with his hands up as he and Jenny almost ran into each other. "Mom! A little plane lost power, and it looks like it's going to land in the upper meadow!"

I said I had to call the fire department as I passed them headed for the phone. All I would be able to tell them was our address and that a small plane had gone down near us. I couldn't explain how to get to the upper meadow. "I'll stay here and show them the way when they arrive," Jenny said to me. "And Van—"

I turned around in the hallway, walked back to her, and put both my hands on her shoulders. "I know. Another plane crash. It's what we talked about last night. It's going to be different this time." I hugged her hard for a second, then let go and went to the phone.

Josh and I drove in the pickup down the paved street, behind the barn, over the wooden bridge, and up the dirt road beside the creek, under oaks and bay trees, climbing toward the meadow. The sun burned just above the surrounding hills as we emerged onto the flat above the creek, and its light turned the grass in the open space to fine gold. At the far end of the field, the plane rested nose down against a three-trunked sycamore tree. Its tail stuck up in the air, and the bottom of the fuselage was exposed. Steam or smoke rose from the far side of it. Wheel tracks followed it halfway across the meadow. There was no motion anywhere.

As we drove toward the plane, I looked for signs of life. A piece of metal shone in the grass and caught my attention for a second, but all was quiet. I stopped the truck hard, and the tires skidded on the dried grass. Josh's door slammed after mine like two gunshots as we jumped out of the truck. A whiff of gasoline hit my nose. A clear liquid dripped out of the front of the engine compartment, and the windshield was broken. Pieces of glass were strewn on the ground under the tree.

I focused on the cockpit. The pilot was inside. I hesitated, then shouted, "Josh, stay back." *Screw you, fate. I'm in charge now.* I stepped on the wheel strut and reached for the door handle on the passenger's side. I pulled the door open and let it hang down. The pilot was draped across the steering wheel. He seemed to be awake, but he wasn't moving.

The smell of gasoline became stronger as I climbed in. I braced my feet on the dashboard to reach for his seatbelt. He lifted his head when he saw me. He was older than I expected, his hair graying and thinning. Blood dripped onto his ear from a cut on his temple. "Leave me here. I'm in bad shape. This airplane could catch fire any second."

"No, I'm going to help you." I unclasped the harness that held him up. I could tell it hurt him when his weight fell against the steering wheel.

He lifted his head a little and looked at me sideways. "Get the toolbox." His voice was weak and gravelly.

I ignored him and shouted out the door. "Josh! Open the other door!" He came around to the pilot's side. Together, we lifted him out and laid him on the brown grass away from the plane. He raised his head and reached up to touch my shoulder. "Go back for the box." I could barely hear him as he croaked out, "If I don't make it, you can have it."

I looked at the plane. It could go up in flames at any second. But fighting fate means taking action. I ran to it. As I put my foot on the strut to go back in, I heard a whoosh and thought the gas had caught fire. I jumped back to the ground. Something had made the sound, but I didn't know what. Gas was still leaking, and the smell was everywhere, but I didn't see any fire. *Fight, Van. Make it do your bidding.* I climbed up onto the wheel strut and stretched across to the toolbox, which was down in the footwell on the passenger side. It was metal, about a foot long, and painted gray. There was a small lock on it. I grabbed it, jumped down, and ran back to them.

The pilot was sitting up. The cut on his head wasn't bleeding anymore, and his face had some color. He pulled a red pack of cigarettes out of his shirt pocket and tapped it against his other hand until one came out of the pack. Then he glanced at the gasoline dripping on the ground, shook his head, and put the cigarette behind his ear. He coughed, looked at the plane for a second, and coughed again. He turned to the right and spat on the ground. It was cherry red and thick, with bubbles in it. He turned to his side again, coughed hard once more, and spit more crimson, frothy blood. He tried to stand up, like he had somewhere to go, then he fell sideways, landing face down in the dry brown grass. His hand clutched at the weeds and dirt before he stopped moving.

I looked at Josh. His face was white with fear.

I turned the pilot on his back. His eyes were open, but he wasn't breathing. I put my fingers on the side of his neck by his Adam's apple. "I can't feel a pulse."

"CPR. I'll push." Josh placed his hands on the man's chest. With his first compression, a fountain of blood gurgled from the man's mouth and Josh jumped back to avoid it. It smelled like rusty nails, so strong I could taste it, like old steel in my mouth.

I felt his neck again, then put my other hand on his wrist. I couldn't feel any movement. "No pulse here. Try pushing again. Not so hard."

More blood came out when Josh pushed. He stopped and sat back on his heels. "He's dead?" He knew, but he wanted me to tell him.

"He's dead," I said, my voice flat, not feeling anything in my shock. "Let's move further from the plane. There's still gas leaking out."

We stood side by side, stunned, surveying the scene. The man on his back, blood thick on his face and on the golden-brown grass beside him. The plane leaking gasoline, its propeller twisted, grotesque like broken arms, dirt and grass plowed up where it had hit. A meadowlark perched on a branch in the middle of the field, his song accentuating the quiet of the morning. Gray-green sage-covered hills waited in hushed repose all around us, and the sun warmed our faces. It seemed so peaceful and so torn apart at the same time.

"I feel sick," Josh said quietly. "I need to sit down." But he just leaned over with his hands on his knees, hanging his head and spitting every so often.

I put my hand on his shoulder. "It's not something you get used to."

I had picked up the toolbox before I stood up, so I turned to set it on the ground next to the pilot before I remembered that he had given it to us. I put it under my arm and draped the other around Josh. When we got back to the truck, I sat on the edge of my seat with the door open. Josh wasn't the only one feeling strange. The numb shock that had washed over me earlier was being overtaken by a dread that seeped into my stomach. Plane crashes were harbingers of great pain for me. Could this time be different?

As soon as I leaned my head back on the seat, I started to dream. Did I fall asleep? I don't know, but strange and confused images assaulted my half-conscious state, full of dust and smoke and howling wind—but also, somehow, hope. I shook my head to wake up and stared up into the uncaring sky. A hawk traced slow circles on thermals high above, taking no notice of us, the morning sun shining golden red through its tail.

Chapter Two

DREAMS

The rest of the morning after the crash was a blur of heat and sweat and emergency vehicles. The toolbox that the pilot had wanted me to rescue sat on the seat of the pickup in the upper meadow while Josh and I helped the emergency crews in any way we could. Then they were gone, and they left us to try to bring our lives back into familiar rhythms. Jenny didn't go to work that day, and Josh and Nate didn't go to school.

I put the box on top of the china cabinet before we sat down for lunch. Jenny asked about what it felt like when the pilot died. I finished chewing my bite of sandwich. "I didn't have time to think about it while it was happening, but afterward, I had a floating sensation like I was above the whole scene, looking at it from the air."

Josh said, "I keep having to remind myself it was real. It feels like a dream."

Jenny looked at the boys, like she wasn't sure she wanted to bring the subject up in front of them, then said, "And it was another plane crash. It doesn't seem so crazy now."

I was too tired to talk about it, so I just waved my hand. "We'll figure it out after lunch."

After we ate, Josh and I both lay down on the living room couches. I was so tired that I thought I would fall asleep immediately, but I kept thinking of plane crashes, especially the first one I had witnessed.

I was about four years old, and my mom and dad and I had driven down the winding dirt road from our cabin in the redwoods of Big Sur to a sandy cove. It was before Pearl Harbor, so it must have been the spring of 1940.

My dad and I lay on a blanket with the sand soft under us. The sun warmed us and the chilly breeze off the ocean lifted his jacket that he had put over me to keep me warm. I was fascinated by the calm effortless flight of turkey vultures soaring on the updrafts of the cliff above. Their wings were spread out, and they didn't move at all—except for the tips—when a gust hit them. That day is my first memory, quiet and calm.

Earlier, we had strolled on the sand, gathering small, smooth rocks. My dad held my hand, and Peppy, our terrier mix dog, was chasing bits of foam and biting kelp pods and tossing them in the air. The waves wet our bare feet, then our feet left dry spots in the damp sand as the water retreated. I put rocks in my pockets until there was no more room and they were pulling my shorts down. Then I handed more to my dad to carry.

He removed some of the rocks from my pockets so my pants would stay up. "Van, all those rocks are going to give you bowed legs." I splashed in the clear water of the creek where it met the ocean until my mom told me my lips were blue and made me dry off and get some food. I didn't feel cold, but I remember my teeth clacking like a wind-up toy as she handed me a peanut butter-and-jelly sandwich. It was a fun game to try to talk with my teeth chattering, and I let my jaw go loose so they would clatter some more.

As I watched the birds' wing tips, fluid in the wind like fingers floating out of a car window, a man appeared at the top of the cliff with a model glider in his hands. He peered over the edge, waved at us, held the glider over his head with two hands, and launched it into the air. We sat up as it sailed, wings rising and falling on the gusty winds, toward the waves where, if it landed, it would be ruined. Then it turned back toward us and sped over our heads. It kept gaining speed as it headed towards the cliffs. It was going to crash. The man surely wouldn't let it crash. But it dove straight into the rocks at the base of the cliff. A wing clipped a rock, and the plane tumbled. I thought it might hold together, then its momentum took it into a larger boulder where it crumpled, and all motion stopped.

My next memory is of standing over the toy plane. Broken edges of the balsa wood frame poked through the shiny yellow and blue cloth covering the wings. Yellow from the plane painted the rocks where it had scraped them. As the man walked up the beach toward us, Peppy barked at him. I don't remember much about the man or what happened after the crash, but the memories of the day are clear in my head, bookmarked by the first plane crash in my life.

Later, my dad lifted me, already wrapped in a blanket, into the car. He was tall and wiry and strong, and it didn't seem like I weighed more to him than Peppy. He bent in to kiss me on the head. He hadn't shaved, and his cheek was rough. He smiled at me, his brown eyes crinkling at the edges, and he pushed my hair back off my face before he closed the door. I remember feeling safe and warm before I fell asleep in the car on the drive back up the canyon.

That evening, we let Peppy out of our cabin as we usually did at night. He heard a commotion in the woods and ran after it, barking. He didn't return that night, although we searched and called. I half expected him to show up on our porch. But he never did.

On the day of my first memory, a plane crashed, and I lost something I loved. That's a pattern I would come to know too well.

I did finally fall asleep on the couch, but it was a troubled sleep. When I woke up, I wandered into the smaller living room, the one without the television. Jenny was in her reading chair with her feet up, staring at the framed drawing of a tree on the wall beside her. She had drawn it her senior year of high school, before her dad's stroke. "I thought I would take advantage of a free afternoon to finish my book," she said, stretching her arms above her head. "I didn't want to wake you up by doing something around the house."

I smiled at her. "Not much reading going on."

"No, I keep thinking about what we talked about last night—especially since, well, there was a plane crash today, right?" I started to pull up a wooden chair, and she moved her feet aside and patted the footstool near her. "I'm glad you told me about your fears. How are you doing now?"

I sat on the footstool and put my hand on her knee. "I'm terrified, to tell you the truth. It's exactly what I was worried about. But you know the floating sensation I described earlier? It was more than that. More like a dream while I was awake. It was chaotic and confusing, but I felt hopeful, like things would be different this time. And I've decided to stop trying to hide in sadness. I'm fighting for what's mine now."

"What do you mean by that?"

"I'm not sure. I'll have to work it out on my own for a bit." I changed the subject. "Why were you staring at your drawing when I came in?"

"It's hard to believe I made that in high school. Was I ever that creative?"

"You're still that creative."

"Last night, I was beating you up for denying your happiness, and I'm doing the same as you in a different way. You can't admit to the good you've made in your life. Meanwhile, I won't even allow myself to explore the parts of me I used to like before I set them on the shelf and forgot them."

"What are you thinking about that?"

She turned back toward the picture on the wall. "I love staring at this drawing. The complexity of the patterns of the bark and branches draws me in. I lose myself in them."

She frowned and swallowed. "Was I ever that patient? Did I ever have that much time? Who was the person who drew that, and is she still inside of me?"

"Are you thinking of finding out?"

"It seems impossible that I could make something like that now." She waved at the drawing with the back of her hand as if to send it away. "Every time I start to think I could, another thought pops up and tells me I'm not good enough or tells me I've already lost my chance."

I smiled. "I guess we're both talking crazy stuff to ourselves, aren't we?"

She crossed her eyes at me, then said, "The question is, can we stop, or will we keep on doing it?"

I spent the rest of the day wandering around the property, trying to do something productive, but it was hard. There were too many thoughts zipping around my head. The plane crash had been so close-up and so violent. Different from the others. I couldn't think straight. Jolts of fear shocked me every time I thought about what happens after plane crashes.

I thought I could distract myself in the orchard, so I got a bucket to pick up fruit that had dropped on the ground, and another for the fruit I would bring inside to eat. I had had a daydream when I was younger of living in a house with enormous glass windows, sitting on top of a low rounded hill in the sun. There would be fruit trees covering the hill in all directions. In my dream, each tree would produce a different variety of fruit, ripening at different times, so I could go out in the morning in June and pick a Snow Angel white peach. In July, those would be gone, but there would be nectarines and Eldorado peaches. I didn't have that. We didn't have the time or the money to hire someone to take care of all those imagined fruit trees.

I did have a small orchard where I'd planted four or five varieties of fruit on dwarf rootstock in the same hole. The dwarf rootstock kept them small, and all the trees planted together stunted them some more, so I could reach the tops of most of the trees without a ladder. I took care of them every day. I enjoyed walking through them in the morning, with dew wetting the cuffs of my jeans. I could pick ripe fruit at almost any time of the summer. It was a quieter kind of success than I had imagined, and every time I found myself enjoying it, I thought about how I hadn't achieved my childhood dream. That took the edge off my enjoyment, and I felt safer. That day, the tranquility I usually found in the fruit orchard wasn't there, though. I couldn't keep the plane crash from my mind. I picked up the buckets and headed back to the house. I was determined that the outcome would be different this time too. But how?

Regardless, I knew that I would choose action over hiding from then on.

Chapter Three

THE NIGHT
BEFORE

The night before the plane crash, Jenny and I had a fight. It wasn't really an argument, more of a discussion, but it had been intense.

After quitting the trucking business with Mike, I kept my head down. I kept my happiness in check. It seemed to be working. We bought some Appaloosa horses and built stalls for them. I leveled the area between the stalls and the house and built a corral where we could train them between taking them on rides in the hills. I bought some tools and started making furniture again, following up on the basics that Ed had taught me. Josh was about to start his senior year in high school, and Nate would be joining him there as a freshman. Jenny had a steady stable of clients, and the mix of time spent with them and time spent alone with their finances worked for her. Things were going well, but as long as I could convince myself I wasn't content, fate wouldn't see me happy. I felt sufficiently hidden.

One Saturday in June, we all went riding in the hills. We started out slow, with the dogs running ahead of us, then coming back, then running ahead again. We rode together up the shady road beside the creek. Just past the upper meadow, we reached the flat loop where the boys liked to race their horses, and they took off. The dogs didn't try to keep up. Jenny and I rode side by side, talking about the events of the past week, breathing the scent of the drying grass, and enjoying the sun on our shoulders. A hawk flew past, shrieking, trying to scare a small animal from its hiding place. Ground squirrels piped warnings as the dogs came close.

When the boys caught up with us again, we followed the creek trail shaded by maples until we reached the top. We continued out onto a promontory among oak trees where we could see west to the ocean. The grass was short under the oaks, and we laid out a blanket and had a picnic. There, under the trees, with the horses grazing nearby, I was content. Like the dogs lounging around, their tongues lolling out the side of their mouths, I hadn't a care. With all of us talking and eating at the same time, I was happy. I felt full and warm. I kept trying to take the edge off it by thinking of what was wrong in my life to keep my contentment hidden from fate, but I couldn't. That worried me.

A week later, I drove down the valley to pick Nate up after basketball practice. Waiting in the school parking lot in the warmth of the car, I read a few pages from the book I always kept there for moments like this. Every so often, I would look up to see if he was coming out. There were kids around being kids, laughing and cavorting. I stopped for a moment and put down the book when I realized that I was more than content. I was happy. I felt my skin prickle; I heard the voice telling me it could all be taken away. So, I thought about the new heater we needed and wondered where we would get the money to pay for it. I thought about the argument Josh and I had had that morning. That pushed the voice into the background. Still, I wasn't sure it was enough.

So, about the fight with Jenny. I had lost my job, but it wasn't about that. I had gone from being a mechanic to starting and quitting the trucking business with Mike to being a mechanic again, this time at an auto dealership in Monterey. I kept getting promoted, mainly because, unlike most of the guys working under cars, I liked doing more than one thing at a time. And I could talk to customers. So, by the summer of 1977, I had been head of the repair shop for five years. But the owner's kid was a mechanic, and he wanted to be head of the shop. You can't have two of those. When business slowed down, they let me go and promoted him.

Before I lost my job, we'd bought the piece of land on the west side of ours. I wanted to have more room for the horses. Someday, I wanted to do that and furniture making full-time, and we would need more land for the horses. So, we took a short-term loan on that property and changed the mortgage on our house to short-term too. That way, we could afford them both, thinking we would get a longer loan when we had more money. We both made more money for a while but kept waiting for rates to go back down. When I was let go from my job, the deadline for the loan was coming up quickly, and interest rates had gone up so much that we might not be able to refinance it. There was a chance we would lose our house along with the new property. But that's not what we fought about either.

Josh had been tough to live with even before he shared his news with us, and we didn't know how to handle his contrary nature. He was coming up on his senior year in high school and was trying out his wings. But like a baby bird that's getting too big for the nest, he was pooping all over the nest before flying away. It seemed like everything was a fight with him, and sometimes it felt like he was just being mean. I guess if he loved being at home too much, he wouldn't ever want to leave, so that was natural. But we couldn't afford for him to go away to college, so he was going to have to live at home for another two years. Then there was his announcement, and for some reason I was the focus of his ire. She just agreed with him, but we didn't fight about him that night.

No, the night before the sixth plane crash, we fought about me. Despite the upcoming balloon payment, and despite Josh being impossible to live with, I was worried that my life was going too well. As much as I denied it, and despite every trick I tried to sabotage it, I was happy. I knew fate wouldn't let that last, so I was trying to hide it under a disguising net of discontent. In the process, I was making everyone else unhappy with me.

Sometimes, on the ocean in the winter, swells from different directions merge and build on each other into one huge swell. Two or even three waves meet just off-shore, and out of nowhere, a sneaker wave larger than any wave that day or that week crashes into the beach. Every winter, we hear of an unsuspecting family climbing on an outcropping where the rocks are bone dry. On a sunny winter day, they're washed out to sea by a wave from a calm ocean. That's what it felt like inside me. A sneaker wave was coming. I could feel it growing. The swells were gathering out there about to break over us. Another plane crash was coming, and something I loved would be taken from me.

In bed that night, I turned to Jenny, who was reading a book, and said, "I'm too happy, and I'm worried."

She didn't even look up. "No, you're not."

That threw me. "No, I'm not worried?"

She set the book down on her lap. "Of course, you're worried. You're always worried. But you can't possibly be too happy. You never let yourself be happy."

I frowned. "I know I don't."

She shook her head. "Why not? You have a wife who loves you, and who I think you love. You have two great kids and friends who you like to hang out with. You have your furniture and your horses, and when you're working, you like your job. You've built—we've built—a wonderful life. And still, you keep going back to what's wrong with it." She reached out and touched my shoulder. "You keep turning away from any enjoyment of what you've built. I don't get it."

"I lost my job." I heard my voice get louder. "We have a balloon payment due in a month. I'm not happy."

Her brow furrowed. "Just a minute ago, you said you were too happy. Here's what I think. You're feeling good about your life despite all the problems that are coming up just now, and it scares you somehow."

She was right. So, I told her. I told her the secret I had been keeping to myself my whole life. "I feel so stupid even saying this. But I need to say it out loud." I took a deep breath. "When I'm too happy, that's when bad things happen. It's been the case all my life. I can't admit that my life is going well because then fate notices and takes away somebody I love."

I saw it in her face. She thought I was making a joke, and she started to get mad at me. Then she saw I was serious. "Wait, do you mean to say that you control your luck?"

I took another deep breath, feeling my heart rate rising. Maybe I should have kept this to myself. "Yes. I know it sounds far-fetched, but I think I do. Or it's more like I keep bad luck from noticing me. Here, let me explain." I started at the beginning, with the plane crash on the beach and Peppy. Then I told her about my dad, and then the plane crash before my mom died. I reminded her that there had been a crash right before we lost our baby girl, and then the Apollo crash when I gave up on the trucking business.

She sat up, crossed her legs, and turned to face me. She looked sad for me. "Could it be that you're generally happy, then things happen? Stuff happens all the time. Could it be that you're not causing the crashes by being happy—that they're just happening?"

I shook my head. "It would seem that way, but it keeps happening. I'm happy, then a plane crashes, then I lose something I love." I sat in resolute silence. I knew it was true, regardless of what she thought.

Her mouth hung open in disbelief. She shut it and shook her head as if she was settling her thoughts. "You're happy, then a plane crashes, then something's taken away? Is that what you're saying? That's how this works?"

"Yes. We were so happy before the trip to Chicago, remember? Then that plane crashed over Lake Michigan, and right afterward, Guppy was gone. I couldn't even make the business go with Mike because I was scared if it went well, something would be taken away. The Apollo fire convinced me to quit the business. It wasn't a plane, but it was close enough. It was like a mobster threatening what could happen if I didn't quit. I couldn't live with it."

She had started crying. "Oh, baby. Is that what you've been doing all this time? Have you been trying not to be happy so you won't cause bad luck? Are you denying all the good in your life so it can't be taken from you?"

Tears were streaming down my cheeks too. I'd never said all of this aloud to anyone. Doing so had cracked me open. "Pretty much. It's seemed to work." I looked down at my hands. I was rubbing them together as I spoke. "But it's building up again. Something's coming. Something's about to happen." I wiped my eyes, and she handed me a tissue. I blew my nose.

She exhaled loudly. "Well, at least I understand a bit more of you now. That's been a paradox to me. After all this time, you're telling me about a part of you I've been guessing at for as long as we've known each other."

I nodded. "Yeah. It feels good to tell someone. I know you're thinking I'm crazy."

She reached over and grabbed my hand. "I don't think you're crazy. Okay, maybe I do just a little." Her smile helped me relax a little. "You have to admit, it sounds kind of crazy—you saying you cause bad things to happen when you admit you're happy. I mean, you're just one tiny person in a huge world, and the idea that your happiness caused the Apollo explosion...it's just..." Her voice trailed off, and she shook her head. "But it does explain things."

I pulled her closer to me. "Like what?"

"Well, I've always been confused about how you go out and build a beautiful life and then hate it while you're living in it. The parts of your life that would make anyone else in the world jealous make you scared. But you keep building it. And you keep pointing out what's wrong with it." She dropped her face into her hands and rubbed her eyes. Then she looked up at me. "How long have we been married, and I'm finally understanding this part of you?"

I sighed. "I was afraid that telling you might drag you into my unhappiness."

"You're already dragging me into it. We feel bad along with you when you won't enjoy the good times in your life." She started rubbing my hand. "By now, it seems like this kind of thinking—whether it's right or wrong—has become a habit, this denying what's right in your life and always looking at what's wrong."

I pulled my hand away. "But what else can I do? Bad things happen when I admit I'm doing okay."

"Or so you've led yourself to believe, anyway." She exhaled loudly. "I don't know, Van. All those things were bad, but they also brought about so much good in your life. Here's an example. Ed wouldn't have been such a big part of your life if your dad had been there, and you wouldn't have learned about furniture making, and furniture making is the place where you find quiet every day. It's the place where your brain finally can stop listening to all the things you tell yourself are wrong with your life." Her words sped up. "And, if your mom hadn't died, you wouldn't have gone to Northern California. We wouldn't have been in the same town at the same time. You and me and what we've built together is the best part of my life, and I think it is for you too." Her gaze softened. "It seems to me like some of the best things in your life came out of terrible tragedies." She reached for my hand again but didn't rub it. Instead, she stared into my eyes. "What if that's just the way life is? What if losses just happen? And what if they can be turned into a beautiful life instead of the other way around? What if you should celebrate the disasters, knowing that something wonderful will grow from their ashes? Something wonderful and unexpected."

Logically, I could see her point. But I was scared to celebrate those things. I felt my jaw harden. "I can't believe that. I can't celebrate the deaths of my parents because they brought me here to this better place. Happiness draws in disasters. Period."

And that was how we left it.

But you don't live as long as I have with a very wise woman without thinking about what she says. That night in bed, I stayed awake ruminating. I tried not to toss or thrash in my wakefulness because she had already fallen asleep. She always fell asleep so fast.

I tried to figure out what I could do to stop hiding like a salamander under a log, hoping fate wouldn't come and turn it over and find me. Maybe she was right. Maybe I was making myself miserable in my effort to not lose what I had. For certain I was making the rest of my family misera- ble. I needed a new strategy. I couldn't accept the idea that tragedies could be turned into blessings; I just couldn't. But maybe I could fight fate. Make it bend to my will. I could meet it head on and force life to go my way.

Then I told myself that was a stupid idea. I fell asleep the night before the sixth plane crash thinking that what I was doing was working fine.

Chapter Four

MAPS

In the dining room that night after supper, I laid a towel out to protect the table and placed the metal box from the upper meadow on it. I had made that table from a huge piece of redwood I found behind the barn just after we moved in. It was twelve feet long and cut from the center of a tree that must have been 300 years old. We all sat at one end of it, gathered around the box. I had cut the lock off it earlier, but I hadn't opened it. I was enjoying the drama, despite my mix of agitation and hope. It was even more fun keeping the rest of the family in suspense.

I put my hands on top of the box and started my speech. "What's in this box?" I said in a dramatic tone, like a magician. Nate and Josh rolled their eyes at the same time. "The pilot knew, but he died before he could tell us. It was so important that he wanted me to go back into the plane that could have caught fire at any moment to get it. And he gave it to us. Whatever's inside is ours now. Let's take a second to honor his memory and then let our imaginations run wild."

"You know, it's not all ours," Jenny said. "No matter what he said to you, we need to find his family. We need to do what's right." She wasn't buying into the anticipation and drama I was trying to build.

I shrugged. "You're right. But in my world right now, he doesn't have any family. It's ours until we find out otherwise. He thought it was important. He gave it to us with his last words. I think it's something special. Let's allow ourselves to fantasize for a minute." I looked at the boys. They seemed excited. "What do you guys think is inside?"

Nate drummed on the table with his hands, then leaned forward. "I still think it's a pile of cash. Hundred-dollar bills."

I pointed at him. "Could be. Or thousand-dollar bills. But I think it's something rare and valuable, like stock certificates or a Van Gogh painting, all rolled up. What would it be like to have a lot of money?"

"If we were rich, I wouldn't have to go to community college next year." Josh sounded almost wistful as he said, "I could go away somewhere and get out of the house. I have the grades. I could get into Berkeley or Stanford."

Nate chimed in. "Ski trips. If you have money, you can go skiing. And vacations to Hawaii. You always know who the rich kids are by their tans. Like Mike's kids. Even when they go skiing, they come back with goggle tans on their faces."

I turned to Jenny. "I would buy you a new kitchen and remodel the house. I would buy that Appaloosa mare I want, then get a new heater for the workshop."

She smiled slowly as she thought. "I'd build a cottage here so my parents can live near us and we could take care of them better."

That made me feel better, like she was joining us in our fantasy world. "Now you're getting in the spirit. We could go on a vacation to Rome and stay near the fountain with the marble horses in it. We could throw coins into the fountain and drink coffee out of tiny cups in cafes on the sidewalk. We wouldn't have to work, so we could travel all the time. I don't think I would look for a new job. I would make furniture full-time and work with the horses."

"I would keep my job," Jenny said. "Being rich wouldn't change my life much. But there's no doubt I would take more time off for vacations."

"Snacks!" Nate jumped up to grab an apple off the counter and took a bite. He continued talking as he chewed. "Snacks and sodas. We could buy a whole refrigerator for sodas and a cupboard next to it with snacks. Not the healthy kind, either. Chips and cookies and caffeine and carbonated fluff."

"I make you cookies," Jenny said.

"Yeah, but those are Mom cookies. Those are special. I want the kind that make you sick after eating because you ate the whole box. Those are what we would buy if we were rich."

We all got quiet for a minute, looking at each other, then I said, "Ready? Let's see what's in there."

"A Camaro!" Nate yelled. "A '68 Camaro SS. Or two—one for me and one for Josh. His would be blue, and mine would be red." He looked around the table. "I just wanted to get that in before we opened the box—in case it's like blowing out birthday candles and you need to get your wishes in early."

Tears came to my eyes I laughed so hard. Nate can always make me laugh like that. After a moment, I yanked the smile off my face and looked around the table again. "Here we go."

I opened the box a slit again, slammed it shut, closed the latch, and lifted my hands up in the air. "We should wait until tomorrow. We're rich right now. Right now, we all have our dreams."

"No!" Jenny shouted. "Do it. I can't wait. Just open it."

I peered at her sideways and smiled crookedly at her. Slowly, I opened the latch and hinged the top back, peeking into the box before letting them see what was inside. It was full of papers. They seemed like they had been jammed into the box until the box was full and the top was locked on them. Papers popped out, crinkled, written all over in spidery handwriting, looking like they would never go back in.

I just sighed, a big, deep sigh. I dug the mess of paper from the box and set it on the table. I turned the toolbox over and shook it above the table to show that there was nothing else in it. Jenny got up to get cookies.

Nate said, "Well, crap. Just a box full of crumpled paper. It's just like my locker, without the gym clothes."

Josh chuckled. "We should have waited."

I picked up the top piece of paper, smoothed it on the table, and inspected the writing on it. It was cramped and contorted. Some of the papers were lined sheets ripped out of a notebook. Others were pieces of typing paper. Most of them were covered in tiny writing that wrapped around the pages. There were arrows pointing from one fragment of words to another, and there were doodles sprinkled throughout. "This is gibberish."

Jenny set the plate of cookies on the table, and both boys reached for them. "Van, remember when we were in San Francisco and that guy in the coffee shop kept telling us how his neighbor was trying to poison him? We believed him for a while until he started making stranger and stranger accusations, then he pulled out his notebook and showed us his notes on how everyone in his apartment building was working together to get him. This is like his notebook, but worse." She reached for a cookie. "How did the pilot seem?"

"We didn't see him for long, but he seemed normal." I had to stop talking for a second. I could feel my face getting red and tears wanting to squeeze out. I gazed up at the ceiling. I set down my cookie and turned to Josh. "It just hit me again that we watched someone die today. He was there, then he coughed blood, and he was gone." I rested my hand on my son's shoulder. "How're you doing?"

He bit his lip. "You know how when you spend the day on the water and later your bed rocks like a boat every time you close your eyes?" I nodded, and he continued. "That's how I feel now. Planes keep crashing and pilots keep bleeding whenever I close my eyes. I'm glad I slept this afternoon."

After the letdown of finding out the treasure was just a bunch of papers, Nate and Josh went to their rooms, Jenny went back to the reading chair, and I went out to the shop. I wanted something to take my mind off the fear that the plane crash brought, but I knew I shouldn't use power tools in that state. My resolve to fight fate this time was slipping away. Hiding hadn't worked. The plane crash had come, and I knew that meant I was going to lose something I loved. I had said I would fight, but how? The only handle I had to grasp at was crumpled papers stuffed into a box by a crazy person. Every time I tried to talk myself into thinking this plane crash might turn out differently, I lost the argument and the icy sharp shard of fear in my stomach grew a little larger. I wanted to crawl under something and hide.

I picked up the framed copy of my dad's map that I kept on the desk in my workshop. Even before he told us he was gay and I didn't react right, Josh and I had been fighting. I kept trying to give him advice, to warn him of possible missteps or let him know what I had learned, and he kept shoving me away when I did.

It all seemed too much. Maps that didn't lead anywhere. Toolboxes of treasure that weren't what they seemed. Kids that we fought with too much, then would leave us too soon. Plans that we couldn't afford. I didn't know where to turn.

I thought back to when we had gotten the map. When I was almost six and we had lived in the cabin in the redwoods of Big Sur for five years, Dad was getting his gear ready to go hunting when he stopped and looked at me. "Hey, Van. What do you think about coming with me today?" I remember running around outside the house for a while whooping and yelling before I came back inside and said yes while jumping up and down with impatience.

When we were about to go, he strode over to get his rifle, and on the rack below it hung a smaller gun. A Winchester single shot bolt-action .22 in a size that I could handle. He nonchalantly picked it off the rack, showed me it was unloaded, and handed it to me. "You'll need to carry this."

That summed up my dad. The rifle wasn't a present, and he didn't make a big deal of it. He didn't make a fuss about much, but he did a lot in his quiet way. I carried that rifle how he showed me, unloaded, all day long as we hiked through the hills. When we came to an open space where the redwoods gave way to a grassy meadow with a cliff at the end, he taught me how to shoot. After setting me up with the rifle against my shoulder, and showing me how to aim it, he kneeled behind me, instructing me. "Breathe in. Now, take up some of the slack in the trigger." I pressed the trigger too quickly, and the gun went off, surprising me.

"That's good. You should be surprised each time it fires. If you're anticipating it, you'll cause the shot to go off-target. Try again." I missed badly again. I growled in frustration, but he said, "These things take time. You can't learn them in a day. We have time to learn this, and you're already doing so well."

"Tell me how to do it right. I want to be as good as you."

"I've had a lot of practice. You'll get it." He put his hand on my shoulder. "Take a breath. Look around the clearing. Smell the wind. Feel it on your cheek. This is fun."

When I smiled at him, he smiled back and said, "Try it again. You're jerking the trigger. That'll make you miss too. Remember to breathe in, then as you're breathing out, take up slack while holding your aim. Squeeze the stock and the trigger like you're squeezing a rubber ball."

When I hit the target for the first time, he hugged me. "You're doing great. You're a quick learner, and you listen well to what I'm teaching you. We have to get home, though."

I wanted to practice more, but he wanted me to finish strong. "There will be lots of days. We'll keep practicing." He ruffled my hair like he was proud of me. "You're going to be good at this, I can tell." Then we unloaded my new gun, and I carried it all the way home, making sure to do it just as had he showed me, taking two steps for every one of his.

That .22 wouldn't take down large animals, but we hunted for rabbits and quail, and with practice, I got better at shooting. Dad would get a deer, and afterward, we would hunt for smaller game. I remember walking home with him the first time I shot a rabbit, carrying it on my shoulder as I had seen him do with a deer, trying to match the way he strode among the undergrowth.

One afternoon, after we had returned from hunting, I was sitting on the porch cleaning my rifle when I saw a man walking toward our cabin. The wind off the ocean seemed to push him out of the wisps of fog flowing up the creek. He had on a leather hat—like a cowboy hat, but smaller. He smiled up at me through a black mustache that covered his upper lip. He was a stranger to me, so I called my dad who was behind the house chopping logs into pieces small enough to fit in the stove. When Dad saw who it was, he strode down to meet him, and they hugged like brothers, slapping their backs and holding each other at arm's length to stare at the other one. Dad introduced him to me as his friend Bobby. They had grown up down the street from each other in Chicago, my dad explained, and they hadn't seen each other in years.

Bobby had hitchhiked across the country through the summer rainstorms and humidity of Missouri, Oklahoma, and Texas on the newly paved Route 66 and across the desert to California. He pushed his hat back and said, "When I reached the ocean, I just turned right, and kept going north until I found you." Back in Chicago, he had been researching lost mines in Arizona and Nevada, hoping to find a place where he could buy a friendly donkey and wander among the red rocks and rattlesnakes up lonely canyons like one of the old prospectors. He wanted to sweat in the dry air with a battered hat on his head and a pick strapped to the top of his pack while Chicago was shivering buried under snow blown off the lake.

That evening, after supper, Dad and Bobby sat at the dining room table, their faces yellow in the light from the kerosene lamp, sipping whisky mixed with water from small glasses. "I was hoping to find something that would send me out wandering with my burro," Bobby said as he smiled over at me. "I wasn't having much luck finding anything when a scrap fell out of one of the old books I had been using for research."

I blurted out, "What was it?"

He glanced at my dad and continued, "It was a book about the Spanish settlements in the west. The area that would become the United States."

"No, what fell out of the book?"

He chuckled at my impatience and pulled a thick amber envelope from his pack. He opened it carefully. Inside, between two pieces of cardboard, was a thin brown scrap of leather with handwriting on it. I could see squiggly lines and symbols drawn on it. He set it on the table and turned it toward my dad. "It's a map. I think it's a treasure map. Look what it says."

On the other side, were words written in Spanish. He read them for us in English. "*My friend hasn't returned. He gave me this map because he knew what he was doing was dangerous. He said he was hiding gold in the cave on the mountainside. He takes chances I won't take. Now that I've written this down, I can forget it.*" He flipped the scrap back over. "I was excited when I read that. It was the treasure map I had been looking for."

Dad leaned in and squinted to read the words written along one of the vertical lines of the map. "You know what this says, don't you?"

"I know. *El país grande del sur.* That means *the big country to the south*. Big Sur. We're going treasure hunting!"

Dad leaned back in his chair with a big grin on his face. "You found a treasure map in an old book, and it says there's gold right in our backyard? I knew I was friends with you for a reason."

I jumped around behind them, chanting "treasure map" over and over as they watched me and smiled. There was gold hidden back in the hills—the same hills we wandered in every day.

Bobby pointed at the map. "I matched the contours on the drawing to the shoreline near your house. This scrap is a map of Big Sur. Since the coastline matches the drawing, that must mean that these two points are the two mountains to the north and south. They're marked with what looks like an S and a P. That matches the Spanish names for the two mountains. If that's true, the cave with the gold is right on the slopes of the mountain to the east of you. Look, it's even marked with an X. I think we should go out there and get rich."

My dad laughed. "Yes, we should," he said as he clinked glasses with Bobby.

My mom smiled at them and shook her head, then retired to the corner near the stove to read under her lamp. After a while, she said it was time for me to go to sleep, and I curled up on my small bed on the other side of the room behind a curtain. I lay there listening to them reminiscing about the old neighborhood and planning their trip into the hills for gold. Then Bobby told Dad a story that I didn't realize until years later had been meant for me. "You know we were rich before the crash, right? My dad was looking to buy one of those mansions out on the lake. We were going to move up into high society."

I heard the top of the whiskey bottle pop open again, and the sound of liquid in a glass. "Your dad was big in the stock market, wasn't he?"

"Yeah. He was buying on margin and making a killing, then it all came tumbling down. We had our house left, but that's all. He started drinking and staying out. He was a mess."

A chair scraped backward, then another, lighter, moved. Someone had put their foot on an extra chair. It was probably my dad. He liked to do that after supper. "Then one night, he comes home, and he wakes me and my mom up, and he looks like he's been sleeping in the streets, and he stinks like alcohol. He says he has something to tell us. He had been out drinking himself into oblivion again, and he passed out after he left the bar. He woke up to someone rolling him over, and he thought he was being robbed. He said he thought it was funny because whoever was robbing him was going to find an empty wallet."

Bobby coughed and lit a cigarette. I breathed in the sharp aroma of the first whiff of smoke. The cabin would stink tomorrow, but for now, it was a good smell. "Then a train whistle blew so loudly he knew it was almost on top of them, and the locomotive thundered by right next to them. He had been on the tracks, and the person he thought was robbing him had rolled him to safety. Car after car passed them, and he felt the wind from each one buffeting him, and it seemed like someone was slapping his face saying, 'Stupid, stupid, stupid!' until the train passed. When the train was gone, the hobo who had pushed him off the train tracks said to him, 'I don't care how bad your life is, you have to keep on. You can't waste it like that.'"

Bobby must have been leaning back in his chair because I heard the front legs hit the floor. "He said he knew then that he had been an idiot. When he came home, he had to wake us up and tell us that all he cared about was the two of us, and the rest was just leaves on the wind." My dad said something to Bobby after that, but it was fuzzy, and their words blended into the crackle of the fire until I fell asleep.

Bobby and Dad spent the next two days in the hills searching, but the gold cave wasn't where the map said it was. Nevertheless, they came back each day, happy to have spent the time together tramping in the brush. They ate huge portions of whatever Mom had cooked and drank more whiskey. Sunday night after supper, Dad stretched his arms over his head, and said, "I've got to go to work in Monterey early tomorrow. It's a drive. I should hit the sack."

Bobby thought for a moment, then said, "Take me out to the road with you, and I'll hitchhike down the coast a little way. I'm thinking the map might match just a bit further south. You should make a copy, though, in case you find another clue. I'll come running if you do."

Dad carefully copied the map onto a piece of brown paper, including the inscription on the back. That night, after returning from Monterey, Dad pulled a hardcover copy of *Moby Dick* from the shelf, opened it to the first chapter, and read aloud, "Call me Ishmael." Then he put the map inside the front cover and set the book back up next to the others. He and Mom seemed to agree that the weekend had been a success. They found riches in the gift of two old friends wandering in the woods, catching up on the news, and drinking some whiskey together. As far as they were concerned, that was the end of treasure hunting.

A few months later, Pearl Harbor was bombed, and Dad enlisted in the Navy. The map inside the book was the last thing on my mind as we all drove together to the bus station in Monterey. I stood by him in the waiting area where mixed-up sounds of other families saying goodbye to their sons and husbands and fathers echoed off the high ceiling and fell down among our sadness. Tears came into my eyes as I hugged him, smelling the clean scent of soap and shaving lotion on his neck. I told myself I was too old to cry. I held on to him for an extra moment, then wiped the tears away with the back of my hand before people saw them.

Chapter Five

MISSIONS

While I was sitting there in my own private puddle of self-pity, Jenny came into the shop and asked me to get a box of her old art supplies and drawings out of the attic. After climbing up the stairs, I ducked my head to keep from hitting the rafters and the roofing nails while at the same time watching where I was stepping among the artifacts we had put there. I found her box behind Josh's fifth-grade California history project about Mission Soledad.

I smiled as I looked at it. His finished product had photos pasted on a large piece of cardboard with hand-printed explanations of what was in each picture. I remember our visit to Salinas for this project. I brought my camera and a fresh roll of film. Josh wanted to be in every shot. It wasn't until we developed the film that we saw the overall effect of his enthusiasm. He was standing beside the gnarled olive tree that had been planted when the mission was in operation. He gestured like Carol Merrill on *Let's Make a Deal* below the wooden cross at the entrance to the mission. He pointed up at the green brass bell in the courtyard and stood with his hands on his hips in front of the altar. It was pretty good for a fifth-grade project. But we had kept it because it was more like a collage of Josh than a mission project, and it made me chuckle every time I saw it. I climbed back up for it after bringing Jenny's box down. I wanted to show Josh his fifth-grade self again. Maybe it would make him smile and remind him we used to be friends.

The next morning, as we fed the horses, Josh and I didn't talk much until we were starting back around with the shovels. It always seemed easier to talk to the horses in the morning than to a person, but that started the words flowing. I was hoping we could start a discussion about our relationship. But as he scratched Nate's horse behind the ears where she liked it, Josh started talking about the toolbox. "I couldn't sleep, so I brought the papers into my room last night. I kept thinking there was more than useless scribbling there. As much as I searched, I couldn't find anything that made any sense. But there were two sets of initials that stood out, especially after you brought my mission project down from the attic."

I tossed the shovel full of manure into the front of the tractor. "What did you figure out?"

"You know what the full name of Mission Soledad is? Nuestra Señora de Soledad. NSS. About the only legible parts of the whole mess of scribbles were the letters 'NSS' and 'SAP.' But I don't know what SAP could be."

It didn't sound like much. At least we were headed in the same direction, though, instead of fighting, so I went along. "Well, let's get this done and then go look."

After we finished the rest of the shoveling, we kicked off our boots on the back porch, and Josh ran to his room. He came back to the dining room where I had poured myself a cup of coffee, and he laid out the papers on the table in a fan in front of us. "Look at this. It's a mess. This was not an organized person. Mom would go crazy if this person lived with us. But here. NSS and SAP. Is there a mission called SAP?" We thought together about the ones we could name. San Juan Bautista, Santa Clara, Carmel, San Jose, San Francisco, Santa Barbara, San Diego.

"There must be more." I thought we had an atlas around, and I got up to get it. When I came back with it, I flipped through the pages until I came to the map of the area south of us. It had the town of Soledad on it but didn't have the mission marked on it. "I bet the missions are in a book on California history. I have one of those." I went to the hall bookcase and grabbed it.

When I opened the book, I was surprised at how many missions there were and where they were located. I knew they were supposed to be a day's ride apart, but I thought they were all in a line, like a highway, running up the state. Instead, they meandered like a creek. There was even one out in Santa Cruz, by the coast.

Josh jammed his finger into the book. "Look Dad! Down below there. There's one I've never heard of. It's up in the hills behind the military base. Mission San Antonio de Padua—SAP!"

A fuzzy connection buzzed in my brain. He started to talk, and I held up my hand. "Wait, I'm thinking." He stopped talking. I jumped up and got the framed map from my shop. Maybe those points on Bobby's map weren't mountains. I opened the atlas again and found the location of the two missions and made small dots on the page. Mission Soledad was out in the Salinas Valley, beside the Salinas River. To the south and west, hidden up a valley behind Fort Hunter Ligget Army Base, was Mission San Antonio de Padua. "So, if we assume that the S and the P on the map mean those two missions instead of two mountains, and the line Bobby and my dad thought was the coast is instead this mountain range, it might make sense."

Josh ran to get some rulers. I put them on the atlas, connecting the dots we had made. "If we make a long thin triangle with those two missions, there should be a mountain right about here. There is. It's called...Pinyon Peak."

"Okay...." Josh said, drawing the word out and leaning in to see better. "You've had that treasure map forever. Your dad thought it was showing the land out where you lived by the coast, but now maybe it shows a completely different area. But it matches the map, and there's a mountain. There might be gold on Pinyon Peak."

"There's no gold in those mountains. Well, not enough to count. It's all in the foothills of the Sierras. But that doesn't mean there's not something there." I felt hope rising inside. "We might be victims of our own dreams, but it makes you wonder, doesn't it?"

"The pilot thought there was something important in the box, but there wasn't anything," Josh said. I could tell he was getting a little excited too. "But with your dad's map, it makes sense. It's not that far. We could drive there and hike in and out in two days."

"No, not that. Hang on, I'm thinking." My mind strayed back to Bobby and Dad and the days they spent in the hills. I remembered the smiles on their faces after their searches despite not finding any treasure. I imagined Josh and me hiking around searching for a mine, then sitting by a campfire at the end of the day, tired and talking about whatever came to mind. Maybe that's what we needed.

The words came out in slow sentences as thoughts came to me. "Why don't we take a horse camping trip down the coast? It could be father-and-son bonding time." Time to remember that we liked hanging out together. "While we're there, we can cut across to the east and check the area out. Pinyon Peak is only thirty miles from here in a straight line, but on trails and taking our time, it would be forty-five miles or a bit more. We could make a loop toward the ocean. It would be cooler, and there would be more water and shade. We could make it there in a few days, and whatever we find, even if we find nothing, we would have had a pleasant trip. What do you think?"

Josh rubbed his hands together and smiled. "I think we should do it. It's been too long since we camped. And maybe we'll find treasure."

That's what I wanted to hear. He still wanted to take a camping trip with me. "Hey, since I don't have a job, I don't have to get time off from work."

As I looked across the table at Josh, I thought about fighting fate. Maybe this was a step in that direction. At least by making something happen, I wasn't hiding from it.

Later, in the barn, we started gathering what we would need. We had camping gear from past trips, and we knew how to pack the horses for a ride like this. The big difference was the pack horses. We were bringing two of them in case we found something. No reason not to be optimistic, I thought.

The other difference was that Nate wasn't coming. His ankle was still swollen, but he could hobble around enough to feed the horses with Jenny's help. It was strange not to be packing up with him. Even though Nate was two years younger, Josh and Nate hung out together all the time. They wouldn't admit it to us or to themselves, but they were each other's best friends. They did chores together. They talked about sports and the future and school, and they rode in the hills together.

Nate's horse was a buckskin quarter horse, short coupled, that could go from a standing start to a full run in a couple of steps and was afraid of nothing. Josh's was an Appaloosa, gray, spotted, regal. When they raced, the buckskin always got out to an early lead and could hold it if the course turned enough. But give the Appaloosa room to stretch out and he would leave Nate's horse behind.

As brothers, they matched like their horses did—which is not at all. But like they knew the horses, each of them knew and appreciated the strengths and weaknesses of the other. Nate was outgoing and sure of himself. He had an easy smile and liked to crack jokes. Girls liked him and the sandy brown hair that fell in his green eyes. Josh was more serious and taller. His dark brown hair was curly at the ends right before it needed to be cut. Then the barber cut the curls off, leaving plain brown hair surrounding a serious face with a solid mouth that looked like it was about to ask a question.

I was putting saddle blankets on top of the pile of gear we had stacked in the tack room when a thought came to my mind. I turned to Josh. "Why don't you grab the rifles and a box of shells?"

His head came up. "What for?"

"We have holsters for them on the saddles, and you never know what we might run into." He started to go get the rifles, then turned and looked at me like I might know something I wasn't saying. I didn't know anything. It was just a hunch. We packed extra water containers, knowing that there might not be much water as we traveled further from the coast into the drier mountain valleys.

The containers reminded me I wanted to check the water tank, and I asked Josh to go make sure it was full and that the inlets and outlets were clear. When we moved in, I ran a pipe from the spring-fed creek that ran past our property to a big wooden tank on the hill above our house. I knew that there was always a danger of fire in the hills, so I laid a large-diameter pipe down near the house and put attachments for fire hoses near the driveway. As I fiddled with the tack, I watched Josh jog up to the tank and check the level. Then he came back down and opened the valve by the driveway, letting water flow down the gravel for a minute before closing it again.

Before going to bed, I spent a little time in my workshop. I had added this room to the back of the house when Josh was small. I'd wanted a place to make furniture in the evenings after the boys were in bed but didn't want to be cut off from the family. Typically, I kept the door open except when I was making too much noise, and the aroma of fresh cut wood wafted through the open door into the rest of the house. It was the first smell that touched my nose when I got home unless someone was cooking something. When they were young, Nate and Josh used to pick up pieces of scrap wood from the floor of the workshop to bring to their rooms so that the smell of the workshop was with them as they fell asleep.

Josh came into the shop that night. I was sitting in my chair in the corner, staring at the ceiling. I looked over at him. "What's up, Bubba?"

He rubbed his eyes, and, for a second, I could see the tired kid who used to come get me so I could put him to bed. "What are you doing? You never just sit and stare."

I leaned back in my chair. "I was just thinking about life. About how life places opportunities in front of you, and you have the choice of picking them up or passing them by."

"Like the map?"

"Nah. I was thinking about you and Nate. You're only with us for such a short time. I'm not optimistic about any treasure, but I'm glad we're going camping." He picked up a scrap of wood and tossed it in the air, catching it behind his back. I watched him for a moment, then kept going, "And it seems like all we do is fight anymore. You know, all I'm doing is trying to help you find out what's best for you."

His relaxed, sleepy demeanor vanished. His eyes focused sharply on me as he said, "And you can't know what's best for me. That's why we keep fighting. You keep telling me what to do."

"I'm not telling you what to do. I'm just trying to protect you. I might be able to keep you from making mistakes like I did. I might know something."

He frowned and shook his head. "No, you don't. You can't. Nobody does. Not even me. How could you know if I don't know? I can't listen to you because you're talking about you, not me."

I felt the frustration rising. I pushed it down. This conversation was so painfully familiar. It was like we had both turned onto a well-worn dirt road with grooves that would catch the tires and turn them.

Josh stopped tossing the scrap. His voice got softer. Maybe not responding was the right thing to do. "Can you try to not tell me what I need to do with my life this week? Back off some, and maybe we won't fight so much?"

I smiled at him. "Sure. But can you admit that I might have some wisdom sometimes that would help you?"

"No. Your wisdom doesn't apply where I need to go." He was smiling too. We were still arguing, but the tone of it was lighter now. "I'm smarter than you think I am. I can figure it out."

"Okay. I know you're smart. I'll leave you alone this week and not tell you what to do."

He tossed the scrap toward me, and I reached out and caught it. "Good. I'm going to bed. We're moving out early tomorrow. You might want to get some sleep too."

I kept my voice light as I said, "Now you're the one who's telling me what's right for me?" I tossed the scrap back to Josh and nodded at him. "That agreement should work both ways. I'll head up in a couple of minutes."

He started to leave, then turned around and stuck his head back in the doorway. "You know, I was thinking... maybe the mistakes are part of the fun, like the bumps are part of a roller coaster."

I watched his back as he turned to go to his room. Where did my kid get that kind of wisdom? But it was easy for him to say. Fate had led me towards crevasses a thousand feet-deep, not over roller coaster bumps. I had to keep fighting so we didn't fall in.

Chapter Six

THE TRAIL

The road up the creek was dark and cool in the early morning as we rode toward the upper meadow. The black licorice medicine aroma of the bay trees permeated what dew remained in the air. Josh was on his gray Appaloosa mare, and I was on mine, which was almost black with white spots on the hindquarters. The two pack horses trailed behind on a lead rope.

As the road gained altitude with the creek, it opened onto a trail between sage-covered hills, becoming drier as the canyon widened and finally ascended into the upper meadow where the plane had been. By the time the sun touched us, we were on the steep long trail out of the meadow up to the top of Bear Ridge. We would follow that trail until White Rock Ridge heading west intersected it and would ride along that until we descended into Wildcat Creek, which flowed to the ocean.

The heat and the moisture in California change quickly as you leave the coast, and the vegetation changes with them. There have been summer days when I've driven in-land from Monterey wearing a sweatshirt in sixty-degree fog, using the windshield wipers in the mist. Then, a half-hour later, after driving up the winding road past the dam and the reservoir in the valley, I've gotten out of the truck at our house in ninety-degree heat. As hot as it gets during the day in these hills, the effect of the ocean almost always drifts inland in the evenings.

We rode down the dry ridge with spindly sharp manzanita and flat tilted rocks on either side of us, the Pacific Ocean disappearing in the distance. The ocean was smooth and one hue darker than the sky, and the two merged without a clear boundary on the horizon. As we descended into the valley, we stopped to let the horses drink at Wildcat Creek. The shade felt good after the dry heat. As we continued down Wildcat Creek toward the ocean, bay trees, oaks, and sycamores gave way to ferns and occasional redwood trees. Then it got cooler, and we were among the giants. The horse's hooves were silent on the soft loam created by years of dropped needles. Coast red-woods can grow huge. I had seen a few in my time logging in Northern California that were twenty-five-feet in diam-eter, but mostly they're like a high school basketball team: tall, growing upward fast and thin.

After traveling through the redwoods for a couple miles, we started up out of the valley to intersect with one of the creeks that ran parallel to the coast along the moun-tain range. It was a steep climb, with switchbacks taking us away from the cool of the redwoods and back onto a sunbaked ridge of scrub and thorns. We paused at the top, giving the horses a break, breathing in the pleasant smell of horse sweat and leather in the heat. I pointed with my chin toward the north. "There's a guy on horseback coming down the trail from White Rock Ridge to Wildcat Creek, the one we were on earlier."

"Do you recognize the horse?"

"Nah. The guy doesn't seem to be in a hurry, either."

Riding horseback doesn't take a lot of thinking. Except for an occasional nudge, the horse finds its own way on a trail. The sound of the hooves on the ground and the subtle rocking of the saddle as the horse walks make a rhythm that creates a space for thoughts to wander in and out of your mind at their own pace. After a while, Josh spoke up. "Dad, I keep thinking about the pilot."

"Makes you pause, doesn't it?" I was silent for a couple of moments, then asked, "What are you thinking about?"

"It seemed so sudden. One moment he was talking to us, and the next he was coughing blood. Then he was gone."

We rode on in the heat for a while, then Josh said, "It could happen to anybody. I know people die, but somehow it didn't seem real to me before. It was only a concept. This was real. It was right there where I couldn't miss it. Suddenly, I imagined something happening to you guys or to me. It's kind of overwhelming."

I turned to look at him. "Scary?"

"No, not that. More like...big. I never thought about me or you guys starting or ending, you know? I just was, without thinking about what that meant. And you guys seem invincible. Since the plane crash, I started realizing that we're not here for a long time. I've lived a fifth of my life already. It changed my perspective."

I paused before answering. Not talking had worked the night before, so I didn't say much. "What's changed for you?"

Josh took off his cap and wiped his forehead before settling the hat back on his head. "It makes me think about what I'm doing. If I could be gone as quick as the pilot was, it would have been awful to have spent the time before it doing something I hated or something useless."

I looked over at a ground squirrel popping his head out of his hole ahead of us. "So, what's the answer?"

"I don't know." He looked over at me. "This is the first time I've ever really thought about dying. It would probably be good to remember the pilot every so often and see if I would regret what I was doing before I died in a plane crash."

I nodded and swatted at a fly. "It might help you do what's important to you earlier rather than putting it off."

"Yeah, or at least closer to what's important."

The conversation drifted away, back into the creak of our saddles and the tang of sage in the afternoon sun. I stared up at a rocky crag standing against the clear sky and felt satisfied. This week was going to be good.

We stopped for the night because we found a nice campsite on a flat spot above Carrizo Creek. Oak trees surrounded a ring of blackened stones for a fire, and there was grass for the horses nearby. After setting up camp, we took our fishing rods out to the creek.

Josh razzed me for getting my first back cast caught in a tree. "Ever eat a pine tree? Many parts are edible." He sounded like Euell Gibbons in the Grape Nuts commercial.

I liked him teasing me like that, like we could be friends instead of just parent and kid.

We worked upstream, taking turns casting, not caring much if we caught anything. We were just enjoying the afternoon sunlight filtering through the trees onto the creek and the sound of water running over rocks. I caught a brook trout and let him go. Then Josh caught one, then nothing for a while. We heard water splashing ahead and came up to a small waterfall. We worked around the edge of the pool above it, casting and retrieving our lines. We slowed as we approached the top where the stream dropped over some rocks and created bubbles in the pond, knowing it was a prime spot for a bigger fish. Josh cast where the stream entered the pool under some overhanging trees. The water stayed still. I dropped my fly behind a log with a rivulet above it, and a fish jumped out of the water to take it. The color on its side told me it was a big rainbow trout. I let it have its way as it ran across the pool. It headed back toward us, and I pulled in line as fast as I could. When it turned to go across the pool again, I applied more pressure to the line. After the fish made a few more runs across the pond, I brought it to the shore.

"It might be a steelhead," Josh said.

I wet my hand and clasped it around the widest part of the fish. "Hard to tell. Could be a big rainbow. He got beat up though, like he hit a snag when he was running." As I took the hook out, I saw that one of his eyes was damaged. "Hmm. Guess we ought to keep it for supper, huh?" We cleaned the fish on the bank of the stream below the pool, then walked back to camp in the waning daylight, breathing deeply the early evening moisture in the air.

As we entered the clearing, the man we had seen earlier came around the trees at the end of the meadow. "Hello, the camp!" he yelled as he rode up on his horse. He was a big man, about forty, with light brown hair. He was good-looking in a salesman type of way—handsome, but not so much that it was what you noticed first. I thought I knew him from somewhere. "Looks like you caught something," he said.

I held up the fish for him to see. "Yeah, Josh thinks it's a steelhead, but I think it's a big rainbow trout. It hurt its eye when we caught it, so we decided to cook it up." I turned to put the fish down on some leaves by the fire area. "You going far?"

"I think I'm done for the day. You mind if I camp here?"

"Make yourself at home," I said over my shoulder. "We'll share the fish with you, whatever it is." There was something about his voice that made me look again as he was getting off his horse. The blonde hair could have darkened, and the frame was about right, if a little heavier. "Are you Russ?"

He turned around and stared at me for a moment. "Van? Van!" Then he smiled. For a moment, his face looked like the kid I played with in the cave by his uncle's mine a long time ago. "How're you doing? I haven't seen you since Eureka." He stalked over to me, shaking the stiffness from riding all day out of his legs. We shook hands, then he grabbed me in a bear hug. "Damn, it's good to see you! We lost contact there."

"Yeah, you kind of disappeared. We were one short in the kitchen poker games, and I had to win sometimes since you weren't there to do the honors."

He squinted, and his smile got lopsided. "Yeah, that. I kind of went on an extended vacation about that time."

I raised my eyebrows. He nodded and looked down. "I got wrapped up in some stuff I shouldn't have. I was kind of hanging around the edges of it, but that was enough to get me sent away for a couple years." He flashed a big smile. "But we're camping, and you're here with your boy. Let's not talk about that other stuff."

I nodded at Josh. "This is Josh. My other son, Nate, is at home with a bum foot." I put my hand on my son's shoulder. "Josh, I knew Russ when we were kids, when both of us were hanging around in these hills. I saw him again up in Northern California when I was a lumberjack there, just before I met your mom."

Russ smiled at the memory, but to Josh, he only said, "We had some adventures."

I held out my hand, and he gave me his saddlebags. "How's Corey?"

Russ grabbed his rifle and the saddle and walked toward a flat spot near an oak tree. As he walked, he kept talking. "He's doing good. Corey decided he needed some discipline in his life, so he joined the Navy. He's still there. He's married and has a couple of kids and runs the warehouses at the base down in San Diego. He's settled down." He looked around the clearing and stretched his back.

"Are you married? Kids?" I tried to imagine him with a bunch of towheaded boys running around a suburban yard.

"No, I never found the right person for me. I'm in Monterey." He took a huge drink from his canteen. "You guys out for a while?"

"Four or five days. Maybe a week. We don't have any real schedule. You?"

"I've already been out a couple of days." He waved his hand back the way he had come from. "Haven't covered much territory, though. I've just been enjoying the quiet. Man, two kids. Up until recently, I was taking care of my little brother too. Wife?"

I put his bags next to a log and looked at him again. It had been a while, and I was glad to see him. "I'm married, and we have a little place up above Carmel Valley with some horses." I pointed toward his horse. "Why don't you get settled in and we'll catch up some more while we're sitting down?" I was glad it was Russ instead of a stranger, but I wondered how him being there would affect Josh and my bonding time.

Chapter Seven

RUSS

I met Russ when I was ten or so and we were still living in the cabin in the redwoods. Dad was away in the war. I was out hunting one day, sitting with my back against a tree and my thoughts drifting amiably through the cool morning stillness when two boys crashed into the clearing. They both had blond hair cut close to their heads, and the hair was choppy. I recognized that haircut. It meant their dad did it outside with their shirts off. He would have scuffed it roughly after he was done with one and turned to the other and said, "Your turn. Get up here." The older one was in the lead. He had baby fat on him. Though he was taller, he seemed soft. The younger boy was wiry and about my age.

I stayed in the shadows, silent and unmoving, watching as the boys tramped along the deer trail with their pants cuffs wet from the dew. Oblivious. I watched them as if I was still hunting. Because I was a kid living in the woods with his mom, I was excited about the prospect of kids my age in the area. But as a hunter, I was mad because there had still been a chance that a deer would show up. Part of me was still thinking about hunting. Halfway across the clearing, they stopped to watch a squirrel in a tree. It was a perfect shot. The bigger boy was turned partly away from me and was behind the smaller one. I could see the sweet spot below his shoulder. If they were deer, could I make a second shot? It would probably be a running shot. Possibly, the smaller one wouldn't know what had happened until I had a chance to lever a second round into the chamber, but more likely, it would run. I decided I could have gotten them both.

I stood up and stepped out into the sunlight. I was apprehensive. I didn't know other kids. Sometimes, if I went with Tom and Cindy or Mom to Monterey, we would visit someone and they would have children. But I didn't go to school, and there weren't any kids in our valley, so I'd really never had the chance to know what kids did.

They turned away from the squirrel and still didn't see me, even though they were looking in my direction. I waved my arm so they would spot me. They startled, like deer. We met in the middle of the clearing in the warmth of the morning sun, standing stiffly, untrusting, them shading their eyes. The big one spoke up. "Where did you come from?"

I inclined my head toward the west. "Down near the ocean. How about you?"

He pointed up the hill. "We're visiting our uncle for the summer, up at the mine."

I had seen the mine before. It was maybe a quarter-mile uphill from where we were, where the trees thinned out. The time I had been there, I'd seen a bunch of steel buildings with a house off to the side, up just below where the rocks got steep. I usually stayed lower, in the redwoods. "I'm Van. What're your names?"

The older one spat off to the side. "I'm Corey." He poked the littler one on the arm. "This is my brother, Russ."

"Our mom sent us up here for the summer." Russ scratched what looked like poison oak on his arm. "She said she needed some time to herself."

"I think she wanted more time alone with her boyfriend." Corey kicked at a clump of dry grass, then reached down and pulled it out and threw it against a tree trunk.

They both had rubber-soled canvas shoes on that wouldn't last long in the woods. The canvas used to be white. "My dad's gone in the war," I said. "He's on a ship in the Pacific. I haven't seen him in a while." That was bragging, but that's all I could think of.

Corey stuck his hands in his pockets and shrugged. "Our dad left us a long time ago, when we were just kids."

I thought it must have been their uncle who gave them the haircuts, then, or maybe their mom's boyfriend. "Is your dad in the war now?"

"No." Corey shook his head and looked down. "He died in a train accident."

"Like a train crash?"

He frowned, then continued. "No, He tried to catch a freight car and missed. He fell under the wheels. We got his belongings sent back to us in a big yellow envelope. No money, though, and no pictures of us or our mom."

Corey was gawking at my gun, and I could tell he wanted to ask about it, but it was Russ who spoke up. "Is that yours?"

"It's my dad's. Since he's away, I'm using it."

Russ squinted. "Do you hunt with it?"

"I was hunting just now, until you guys scared the deer away." They glanced at each other.

Russ' eyes got bright. "We know where there's black widows. We catch them and put them in jars. Want to see?"

They seemed all right. Maybe we could be friends. "Up at the mine?"

"Behind it," Russ said. "There's a chalk wall there. They live in the cracks. We'll show you."

I followed them up the hill, out of the trees, and across the scrub and grass to the mine. The mine buildings were at the top of an open meadow. Abandoned machinery rusted in the field below. A large wheel with a cable on it rose on a steel tower above what must have been above the opening of the mine. Corrugated steel buildings rusted red enclosed the bottom of the tower. At the far end of the clearing, a small unpainted house squatted near pine trees. A truck was parked in front. Nobody was out. Maybe they were all in the mine.

We walked over to a shed by one of the buildings, and they showed me the jars with black widows in them. Then we went out behind the mine where a crumbling limestone cliff rose. Corey and Russ showed me how, when they pulled pieces of the rock out, they could find spiders in their dark homes and coax them with a stick into a jar. I always thought black widows had orange hourglasses on their backs and was surprised that they were calling these shiny, bulbous spiders black widows. I'm not a fan of spiders, but they were pretty bugs, and I felt a little sorry for them, being jolted from their comfortable, dark hiding places and put in a jar. When I asked about the markings, Corey held a jar up so I could see the belly of one of the spiders, and there it was, the hourglass. It wasn't as good of a warning system as I had thought it would be. You had to be able to see the bottom of the spider to see it, and by then you would be too close. I didn't help them catch any.

When I was leaving, Russ yelled after me, "If you come back, we'll show you the Indian gold cave."

That made me turn around. I thought of Bobby's map. "What's that?"

"We'll take you there when you come the next time."

I raised my chin toward him. "Okay, I'll head back up here in a few days."

I couldn't wait a few days. That night, I grabbed *Moby Dick* off the shelf and pored over Dad's copy of Bobby's map. The Spanish cave on the side of the hill marked on the map could be up near Corey and Russ's uncle's mine. Corey and Russ could have found the gold Bobby and Dad were searching for. I imagined sitting in the cave with them, pouring gold coins over our heads like water, then filling my pack and hiking back down the hill to our cabin and spilling them out on the table in front of Mom. She would be amazed. We could even send some to Bobby in Chicago.

The next day, when I knocked on the door of the little house by the mine, Russ answered. He wanted to practice shooting before we went up to the cave. I had my rifle with me, and Russ said he could borrow one from his uncle. Both rifles used the same cartridges, and his uncle had boxes of them stacked on a shelf in the pantry, so we could shoot as much as we wanted. Russ had only shot a gun a few times before, and I had to show him the skills my dad had taught me. But he had a natural eye, and he was able to hit most of the targets we set up by the time I mentioned the cave again. "I want to keep practicing until I can shoot as well as you," he said as he sighted on a can and missed. "Then I want you to show me how to hunt."

I hit a can, and it flew back against the tree behind it. "You should knock off another one, then let your body get used to what you just learned. My dad taught me that. You stop right after you do it right, and then you sleep on it. The next day you do it more naturally."

When we went back to the house to put the gun away, Corey came out and said, "Let's go to the Indian Gold Cave."

"Why do you call it that?" I asked as we started up the trail behind their house.

"We found an arrowhead right outside the entrance. Probably the Indians were hunting and digging for gold."

The night before, I had fantasized about the treasure in the cave. I imagined stalactites dripping from the ceiling as we slipped down steep slime covered slopes into the depths of a limestone abyss that had been carved over the millennium by rushing water. We would have to go deep into the darkness of the earth. We would find a chest of gold coins and jewels guarded by a skeleton holding a sword with the bones of his hands. We would emerge from the cave triumphant and would share the treasure with everyone we knew, but still there would be enough that we would be rich.

When we arrived at the cave entrance, all I could see was an opening that had been dug out of the sandstone of the hillside. At first, I thought Russ and Corey had dug it.

We had to crawl on our hands and knees to get in. It didn't go too far back, maybe fifteen feet, so I saw the whole dirt tunnel in just a few minutes. There were no stalactites or treasure chests or grinning skeletons, just dry sandstone and dust, left by somebody a long time ago giving up digging.

Russ wanted to play a game of make-believe where we were settlers hiding from an Indian attack. I started to go along with it, but Corey said that he was bored and that we were being babies playing silly games, and he left. I kept playing with Russ. He was fun do things with, but I had to stop wrestling with him because he took it too seriously. One day, he got me in a chokehold that he held a little too long and a lot too tight, and I thought I would pass out. Most of the time, though, I was just happy to have someone to hang around with.

We fell into a rhythm that summer. Every couple of days, between hunting and working in the wood shop with Ed, our neighbor, I would head up to the mine. Russ and I would practice shooting some days. He got good fast. He was a better shot than me if he had a lot of time to set up the shot and to lean against a tree or a rock. I was better than him when we were shooting quicker or from a crouching or standing position. I started showing him how to hunt, but he didn't like to get up early, so he didn't have much chance to see any animals. He got pretty good at tracking, though. Other days, we would go up to the cave and play make-believe. It was hot on the hills in the afternoons, but the cave was cool. So, we would lie down in the shade inside the entrance and make cities out of rocks and attack them with cannons and catapults we made from sticks.

One day in early August, hot Diablo winds were howling from the east. Usually, cool breezes flowed gently from the ocean in the west. On a few hot, dry days in late summer or fall, the Diablo winds arrived, and with them came the danger of fires that moved with the wind as fast as a man could run. When this happened, the grownups got worried about fires, and everyone was grumpy. Russ and I were hiding from the wind and the heat by lying in the cool of the mouth of the cave. Russ took his shoes off because they were getting too small for him.

"I think you're getting too big, not the other way around," I said.

He tossed a rock at me. "Shut up."

We were playing a game where we pretended to be kings of the city we had built from sticks and rocks. In our game, we had to destroy our city because the people in it were disobeying us. Russ was about to roll a boulder down the hill from our castle to punish them when the hillside shook. The earth jolted left then back right again. Our city fell over. Loose rocks tumbled down onto our heads. Dust filled the air. Russ yelled, "Earthquake! Get inside the cave. The rocks are coming down the hill!"

I grabbed his wrist. "No! Outside!" I pulled him out into the stones and pebbles raining down from above. We slid down the hill, covering our heads in case a big rock came down. Then the earth tilted. The first jolt had been left and right, quickly, like shaking your hand to get a fly off it. The second jolt rolled like the back of a cat stretching. The earth rose before us in a wave, then the wave came toward us, lifting us on its arching back while in front of us it lowered again. We cowered at the bottom of the hill behind a tree, covering our heads and faces as rocks rolled over us from above. The rumbling went on for a long time. It was probably less than a minute, but with the earth rising and falling and shaking around us, it felt like forever. Birds flew into the air. Down below, the dogs were barking.

Afterward, it was eerily quiet and still. The winds had stopped. Clouds of dust hung in the air as if a convoy of trucks had passed on a dirt road on a windless day. I looked Russ over to see if he was okay. He was covered in dust and his eyes were wide with fright. "My shoes are in the cave," he said.

We climbed the hill to the cave. It wasn't there. The entrance that had been a frowning mouth gaping open in the face of the hillside was now a stern scowl, lips pulled tight and thin. The hole, dug out of the dirt and rocks, that had seemed so solid minutes before had collapsed.

"We were going to hide in there," Russ said.

"Yeah. I know. We would be flat."

Russ shook his head. "We should go see if everyone else is okay. We should let them know where we are."

Russ picked his way down the hill in his socks. After a while, I gave him one of my shoes, then we switched feet halfway to his house so each of our feet only hurt a bit. Diablo winds and collapsing caves: We had survived them both this time. But the winds came every year, and the earth moves all the time in California.

Chapter Eight

GLENMORANGIE

Josh started the campfire while Russ got his tent out. There was a grate by the rocks that we could use to cook the fish. We were pulling out food when Russ walked over carrying a can with a yellow label, a bottle of whiskey with a red label, and a dry salami. "I thought I would contribute a bit. Priorities, though. Anyone want a nip of single malt before dinner?"

"Yes, sir!" I held out my cup. I told Josh he could have some too if he sipped it slowly.

Russ held up the can, showing us the label with a picture of peaches in syrup. "That's for dessert." He cut a piece off the salami and handed it to Josh. "Appetizer." Then he cut some for me. "So, Van and Josh. What are your plans back here?"

I took a sip from the tin cup I always carried with me on camping trips. "We're out for a father-son camping trip while the weather is so hot. Josh is going into his last year in high school, and we might not get too many more chances for time together. What are you up to?"

Russ took a healthy slug of the whiskey—much healthier than mine—and then held up the bottle ceremoniously. "Glenmorangie Scotch Whiskey. It's so smooth. I always take it out camping with me. You can sip it with anything." He took another big slug and rolled it around in his mouth. "I'm just camping, too. No real agenda. I thought I might head down toward the mine where we hung out that summer. It's abandoned now. It might be fun to see what's there."

We ate salami and bread while cooking the trout over the fire, sipping whiskey and telling stories. Russ told good stories, and they got more interesting with more whiskey. It seemed that Russ had been a lot of places. A lot had happened to him, and he loved to talk about all of it. He reminded me of a guy I knew in the lumber camp who wove a long story about what had happened to him that weekend. Just as he finished, another man walked up to the campfire where we were sitting, heard the end of the story, and wanted to hear the beginning. The guy begged off, saying that everyone had already heard it. I remember saying, "Tell it to us again. It'll be better the second time." And it was. That was Russ. He made even the most mundane stories interesting. The way Russ drank, I was pretty sure there were more bottles of whiskey in his saddlebags.

When Russ asked Josh what his plans were for after high school, Josh thought for a moment before answering. "I'm not sure. People think they know what I should do, and I keep telling them what's right for them isn't what's right for me." I had done a good job of not telling Josh what I thought he should do that afternoon, so I kept quiet. "But I haven't figured out where I want to go yet. I want to make a difference and care about what I'm doing, not learn what someone else is telling me I should be learning. But what if I never find out for myself and realize I should have listened to someone else?"

Russ sat contemplating for a moment, nodding his head. He took another sip of whiskey and said, "I think that's what makes life worth living. If you can follow the path of what you care about, you'll have a full life. Never let someone else tell you what's important in your life."

Josh leaned forward. "Okay, I know listening to other people's dreams is boring, but I have to tell you one I had last week. It seemed like it had a message about following your own path. You want to hear it?"

Russ shrugged his shoulders. "We don't have much else to do, so go on ahead."

"I dreamed I was in a wooden boat, like a big rowboat, way up in the jungle in the Amazon with three or four other people, going down a river. We came down to a waterfall—a huge one, like Victoria Falls. I could see the edge of the waterfall with the river disappearing over it and the land further out, way down below." Josh stood up by the fire and paddled, as if he was in the dream. "We were all paddling backward as fast as we could to try to not go over, but the current was too strong. We were pulled over the edge, and then my dream jumped. I was on the shore below the waterfall and the debris from our boat was around me, and my buddies were washing up on the shore, drowned. I was the only survivor." He looked at us across the campfire.

"What happened next?" I wondered if the dream had something to do with feeling alone, maybe abandoned, after what he had told us earlier in the week.

"I started hiking through the jungle, heading in the direction I thought would bring me to civilization. Voices kept coming out of the jungle telling me where to turn." He looked into the night, as if the Amazon wilderness was all around him. "But I kept telling myself to make my own decisions, and to head where I thought was right. Every time I came to a choice in the dark of the trees, with the voices telling me from all directions where to go, I would say to myself, *Trust yourself; keep moving.*" He sat back down and took a sip of his whiskey. I tried not to notice.

"It became like a mantra. I hiked through the jungle for what seemed like weeks in that dream. I was slipping on muddy roots and getting caught in vines hanging from trees and crossing rivers with crocodiles in them." He paused and looked at Russ, then at me. His voice got softer. "The whole time I kept saying over and over again, *Trust yourself; keep moving.* I came to a clearing, and I saw buildings on a hill rising over the trees ahead. I knew I had made it out. Then, at the end of the clearing was a dark-haired Amazon woman. She was tall, with a bow over her shoulder. Dressed in leather. As I came nearer, she said to me as she stared into my eyes, 'I'm telling you this story because you need direction. Trust yourself; keep moving.' Then she walked past me and into the jungle."

I was sure the dream was about the direction his life was taking. He and the Amazon woman walked past each other. It seemed symbolic. Then Russ said, "'I'm telling you this story because you need direction.' A guy down in Mexico once said that to me." Russ opened the can of peaches and passed it to me. "I'll tell you what he said." He took a deep breath, as though it was going to be a long story and he had to prepare for it. "I was outside La Paz, way down on the tip of Baja on the Gulf of California, in México. La Paz isn't like the border towns. It's in a corner of a crescent moon bay, like Monterey, but the bay is twice as big as Monterey Bay, and there's an island out in the middle. Nothing was happening except for fishing boats going out and coming back in. It was June, and it was humid. I was sitting at a bar, sweating under a roof made of palm leaves, daydreaming as I gazed at the ocean, hoping for a breeze. I had just finished a snapper, pan-fried in garlic and butter, whole, with the eye staring at me as I ate it. That may have been the best fish I ever had until this one you all caught today."

Russ poked the fire with a stick. A few sparks rose, then he added the stick to the coals and flames rose from it. "There was an older guy who had been sitting at a table out by the edge of the bar the whole time I was there. The remains of a snapper were in front of him too. He was like a lot of the guys who leave the states to live down there all the time—too tanned and too well fed. He had that puffiness from drinking too much for too long. I passed by his table on the way back from the bathroom, and he waved at me and pointed toward the bones on his plate. 'Best snapper in the world, don't you think?' he says.

"I turned toward him, smiled, and said something like, 'If they served it with an air conditioner, it would be perfect.'

"So, he says, 'You know why I sit at this table over here in the corner? It's because it always gets a breeze at this time of day, if there's any moving at all. I can feel the start of a draft on my back now. Why don't you bring your beer over and share the wind?'

"So, I got a couple more beers from the bartender and brought them over to the table. We talked a while about fishing, then he said, 'I'm gonna tell you a story. It's a cold story and we need cold stories today.' But it wasn't just a cold story. It seemed to be about me, telling me what to do next, telling me how to deal with my stepdad."

I looked over at Josh. His eyes were fixed on Russ as he continued. "This guy in the bar was out in the Yukon with his dog sled, tending his trap line on a dry day in late winter, early spring. They came around a bend, and there, blocking the trail, was a huge grizzly bear. The dogs were snarling at the bear and trying to get at it. He had the brake on, waiting for the bear to decide to turn the other way and leave them alone, but the old grizz must have been in a bad mood or woke up hungry because it waded into the dogs, tearing at them and knocking them aside. He had taken his rifle off the sled when the bear appeared, so when the bear started for the lead dog, he shot it. But it just kept coming. It swiped at his head with its paw, ripping his scalp open and knocking him out." Russ looked wide-eyed at me, then at Josh.

"When he came to, the bear was standing over him and the dogs were quiet. He stayed still, with its breath on his face. The bear snuffled breaths in and snorted out snot and foul-smelling anger. It swatted at him again and turned away and disappeared into the bushes, huffing as it went. He didn't move until he couldn't hear the bear anymore, then he went to see what he could do for the dogs. The bear had ripped them apart, and if they weren't dead, they were dying. So, he put together a backpack. He knew he had a trek in front of him—three days or so—but he was happy to be alive. After an hour or so of walking, he was on a trail beside a cliff when the bear came charging out of the bushes at him. He dropped to the ground before it hit him, and the bear's momentum kept it going past him over the cliff. He watched it lose its footing and bounce down the cliff from rock to rock and hit a tree. The bear didn't move, and he thought it might be dead, so he started walking again. As he hiked, he kept thinking he heard something behind him, and thought it was the bear, though he never saw anything."

Sitting by the fire sipping whiskey with my son and Russ, I looked up into the sky and felt deeply peaceful. Russ's story was going on, and I didn't know what it meant, but it didn't matter. I was enjoying it all. I might have missed part of the story as my mind wandered, but I caught back on fast enough.

"That night, the man climbed up a tree and settled into a spot about twenty feet up where three or four limbs came together in a cradle. He tried to sleep, but he spent the night shivering. The next morning, when it got light, he saw huge grizzly bear footprints around the base of the tree. He walked all the next day thinking something was behind him. Again, in the morning, there were footprints at the base of the tree he had climbed. The bear wasn't giving up.

"When he got back to people and houses, he slept in the warmth of a cabin with the door barred, but he woke up during the night dreaming that the bear was snuffling at his head again. He smelled its breath on his face and felt its anger inside his head.

"He said he had that dream a lot over the years. He told me that the bear was still following him in his dreams, and he didn't think it was ever going to give up until he killed it. Then, get this. He said, 'That's my story. I think it might help you.' Just like your beautiful Amazon lady."

I was a little puzzled. Russ had said the story was about him and his stepdad, but I couldn't see it. "You said the story was about you and your stepdad. Who's the bear?"

He didn't answer directly. Instead, he started what seemed like a reminiscence. "That man's a real piece of work. He married my mom when I was fifteen. He brought his kid with him, too. Stevie. When he drank, he would whack the kid or my mom, whoever got in his way." He held up his cup. "He's a whiskey drinker. I guess that's where I got the appetite, stealing from his bottles. He didn't drink good booze like this, though. He was a volume drinker. Whatever was cheap and plentiful was his poison of choice." He stared into the dark for a moment, and said, "Maybe another time. I'm still thinking about that one."

As the fire was about to burn out, I kicked Josh and nodded toward the tent. Then Russ started a new story. "The kid, Stevie, was a weird guy. Even after he grew up. He was younger, five or six years younger than me. He was super smart, but he didn't take care of himself very well, and he didn't like to leave his room. My stepdad left my mom right about when I graduated from high school, and he left Stevie behind with us. Stevie and my mom got into a routine after his dad left. She made him food and reminded him to shower every so often, and he didn't go much of anywhere. Mom passed away last year, and Stevie came to live in my spare bedroom. The only place he ever went was to the library, or to somewhere to follow up on one of the crazy theories he had.

"Earlier this summer, he got a burst of energy. He wanted to go to the Mojave Desert to find a lost mine he had researched. Remember now, this guy doesn't leave his room. I told him it was too hot, but he said he wanted to do it. He had read up on it and convinced himself he could find it."

The words *lost mine* caught my attention. Was Russ's stepbrother researching the same mine Bobby had been? Was that why Russ was out here? What about his stepfather? I listened more closely. I wasn't sure how I felt about Russ. I had liked him as a kid, and again in Eureka, and now he was good company to sit around a campfire with. But there was an edge to him, like he could decide without warning to do something, and we would be dragged into it with him. I couldn't quite relax.

Russ continued. "I decided I had to go with him. We parked the car and hiked into the desert early in the morning, looking for a lost mine. He kept getting more excited, saying how we were on the right track. We hiked all morning among the cholla and the small spiny yuccas. When it got to midday, I made us stop and get under shade of a small pine tree to wait until it cooled down because it was over a hundred degrees. I fell asleep, and when I woke up, he wasn't around. He had gone up one of the canyons while I was napping. The problem was there were three or four he might have gone up and I couldn't tell which one. He had taken most of the water, so I thought he would be okay for a while. I started yelling and searching, but there were too many directions he could have gone. After a while, I was overheating, and my water was just about gone. So, I left to get help. Almost didn't make it." He shook his head, like he was back there baking in the sun. "For a while I was so tired, I lay down in the shade of a bush to sleep for a moment. I remember I was dreaming of playing in a cool stream. When I woke up, the sun was directly on me. I almost didn't wake up in time.

"They didn't find Stevie until the next afternoon. He had gone almost three miles up a canyon. He was curled up as if he were asleep next to a rock, just like I had been." He took a deep breath and exhaled slowly. "I couldn't save him when it counted. He drove me nuts, but I miss him."

Josh looked puzzled. "Stevie died out in the desert?"

"Yeah. I almost did too. But he was up the canyon in the heat, and I feel responsible."

"What about your stepdad? Stevie's dad?" I asked.

Russ shrugged. "I couldn't find him. Stevie knew how to find him, but he hadn't told me. I knew he kept his plane out at the airport in Monterey, but that was all. He showed up at my house later, though, just a while back. Not a nice person."

We all sat in silence for a couple of minutes, then Russ spoke up again. "Hey, you guys look beat. I think I'll sit by the fire for a while longer. I'll make sure it's out before I turn in."

Josh and I exchanged glances over the fire. Russ's stepbrother was looking for hidden gold, and he died out in the desert with Russ. It sounded like an accident, but it still made me wonder.

Chapter Nine

CONDORS

J osh and I were up at first light. We had our horses packed up with everything but the coffeepot when Russ emerged from his tent, rubbing his eyes and coughing in the morning light. I pointed toward the fire. "You want some coffee? We left the pot for last in case you decided to show yourself."

Russ stretched. "Coffee sounds great."

I tightened the cinch on our horses. "Want to ride along with us for a while?"

"No, I'm not moving too fast this morning. Besides, I want to get down to the old mine site. I haven't been there since we were kids that summer." He emptied the last of the coffee into his cup and handed me the pot. "I think about that sometimes. You and I almost died in that earthquake in the Indian cave. One moment one way or the other, you know?"

"I know. That cave seemed so solid too."

We said our goodbyes and rode up the trail, leaving him sitting by the fire.

Josh and I stopped for lunch in the shade with the creek murmuring beside us. Toward afternoon, we rode up switchbacks through a low pass and wove our way down into a shallow flat valley of dry, golden-brown grass dotted with dark green oak trees, their branches sometimes touching the ground.

As we rode down the slope into the valley, we saw turkey vultures soaring and landing behind a spreading oak near the center of the valley. "Something dead over there," Josh said. "Might be a deer." We watched with interest as the birds gathered. When we rounded the corner and could see what was on the ground, Josh said, "That's why they call them turkey vultures." The birds on the ground looked like wild turkeys standing around a carcass. "Looks like a deer from here."

When we got within a hundred yards of the vultures, most of them rose into the air. The rest hopped away, hissing and grunting. At first, I thought we had scared them, but then we saw two huge birds, twice as big as the turkey vultures, gliding toward the carcass like B-52s. As they flared their wings to land, we saw their white undersides. "Condors!" I said to Josh. "Man, look at the size of them. I've never seen one in the wild before. I thought they were only further south." We watched for a minute, then kept riding.

I stopped when we were just past the carcass and turned to look back at it. Something wasn't right. Its legs were splayed at an odd angle. "Hang on, Josh." I turned my horse around. "I want to look at something." We rode back up toward the condors. One of them spread his giant wings and started toward us. They weren't giving up their lunch. That was okay. I saw what I needed to see: The deer had been staked out on the ground and skinned alive. I had seen that before, when I was a kid hanging out with Russ and Corey.

I was headed up to visit Russ one morning later that summer we hung out together as kids, and I saw a rabbit that had been cut and maimed. The amount of blood at the cut edges of its fur told me its heart had still been beating when it was sliced open. Its entrails had been taken out in one piece and laid to the side still attached, prolonging the time it lay alive. I stopped looking after that. I had seen enough. I had been seeing small animals tortured like this—rabbits, squirrels, birds—every once in a while that summer. It had started before Corey and Russ showed up.

This wasn't hunting. This was different. I caught animals in snares. I killed rabbits and squirrels. There were times when a snare didn't kill an animal when it caught it, but I always did everything I could to minimize its suffering. I thanked each one for dying so we could live. And we ate them. We didn't leave them in the woods. Whoever was setting these snares was keeping them alive and playing with their deaths, then leaving them after he was done with them. It was a man, or someone with man-size shoes. It worried me, but Dad wasn't around, and I didn't want to discuss it with Mom or Ed, since they might not let me wander by myself if they knew.

When I reached Russ and Corey's cabin, Russ was out on the front step throwing his knife into a board, trying to make it stick. The rabbit was on my mind, so I asked him if he knew anything about it. His face snapped into a snarl. I'd never seen him do that before. "It's practice. Those animals are just practice. After that, it'll be a person. Maybe a little boy." I slid my hand closer to the knife on my belt and backed away.

I took a few more steps back. "I've got some things to do. I'll come back later, okay?" I headed down the hill toward the simplicity of the forest.

I knew it wasn't Russ. The footprints around the torture sites were the same as they had always been. A lone, man-size person was feeding something sick inside himself. But Russ was involved somehow—why else would he have reacted so strangely? Maybe it was his cousin or his uncle. They were hardly ever around when I was there. They were working in the mine or in the ore processing areas, and we weren't allowed near those. Maybe Corey was doing something with his cousin.

After that incident, I figured I ought to steer clear of both Corey and Russ for a while. I stayed away for a week or two, and by the time I went back, Corey and Russ had gone home. I didn't see either of them again until a lot of life had gone by.

Once we were riding again, I told Josh about the tortured animals I'd found when I was a kid. "I didn't think it was Russ or Corey back then because I could tell the person doing it was bigger and older. I always thought it was their cousin, Frank, and Russ confirmed that when I met him in Eureka ten or eleven years later. Maybe Frank's still around. It makes me sick to think that he's been doing that all this time." I pulled the horse's head up from where it was grazing. "We'll have to be aware." The trip had just gotten a lot less relaxing.

After we had ridden a half hour or so, Josh pulled up to let his horse drink where a stream crossed the trail. "Do you think the pilot might be Russ's stepdad?"

I looked down at my horse drinking. I hadn't gotten that far in my pondering, but it made sense. "He could be. I wondered last night about his little brother. I almost said something. His brother sounds like the type of person who would have written all the notes in the toolbox. And his stepdad had an airplane."

Josh had a serious expression on his face. "We should ask him if we see him again."

"You're right." I took a drink from my canteen. "I've been thinking. Russ might not know about the crash since he's been out here this whole week. It's strange that a plane crashes with a clue to a treasure, and then we run into Russ, whose stepbrother might have written the clue. All the parts should come together, but I can't fit them in my mind." As the horses drank, I noticed what I thought might be a shortcut. I shook my head to clear it and pointed to the left. "Let's cut up this valley. There isn't a trail, but people have gone this way. It should take us to the bottom of the high valley below Pinyon Peak."

Following a series of game trails, we made our way up the creek among oaks and California buckeye trees with their round seeds as big as baseballs. They were already dropping their leaves and going dormant for the rest of the dry season. The trees would green up as soon as the rains came, and in the spring would be covered in towers of light pink flowers and bees. On the hillsides above, the poison oak was turning bright red. It grew in great clumps, sometimes climbing the trees to get closer to the sun. As we rode, Josh asked me about what Russ had called his "Extended Vacation." I stopped in a shady spot. "It might have something to do with his poker playing days. When we ran into each other in Eureka, he was still kind of wild." I hadn't thought about those days in a while, but Josh's question brought me back to them—back to the time right before I met Jenny. The days when Al and I were still chopping down redwoods for a living.

Chapter Ten

POKER

I was in the department store in downtown Eureka hunting for new work boots when a hand tapped me on the shoulder. I turned around to see a man my height and age with blond hair. He was built thicker than I was and stronger through the chest, like he lifted weights. I recognized him, but I wasn't sure from where. He stood, grinning, hands on his hips, waiting for the pieces to click together in my mind. "Russ! Man, it's been forever! What're you doing here?"

His smile grew even larger, and he stepped back to look at me. "Wandering. Making money." He slapped me on the arm. "I can't believe you're here in Eureka! I love it. Want to grab a beer?"

I smiled back and nodded. "Yeah. How's Corey?"

"Let's get that beer. I'm thirsty. I'll catch you up on what's been happening."

We walked down the street to the first place that had a beer sign in the window and went inside. We sat down at a table in the corner, and after Russ had downed half his glass in one long gulp and wiped his lips with the back of his hand, he said, "I need to apologize to you. What I said to you about some little kid being strung up next? That was wrong."

I shrugged. "I knew it wasn't you."

He smiled at me like I had given him a gift. "How did you know?"

I almost told him about the size of the footprints and the animals I had seen before they arrived, but I saw the way he was looking at me. His face was asking me for the second part of the gift, and I was holding it in my hands. I gave it to him. "That's not who you are, Russ. You're a better person than that."

His shoulders dropped, and he sat back in his chair. "It was my cousin Frank. He kept saying that to me and threatening to kill me or Corey out in the woods like that, slowly. When you asked about it that day, I just busted out and said to you what he had been telling me. But that kind of screwed things up with you and me." He took another gulp of beer. His glass was almost empty. "You didn't come back, and Corey and I went home the next week. We talked about it, though. We made a promise to each other never to go anywhere alone with Frank." He leaned forward. "We never went back there again. Frank's dad was my mom's brother, so we saw them when they visited our house. Not up there, though. Too weird, you know?"

If Frank was the one doing those things to the animals, I was glad I had stopped going up there. In all the times I had been at the mine that summer, I hadn't met him. "How's Corey?"

Russ pursed his lips. "I'm not sure. He took off as soon as he could because the stepdad's an asshole. He's been away a couple years. I left after I graduated high school. The stepdad was gone by then."

I shelled a peanut and tossed it in my mouth. We were supposed to throw the shells on the floor, but nobody had. I didn't want to start the mess, so I piled them on the table. "What's Corey like?"

"Still soft. He's as tall as me, but people push him around. He's a momma's boy, but he's all right. But boy, can he talk. If he wants you to do something, he'll keep talking at you until he finds the right angle, then he'll hammer on that angle until you start to think it's not such a bad idea, and you go along. He's tougher than he looks, though." Russ reached for a peanut and added the shell to my pile on the table. "How are things with you?"

I shrugged. "Partly total crap and partly pretty good."

He tilted his head. "What's with that?"

"Well, my dad died in the war, and my mom died of cancer last year, so that's the shitty part. Other than that, I'm doing okay." I said it without thinking, but when I stopped to see if it was true, I was surprised that it was. I was doing okay.

His brow furrowed. "Aw man, that's awful."

"Your dad died in the train accident. You know what it's like."

"Yeah. He left us first, and I was so mad at him that I thought he deserved it, you know? I was burning up with anger at him for leaving us, then for going and getting himself killed on top of it all."

"Yeah, I'm kind of mad at my dad for going off to war. I mean, I shouldn't be, but I am, so there it is."

Russ shifted in his seat and ran his hands through his hair. "Here. I'll tell you something that happened to me. Maybe it'll fit with you too. I don't know if you saw it, but when we were kids up at the mine, I was pissed off at everything. When we weren't hanging out, I was heading more toward Frank's way of thinking. I was looking for something to take my anger out on."

He moved his bottle around on the slick table, making wet rings, his head down as he talked. "When we got back home, I was out in the park one day, throwing rocks at squirrels. Then this voice behind me says, 'You need to forgive them.' I turned around, and there was this guy sitting on a bench. He had been watching me. He was missing a leg, from the knee down. He says it again, 'Whoever you're mad at, you need to forgive them.'

"I said in a sarcastic way, 'Did you forgive the people who shot off your leg?' I was in kind of a bad mood, and I didn't mind who I pissed off. He nodded at me and said, 'It might surprise you, but I did.' I asked him how. He said, 'I keep imagining them as people trying their best to make it through with whatever they were dealt. I know that boy who fired the bullet that took off my leg was as scared as me. That made him real to me, and I felt sorry for him, and then I could forgive him. He was just doing what he could do.'"

Russ stared across the bar at the reflection in the mirror of someone coming in the door. I looked too, like there was something to see, then he looked back at me. "After that, when I went home, I imagined my dad scared, with two boys and a wife and not knowing what to do, and I had some sympathy for him. I forgave him partway

for running off on us. But I can't forgive him all the way."
He had been spinning the cardboard beer coaster, and he
knocked it flat on the table. "I would never do what he did
to a kid of mine—up and take off like that."

I went to the bar to get a couple more beers. As I sat
down, I said, "You know, my dad wasn't much older than
me when he went off to war. What kind of decision would
I make in his place?" Russ and I clinked the necks of our
bottles and drank. "I'm not so pissed off at him these days.
I'm madder at fate for all the stuff it's piled on me. How do
you put yourself in God's shoes and forgive him for killing
off your mom?"

Russ raised his eyebrows. "You got a point there. You
can't say that fate's just struggling through every day just
like you are. It's hard to feel sorry for fate."

I drank another swallow, shook my head, and tapped
him on the shoulder to break the moment, "That's some
deep shit we got ourselves into. Think we'll remember any
of it tomorrow?" He laughed and shrugged. I figured it
was a good time to change the subject. "So, what are you
up to around here?"

"Poker." His face lit up. "I'm playing poker and making money at it. And having a good time. Want in on it?"

Ed had showed me how to play poker. He said every guy
should know how to play because everywhere men hang out
there's a poker game, and you don't want to be losing money
when you're passing time and drinking. He taught me the
odds of all the combinations and made me rattle them off
when we were playing against each other. After each hand,
we would dissect the play and talk about whether it had
been smart poker or not. He showed me how people cheat

too, because that's part of the landscape wherever cards are played. He also gave me one piece of advice: "Never try to make money at cards. Play with your buddies and win or lose a little. But if it ever gets to the point where you're betting a significant part of your income, run away."

Thinking about Ed's words, I told Russ I didn't play for real. "I only play for fun. No big money."

"You'll like the game going on tonight, then. It's twenty dollars to buy in, so we're betting nickels, dimes, and quarters. You should try it. It's a good time."

An hour later, we were sitting at the kitchen table of a house just a couple blocks from Eureka's main street. The other players at the table were good, but they played a loose, fun game with a lot of chatter. They seemed to like Russ. I liked them. By the end, Russ had taken most of their money, but they didn't seem to mind. I added ten to my twenty and felt good about that. They invited me back the next week, and I said I'd come. The warm yellow kitchen with cold beers, salty snacks, and easy camaraderie was just what I needed.

A couple of weeks later, as we were leaving that same house, Russ asked me if I would come with him to a bigger game that Thursday night. He explained that it had a hundred dollar buy in. "I don't do that," I said firmly.

He put his hand on my shoulder. "Please. I need a fifth player, and you're good. You won't lose money, I promise."

I stopped in the middle of the sidewalk. It wasn't that cold, but it felt cold with the mist in the air. He stopped too and waited for me to reply. "Look, it's too much money. A hundred dollars is getting dangerously close to what I make in a week. It's too much pressure."

"I'll cover your buy-in. I need you there. I don't know these guys, and I need a friendly face in the room. Please." He put his hands together under his chin, like he was praying.

My eyes narrowed. "You'll cover my buy-in? I don't have to put up any money?"

He nodded a bit too quickly. "Right. Whatever you win, over the buy-in, you keep. If you lose, and you won't, it's on me." He started walking again, as if I had said yes.

I should have said no. Ed had been clear about the rules. But I was coming out ahead almost every time I joined the kitchen games. I could have beaten Russ too, but I played very conservatively and let him have pots I could have taken. I wanted to know if I was good enough to play in a big money game, and Russ was offering me a no-lose way to find out.

That Thursday night, we climbed up a set of dimly lit outside stairs behind a brick building to a steel door. Russ knocked, and we were let in. The atmosphere couldn't have been more different than where we had been playing. The room was dark, with lights over a table in the center. Three guys were standing by a bar in the corner, making drinks. Two of them looked like businessmen, and the third looked like a gambler. The way he rubbed his hands he could have been a kindergarten teacher, and I would still watch him when he shuffled. One of the businessmen was a bit fat, and the other one's shirt was tight around his shoulders and chest, like he lifted weights every day.

As soon as we introduced ourselves and got a couple of beers, the other guys sat down, and we started playing. The one who looked like a gambler, who was confident and moved his eyes around a lot, played like the guys in the kitchen. Maybe he was a kindergarten teacher after all. He took a lot of chances and bluffed when he had nothing in his hand. The fat businessman would only bet when he had a winning hand already made. The weightlifter was the dangerous one. I stayed out for most of the hands or bet small and got out. I was watching. Russ played his usual game. He was aggressive and smart and folded when he was beaten. We started to get into a rhythm. Cards flowed around the table. Money flowed around too. Some of it stopped for a while, then it moved on again.

Later in the game, when Russ had about doubled his money and I had won a few small hands, the kindergarten teacher spilled one of the black Russians he'd been sipping all night. It wasn't much, but it made the deck sticky, so the businessman got up to get a new pack of cards. We wiped and dried the table, and he made a show of working to open the cellophane wrapper on the deck. He handed it to me to cut the cards, and I watched him slip the deck back to its original order after I cut it. I glanced at Russ and tried to catch his eye. He wasn't paying attention to me. So, I leaned in and said, "Guys. I'm getting tired. I need to leave soon."

Russ looked at me then, but he wasn't seeing me. He was staring at me, trying to tell me that he was winning and we had to stay. I gave him a small shake of my head and the businessman started dealing. I heard the sliding sound of a card being dealt from the bottom of the deck on two of the cards I was dealt, so I wasn't surprised when I saw a pair of queens in my hand. The next time around I heard the slip again, and I had a third queen. All I knew was that somebody—not Russ—had been dealt a full house or a flush, and I was supposed to bet big on my three of a kind. It was time to leave. I folded, keeping my head down but noticing who was surprised. The businessman and the kindergarten teacher were surprised. I changed his occupation back to gambler. The weightlifter seemed not to notice.

I got up. "Hey guys, I'm not feeling good. I think we should go. Maybe something I ate. I want to be away from people before my stomach erupts." Russ pleaded with me to stay a few more hands. I told him he was my ride, so he had to come with me. He stared hard at me and seemed to get that I was trying to tell him something, so he got up to leave.

As soon as we got out the door, I turned to Russ and said, "Run!" He followed me down the stairs, around the building, and over to the next street where I had parked the truck. When we arrived, he'd asked why we didn't park next to the building. Now he knew why. We needed to get out of there before those guys came after us. I told him about the false cut and the bottom dealing. "The kindergarten teacher spilled his drink on purpose, Russ." He didn't understand why I was calling him a kindergarten teacher, and I didn't explain. I told him the businessman was working with the kindergarten teacher. I didn't know about the weightlifter, but he seemed innocent. "I'm not going to any more games like that. Too much money." Ed had been right.

When I went back to the kitchen game the following week, Russ wasn't there. The rest of us joked and played loose poker and had a good time. The week after that, Russ came in late, and he was a mess. He pretended that his face wasn't covered with purple bruises, got a beer, and sat down at the table. We all stared at him. "Let me drink this, then I'll explain," he said.

After we counted out the chips and distributed them, Russ started talking. "So, I got invited to a game with a five hundred dollar buy-in. With the money I won the other night, I figured I could swing it. I knew two of the guys who would be there, and they had seemed okay." He picked up a potato chip, chewed it, then got another while we waited. He was enjoying keeping us waiting. "They said they had a new guy from out of town who wanted to play a big game. It went down a lot like the other night with you, Van. One of the guys I had played with before dropped his hand when he reached for his drink, and when he went to try and catch it, he bent one of the cards. The other guy got a new deck and unwrapped it. I figured I could just fold out of a few hands until they didn't know where the cards were. That was my plan, until lady luck stepped in."

"Lady luck?" one of the guys asked. "What happened?"

Russ shook his head. "Just like Van, I got two jacks. I even heard the slipping sound Van talked about. I thought it would be worth it to see them deal me another jack if the pot didn't get too big. Nobody bet much that round, so I waited to see what I got. I heard the sound of the other jack being dealt from the bottom of the deck. And then it happened." He paused for effect, looking around the table. "Without the slipping sound, I got another one. I had four jacks. They thought I had three. I was sure somebody had a straight or a flush. They would keep bidding the pot up, thinking they couldn't lose. I thought about folding, but

I couldn't help myself. I planned my escape route instead. We were on the first floor, and there was a fence behind the building. I could jump over that. I was sure I was faster than any of them. We were playing for cash. I could jam it in my pocket and run."

He looked around the table at us. We waited, silent. "So, I did it. I bet and they raised. I re-raised, and they called. I had four jacks, and the big spender from out of town had a flush. One of the guys I knew, the one that hadn't dealt the cards, had a full house. They were trying to take from both of us—in one hand! Incredible." He shook his head. "Anyway, I gathered the money and stacked it on the table. Then I told them I had to use the bathroom. I picked up the cash, took three steps toward the bathroom, and ran for the door. I got it unlocked and slammed it shut behind me. I was thinking I might make it when I ran face first into a wall. Only, it wasn't a wall; it was a fist. There were two big guys outside, and they hit me a couple of times before the two guys I knew came out. They started kicking me and took all the money back. Then they stood me up, and the two big guys hit me some more." He pointed to his face. "You can see their handiwork."

We played cards that night as usual. One of the guys called Russ "a smooth operator," then someone else said, "Nah, I think we should call him 'Brickwall' from now on!" That one stuck. We shortened it to Brick for a while, then Brickhead, and finally settled back to Brick. He didn't seem to mind that.

A couple weeks afterward, Russ stopped coming to the poker games, and nobody knew where he had gone. But I kept playing cards in the warm yellow kitchen. I was glad I hadn't gone with him to the big game. I was learning to trust my own judgement. I wasn't trusting luck, though. You can get lucky and be dealt the fourth jack, and you can still run into a brick wall.

Chapter Eleven

PINYON PEAK

As the horses picked their way slowly through the brush, and I told Josh about the poker games, it made sense Russ had gotten into trouble and had to take an "extended vacation."

"Brickwall," Josh said, shaking his head. "I have some friends who could use that as a nickname."

"Yeah. Probably best not to bring that up with Russ. He seems like he's comfortable telling us stories, but he might not like me telling them for him."

We were doing exactly what I had wanted to on this camping trip. We were sharing father-son time. It felt like we were finding the rhythm of our relationship again. But going back to how we were wasn't enough. We had to find a way to be comfortable together with Josh's new vision of his life, and we hadn't done that. I hoped we would, and I knew that it was up to me to make it happen. For the moment, though, I was happy we were finding our old selves. Our new ones might grow from that base of trust.

The creek wound up onto a small meadow. As Josh and I rode out into the open, two bearded men with rifles emerged from the brush and blocked our path. "Turn around and go back the way you came," the bigger one said. "This is private property."

Josh drew a breath, like he was going to say something, but I shook my head and he let the air back out. We sat on our horses, silent for a moment, staring at the men. They were in their twenties, one short and one tall, and both with long hair. We knew we were on National Forest land, but when men with guns in their hands tell you it's their land, it's best not to argue. So, I nodded and turned my horse back toward the creek.

When we had gone a little way, Josh stopped in front of me. "What was that about?"

I shrugged my shoulders. "I don't know. I've heard about people growing marijuana way back in the hills like this. That's all I can think of."

Josh spit out a bug that had flown into his mouth. "So much for our shortcut."

I nodded slowly. "Yeah. I guess we'll have to go the long way along the Lost Valley Trail. We weren't sure we could get through that canyon anyway."

The Lost Valley trail was at times narrow and rocky, with manzanita scraping our legs as we passed, and grasshoppers buzzing and flying when we rode by. Other times it dropped down near the creek and we could water the horses.

Josh and I rode into the late afternoon, wanting to get near the high valley below Pinyon Peak before we stopped for the night. Ascending out of the Valley of the Condors, as we called it, the trail wove along the ridgelines and headed away from the ocean. We climbed a steep exposed section with switchbacks crisscrossing the rocky spine of the mountain until we topped out at a steel fire lookout tower on Serra Peak. Rust marks stained its concrete footings which were set among granite boulders that fell away steeply in all directions.

To the west, we could see the Valley of the Condors, then a shorter ridge, and beyond, the Pacific Ocean. It shined silver and gold in the afternoon sun. To the east was a dry valley and Pinyon Peak in the distance. Bobby's map showed the gold mine on the south slope of Pinyon Peak. In the waning daylight, we followed the semicircular route along ridges heading east, then we rode down a long slope into the valley below Pinyon Peak.

A dry camp was all we got that night. We snacked on jerky and nuts and temporarily set up the tent until we could find a better place. We watered the horses and ourselves from jugs we had filled earlier in the day.

After laying out my sleeping bag, I crawled out of the tent and turned around to see Josh sitting on a rock, studying our maps and toolbox papers. He pointed to the east. "The draw on the south side of Pinyon Peak is where the X on the map is. I'm reading the scribbling one more time to look for any more clues that might pop out at me." I left him to it and walked over to hobble the horses in a pasture where they could graze.

When I came back, Josh looked up from the papers. "You and Mom met in Eureka, right? Was that after you were hanging out with Russ? What were you doing up there anyhow?"

He knew a lot of the stuff you tell kids when they're young—the sweet stuff about how we met when she was a waitress in her parents' diner and how we fell in love and got married soon after. I was silent for a while as I thought about what I could tell him now that he was older. What was I doing in Eureka? That story went back to my mom and the bakery, but it really went farther back. It went as far back as my dad and Ed and the war. But first, I'd have to explain to Josh who Ed was.

My parents met Ed when they were looking for a cabin in Big Sur. They had heard that there were abandoned mining cabins deep in a canyon among the redwoods. My mother had grown up on the Menominee Reservation in Wisconsin and loved the stillness of the trees. Though they didn't talk about it much, my folks had left Chicago because people didn't approve of a reservation Indian marrying a white man. They thought it would be better in California, but after a while, they found they felt more comfortable away from the stares that accompanied them whenever they were together in public. They decided to move to a more secluded location. When they inquired about the cabins they had heard of, people said they should ask Ed about them.

Ed was a slow-moving, thin man of fifty or so who always had reading glasses perched on the top of his head. He lived alone in a cabin where the road ended. The canyon above him got steeper, and the trees blocked the sunlight most days. When my parents hiked up to meet him, he told them about the old miner's cabins further up the length of the canyon. "They're in varying states of disrepair," he said, "depending on who was in them last and how handy the miner who built them was."

Ed's cabin was made of split redwood. It sat on a flat open area above the creek, with dark purple and pink hollyhocks growing beside the front steps. The canyon was wider there than it was farther up, and he had built a workshop behind the cabin, where he made furniture from the hardwoods he harvested and cured. "We thought of Ed as just a nice old guy living alone in the redwoods until he showed us his shop," I remember my dad saying. "As soon as we saw it, we realized we were in the presence of an artist." Dad talked about the care Ed took with each piece. Mom said that if you could have hung them on a wall, they would be artwork, but they were also pieces of furniture that you used every day.

Years later, Mom told me about going into his house that day. "He was making a table out of white oak, I remember. I was so taken by the beauty and simplicity of it that I wanted to settle down and live there in the warmth of the workshop. The smell in the air was intoxicating, like bourbon with a hint of vanilla." The dimple on her left cheek appeared as she smiled at the memory. "And, when he took us inside his house, it was like we'd strolled into a cozy, inviting museum. Each piece of furniture was at home in his cabin, but every one had a secret that showed itself to you if you looked. One had a carved area that got more intricate the closer you came. Another had hidden compartments. One had too many feet. You knew there was something different about that one but couldn't figure it out until you examined it closely." Later, I learned that this would be the theme of all Ed's pieces. All of them invited you to get to know them better, and when you did, you invariably found a delight you wouldn't have known about otherwise.

Ed helped Mom and Dad find a cabin a couple hundred yards up the steep side creek, nestled up on the hillside, so it got some sun in the winter when the bottom of the canyon was shaded all day. It had a tin chimney and two glass windows that were still intact. A portly cast-iron stove sat in the corner, which was a miracle because it would have been too heavy for Mom and Dad to carry in. I spent a lot of evenings in the warm embrace of that stove. Sometimes when we were cooking, it warmed the cabin too much, and we had to open the door to let some of the heat out.

That was where Mom learned to bake with sourdough. Tom and Cindy were our neighbors down the creek. Tom's left foot turned inward and had since he was born, so he didn't go to war. He was as capable as if it didn't, and I always thought they were missing out by not taking him. He was the baker in their family. He could tell when the bread was just right by touching it or smelling it, or because it had the right sheen to it. He and Cindy had been bakers when they lived in the city. When they moved to the canyon, they started making big batches of oatmeal raisin cookies every Wednesday and Thursday and driving them up to Monterey on Friday. They made everything with sourdough. There were always buckets and pans of dough sitting around in various parts of their cabin, covered and rising. Others were recovering in the cool of the creek house they had built to act as a refrigerator.

Cindy taught Mom how to make sourdough bread, and after that, sourdough pancakes and muffins. One day, she mentioned that the pail of blackberries she had gathered would be worth more and would survive the trip better if they made them into a pie or a pastry, so she and Mom worked together to get them done in time to go to the city.

One Thursday during the war when Dad was gone and Mom and I were living alone in the cabin, I wandered down the creek past Tom and Cindy's cabin to see if there were any broken cookies for me. There were always a couple. I never questioned why Cindy broke one or two each time she started cooking but never again in all the later batches. Maybe I was lucky that way. I headed on down to Ed's house to check in with him before going out hunting. Ed was in front, glasses on top of his head like usual, about to get in his truck. He reached down to tie his boot, then rolled up the sleeve of his flannel shirt. "Hey Van, want to come with me? I'm going down the coast to get a tree a rancher cut down."

I looked in the back of his pickup. "For furniture?"

He tossed me an apple and picked one out of a bag on the seat for himself. "Yup. He got a hold of me because he had to remove a maple tree to make room for his new barn. He knew I would want good maple wood."

"He's giving it to you?"

"He said it was that or use it for firewood, and I couldn't let that happen."

"If we'll be back before supper, sure. I'll go tell Mom where I'm going and drop off the rifle."

Ed and I drove down the coast on the paved road that had been recently built. Then we turned inland and up a dirt road to a cattle ranch in the hills. When we arrived, the maple logs were stacked at the edge of the cleared area. The rancher used the loader on his tractor to lift the wood into Ed's truck. There were too many logs to take in one load, but the rancher simply shrugged and told us they weren't going anywhere.

Back at Ed's house, when I went inside for a glass of water, I took time to look at the maple cabinet he had made. "These all were once logs like we got today?"

"All of them. I buy some of the wood, but usually I use local timber."

It was one of those flashes of awareness that seems to happen to kids, when something that has always been there changes and has meaning. It was like understanding for the first time that chickens came out of eggs: Each chair or door was made by Ed's hands. I touched a carved design on his desk and pulled a drawer out, marveling at how smoothly it opened. "How did you do this all by yourself?"

He smiled. "It takes a lot of patience, but it's a skill you can learn with practice."

The next day, after my schoolwork was done, instead of taking my rifle and heading up the canyon, I walked down to Ed's house. Ed was sitting on his front porch eating his lunch and looked up when I appeared around the corner. He was in the shade, but the sun was warming the knees of his jeans. He had been staring into the trees, seeming to be deep in thought. He raised his chin in greeting, and said, "I have some extra food if you want a bit."

After we ate, I followed Ed to his workshop, and he showed me the table he was working on. He pulled his glasses off his head and put them on. Then, he ran his hand over the smooth surface of the tabletop, examining it. "This is to replace my kitchen table. I sold it last month. Sometimes people want me to build them a piece like what I already have, but smaller, or with more drawers. Then I make it for them. Every so often, though, someone wants exactly what I have in my house, so I just let them have it." He picked up two pieces of wood that fit together in a dovetail and slid them apart. "The upside is that I get to improve it after having lived with it for a while. I have a few ideas I want to try on this new model, so I'm kind of excited about it."

I asked him if I could watch for a while, and he motioned to a corner of the workshop where sunlight was coming through the window. As I sat there, he said, "I'm testing a new way of joining the legs of the table to the top. I need to make a couple of trials before I attempt it for real." He returned to his work, then paused and looked back up at me. "Do you want to carve some dowels for me to use?"

Two hours later, I had made a small pile of dowels and had lost track of time, noticing its passage only when the sunlight that had been streaming in the window stopped illuminating the carving I was doing. I looked at Ed, and he smiled at me. I breathed in the agreeable smell of the wood chips and said, "Can I come back here more?"

Ed nodded. "Any time. Of course, I might put you to work if you show up."

The next day, Ed showed me how to carve a different dowel and I worked on that with him in comfortable silence, interrupted every so often by whatever thought came to our minds. I went out hunting the next morning, but the day after I appeared on Ed's porch around lunchtime with blackberry muffins in a towel my mom had handed to me as I hurried out the door. I still spent a lot of my afternoons in the hills, but when Ed saw me in his doorway, he would smile and nod toward the workspace in the corner that he had set aside for me and the project that I had been working on the last time I was there.

Josh had been sitting quietly as I told him about Ed and the maple tree. "Is that where you learned to make furniture?"

"It's where I got my start, for sure. If I could make something that Ed would like, I think I would have succeeded."

In the morning, with the sun still behind Pinyon Peak, Josh and I found a trickle of water in the creek, running over the lip of a rock basin. It was almost not flowing at all, but when we dug into the sand behind the lip, water seeped into the hole. "That'll do the trick," I said.

Leaving the horses to forage in the meadow, we set out on foot to search for the gold cave that was marked on the slope of Pinyon Peak. There wasn't much to go by, since the map didn't have any details, and the area was huge. We followed deer trails when we could, but deer can leap over manzanita bushes. We couldn't, so we had to fight our way through between them, getting scraped and poked by the stiff branches the whole time. The sun beat down on us, little flies flew straight for our eyes, and bigger flies tried to bite us anywhere our skin was exposed.

I had just gone around a bush when I felt a sharp jab on my neck, then another on my wrist. Josh yelled, "Bees!" We had stumbled on a yellow jacket nest. We both ran uphill, bucking like broncos as we slapped at our faces and arms. When we had put enough distance between us and the nest, we both started laughing. Josh was snorting as he mimicked me, flailing around in the air and yelling, "Bees! Bees! Run for your life!"

A bit later, we were stopped for a moment by a dry creek when something caught my eye. Under a small tree was a piece of wood with an arrow carved into it. It was held up by another piece of wood, and there was a mound of rocks piled up in front of it. "It could be a clue," I said.

"But we're not on the side of the mountain."

"I don't think the map's as accurate as we want it to be. I think we should look around a bit." I walked in a large circle while Josh started moving the mounded rocks to see what was below. A few feet away from the pile of stones, I found a plank with a name carved into it. I brought it over to where Josh was working. "I'm thinking you might be right."

Josh stood up and wiped his brow. "What'd you find?"

"Not sure. This seems more like a grave marker than anything else. And if that there is a marker too, then those rocks might just be a grave."

Josh stepped away from the pile of rocks in a bit of a hurry. "It is the right shape."

"I think we should remember where this is. We can come back if we don't find anything else."

I nodded. "I'm always in favor of leaving graves alone. We're not finding much, and it's hot as heck out here. I hope something interesting shows up soon, or we might have to find out if it is a grave." I reached over and bumped his shoulder with my hand. "At least we're out having an adventure, right? Nate'll be jealous when we tell him about the cowboy grave we found."

He smiled. "Yeah, it's better than shoveling out the stalls."

Late in the afternoon, up a brush-choked ravine below Pinyon Peak, I saw a rockslide partway up the hill. I pointed it out to Josh. "Someone was digging there. See the dark spot at the top, and the darker colored rocks below it? It might be something."

We decided to work our way up there, fighting through the thick, sharp bushes until we reached the spot. It did look like someone had been digging there, but since the hill above had slid down, it was hard to say how recently. As Josh reached for a rock to start clearing the entrance, a rattlesnake buzzed.

That sound sends adrenaline through you and makes you jump more than you should, sometimes getting you into trouble from the jumping. You know it's somewhere near, and you don't want to be close to it. So, we both jumped back and slid down the hillside among the rocks. When we recovered our composure, we saw the snake coiled to the left of the entrance. "I'm going to grab a stick and see if I can toss him down the hill with it," Josh said. The stick he found was about four feet long and sturdy, with a tapered end. The snake was still coiled and angry, rattling when he came close. I watched as Josh moved smoothly and quickly, poking the thin end of the stick into the center of the coiled snake, below the head. The snake struck at the stick twice in rapid succession, like shots. Then Josh twisted the stick so the angled branch was under the snake and flung it into a bush below.

Where had he learned to do that? "Dang. You hooked that snake like an expert."

His eyes were wide, like he was as surprised at his success as I was. "I hope that's the only one."

"Don't count on it. Let's put on the gloves and toss some rocks."

As we dug together, sweating in the heat of the afternoon, I was reminded of the hours the boys and I spent on the beach when they were young, digging holes in the sand, making elaborate sandcastles, burying each other. All for no reason other than because it was fun. This felt like that, since we knew this could be a dead end. Whatever happened, it was time together.

There were the remnants of sandstone below the hole, though, that were darker than what was on the surface, like they were part of the layer of darker rock with quartz in it that ran straight across the opening. Mixed in with the darker sandstone was a lighter rock that contained a few fossils of seashells. Josh set these aside as he found them.

The rockslide that had covered the opening included some boulders a couple hundred pounds in weight. We worked together to push those downhill, watching as the rocks bounced out of sight in the brush below. We'd brought a short shovel and used that to dig the loose dirt from between the stones where we couldn't move it with our hands. At one point, Josh picked up a flat rock weighing twenty or thirty pounds and we heard an angry hiss. Josh didn't think; he just dropped the rock on top of the snake. "Damn, there's more of them." After that, we each kept a pile of rocks off to the side within easy reach.

The sun had gone behind the mountain on the west side of the valley when the hole was large enough for a person to fit through. We could see a little way inside the tunnel. It was only three or four feet tall, but it was supported by tree trunks. My heart leapt: Someone had been mining there! They had gone far enough into the hillside that they needed to support the roof with timbers. Maybe there was something to the map after all. Josh did a little dance while sliding down the hill, singing, "It's a mine! It's a treasure mine! We're going to be rich!"

Josh wanted to go inside right away, but I vetoed that. I made us clean the entrance until the hole was almost the width of the opening inside. Then I told Josh we were stopping for the day. "We'll go inside in the morning, when we're fresh." The disappointment showed on his face.

The hike down the canyon was easier than it had been on the way up, in part because we knew where we were going. We stopped every hundred yards to gaze back up toward the mine site. The terrain looks very different from different angles, and we wanted to be sure we could find the mine again in the morning. Josh brought all the snail and clam fossils he had been gathering down the hill with him. He joked that the person who made the map wanted to be able to go back and get all the good fossils he had left behind. The sky was turning indigo blue as we washed off at the water hole below our camp.

Josh was excited as he built a fire. "It's the one on the map, I'm sure. I can feel it."

I had seen enough of life to understand how often what you think is leading to riches turns out to be a dead end. I didn't want him to get his hopes up. I didn't want to get my hopes up either. I sat next to him on a log. "I would like this to be real so much it makes me want to go back up there this minute." I paused a moment, deciding whether to go on. I was used to keeping painful memories to myself, but maybe it was worth telling him about this. "You were still too young to understand what was happening when Mike and I started the trucking company together." I felt my voice cracking. "The pressure was too much, and I backed out. You know the end of the story, though." He looked at me but didn't say anything.

I rubbed my face with both hands, feeling the anxiety knot my stomach up again like it had ten years earlier. "The company that we began together—Mike made it a huge success. We would have been a success together, if I'd have stuck it out. You guys would have been taking ski trips with your cousins and going to a four-year college." I looked over at him. He was listening. "I feel like I was a coward during that time—for not pushing through my anxiety. I can't help thinking that my cowardice continues to affect you guys." I was feeling cowardice creep back in at that moment, thinking about going into the mine. But I had said I was going to fight fate. I had to see this thing through, for me and for Josh. "If there's treasure in this mine, it might help to make some of that right. I need to fight this time. I need to take charge of our fate."

I looked out into the evening darkness rising around us. I wanted to stop right then. I realized I had been holding my breath, so I let it out slowly. I was terrified of not finding treasure. And I was equally afraid that we might find it. Both outcomes brought with them possibilities for disaster.

Josh stopped stacking sticks and looked at me with a serious expression on his face. "Dad. You're not a coward. You're brave all the time. You climbed into the plane after the pilot when it might have caught on fire."

"No." I shook my head. "No." I looked at the ground, then looked up at him. "Josh, I went into that plane in part because I was trying to convince myself that I'm brave—and also because you are. You would have gone in there if I hadn't, and I couldn't let you do that. You know what's right to do, and you do it." I could feel tears welling up. "I'm proud of the person you're becoming. Part of what I'm proud of is that you're determined to figure out for yourself what's right for you."

I got up from the log and picked up some larger pieces of wood to move next to the fire. "I need to push forward. We may find something tomorrow, or we may not. Either way, it won't solve the problem of me chickening out back when I had a chance. But it could help me change my path going forward—especially if there's anything in that mine." I was glad I said it out loud; it meant I was committed. "Let's eat and get some sleep and get up there as early as we can in the morning."

Josh nodded at the pot on the fire that hadn't boiled yet. "While we're eating you can tell me more about you growing up. How did you end up in Eureka?"

"Well, I told you a little about Ed, but I didn't tell you about the time after my father died. It's a long story."

"Dad. All we have is time."

I smiled at him and sat back against a rock, sipped from my canteen, and thought about the day my world fell apart.

Chapter Twelve

RAGE

A dark blue sedan pulled up to Ed's house one day around lunchtime. It parked in the flat area where the dirt road widened. Two men in uniform got out, and Ed went to meet them. I followed. They asked for my mother, and Ed said he would take them up to the house. Ed raised his hand to Cindy as we passed her cabin. She didn't wave or say anything; she just nodded. We led the men up the creek trail until we got in sight of our house, then Ed motioned them forward.

My mom came out the door as we were climbing the path from the creek to the house, and when she saw them, her face fell. I listened as they told her my dad had been killed. My mom turned away for a moment with her face in her hands, then I saw her straighten her shoulders and take a deep breath, and she turned back to them and asked them what had happened. They said my dad was killed when a Japanese plane crashed into the ship he was on. He had tried to rescue another man who was trapped in the fire that erupted afterward, and they both had perished.

I knew then what my mom had known when she saw them coming up the path, and what Ed had known when they got out of the car. My dad was gone, and he wouldn't be back.

That was the second plane crash, the one that would weigh on me the rest of my life. The official papers praised him for his bravery, but for Mom and me, he had been taken from us, bravery be damned.

It was the spring of 1945. I was almost ten years old. I started to spend more time in the hills alone. Days when the rage inside that I couldn't name grew until I thought I would explode, I ran until I was exhausted, uphill into the dry brush, carrying my rifle and a small pack. I ran until I had no room in my body for feelings because I didn't have the strength for them to exist. I would curl up and sleep like an animal under a bush and wake up with remorse. I would wake up wondering why there was so much pain. It felt like somebody wanted me to suffer, and I was mad at them for it. Like it was personal. Like my whole world was pain, and I had to break out of it. I shouldn't have let the anger take over, but there was freedom in not holding back, in turning my body inside-out and baking dry the turmoil in the sun and sweat and exhaustion.

In the self-centered world of a kid, I focused on my own pain, so I left my mom to deal with her loss herself. As I think back, I understand that what had been bearable solitude while waiting for his return became stark loneliness for her. After Dad's death, she was determined to continue living in the cabin in the redwoods, but it was hard without him. It had been their project, and now, instead of feeling like an adventure, it must have been an ongoing chore that she slogged through every day. I couldn't be her partner like my dad had been. All I could be was a kid, same as always, and my emotions were straightforward and blunt, without a lot of nuance. Hers must have been so much more complex.

I started spending more of my afternoons in the quiet of Ed's shop, working on furniture and only talking when I wanted to. Ed never pushed me, but when I decided to say something, Ed listened. When I asked to try larger projects, Ed helped me get set up and gave me guidance.

Ed's woodpile grew to monumental size because there were days when all we did was chop wood, without words, side by side. After a while, he saw that swinging an ax wasn't enough. "I'm worried about you running in the hills so much, and if we keep chopping wood, we'll fill the yard with stacks of logs. I have an idea." He filled a canvas duffle bag with sawdust and hung it in the yard. He gave me a pair of leather work gloves and showed me how to punch. "This is a jab." His fist flicked out and hit the bag. "It's the workhorse of punches. It's straight, with no wasted movement, and sudden. After that, I'll teach you how to throw uppercuts and crosses, and we'll do combinations of those." Almost every day after that, when I left his house, I couldn't raise my arms.

On the days when I wore myself out on the punching bag, I didn't need to go running out in the hills so much. After I had beaten up the bag, Ed and I would play a game of hitting the other one's hands before they could react. Ed taught me to punch straight from the shoulder and how to use my legs and body to put power behind the punches. I complained that Ed was cheating because I was tired and couldn't move as quickly. "You're as fast as I am even when you're tired, Van," he said. "The punching bag only makes the contest fair."

When we were outside, he and I played a game of tossing small pieces of wood at each other to see if we could catch them. Part of the game was trying to be creative in where the scraps came from, and other part was making the toss at surprising moments, such as when the other person reached for a piece of bread or was bent over to pick something up. A chunk of wood might come from anywhere and appear in front of you. You would have to decide in an instant if you could catch it and how.

Whenever Ed sensed the restlessness building up in me, he would suggest a game. We played baseball with the pitcher throwing wood chips and the batter trying to hit them with a thin dowel as they fluttered and spun through the air. The odd-sized scraps dove and curved as they flew, and they were devilishly hard to hit, especially with a three-quarters-inch wood dowel, but the wild hacks we took at them made us laugh. When someone connected, we celebrated. Over time, we found we were able to hit the chips more often. We started trying to catch the chunks as they flew back at the pitcher, and we made up a game with points for hitting the chips over the pitcher's head or at him if he didn't catch it.

We had contests of throwing rocks at cans set on stumps. We stood by the creek trying to hit a tree a hundred feet away with smooth stones we picked up from the creek bed. My anger came less often. Although I never quite got over the need to beat it out of me with a long run in the hills, I worked a lot of it out at Ed's house.

We were throwing rocks at trees one morning when Ed told me a story from when he was younger. "My wife, before she died, was a strong woman. And she could read people. I was about to get into a business deal with a guy, and I brought him home for supper. After he left, she told me that he was a cheater, and he would cheat me too." He threw a rock and missed the tree, then picked up another one. "I couldn't see it. He seemed like a stand-up guy to me."

I lofted a rock over the creek. "What did you do?"

He paused and smiled at me, then continued. "I listened. That's the thing. She was smarter than me about so much. I told her I would be more careful than usual. Sure enough, he started stealing money. I found out before he got very much because I was watching out."

I thought about my mom up in the cabin. "My mom and dad worked on things together like that. They listened to each other's opinions even when they didn't agree with them."

He gazed out into the woods before he answered. "The best thing I did in my life was marry someone who could be my partner, someone who I could change with. And my biggest regret is that we didn't get to grow old together and see what we would have grown into."

I didn't get to see my mom and dad together for long, but what I remember of them seemed like what Ed was talking about. I didn't know it then, but that story stuck with me for a long time and affected what I looked for in a girl.

One morning, I woke to warmth and sunlight, which was unfamiliar in our glade where the fog stayed sometimes all day in the summer. I also woke that day to the familiar rage that wanted to hurt something. It filled the room and overwhelmed me. I felt out of control, and I knew I had to run. Mom saw I was in a mood as I grabbed some food, and she didn't talk to me other than to say, "Good morning." I nodded to her and picked up my gun on the way out the door. And I ran. I pounded up the hill until my breath came in great gasping gulps, then I stopped and thought I would throw up. I wanted to be sick because maybe the despair in my gut would come out with it, but nothing came out. I started running again.

When I reached the top of the mountain and threw myself down in the dry bunch grasses there, I stayed for a while smelling the earth and the sweet roots of the grass, reveling in the serenity. I sat up and gazed over the ocean in the distance. I searched inside for the anger, knowing it was there, knowing I would recognize it as it peeked out from where I had banished it with exhaustion. I sat waiting, wordless, thoughtless, watching the sky, light blue, meet the ocean, darker stronger deeper cooler. I noticed myself waiting for the rage that had overwhelmed me to return. But I saw I wasn't the rage. I was the one waiting for it. The back of my neck tightened, then the tightness crept up to my scalp and a sour heat rose in my stomach—all signs of the anger coming back. I knew it would threaten to overcome me. I was curious to find out where it would go, but now it was separate from me, not me. I asked myself, "Who am I if I'm not what's happening to my body? Who is watching the anger rising? Is that me?

Am I the one watching it all happen?" A stillness washed over me, and I fell asleep with the grasses waving in the wind, brushing against my face.

When my eyes opened and I rubbed at the stems of fescue that were sticking to my cheek, I knew I had changed. Back on that day at the beach when I was four, I became aware of myself as a person separate from my parents, when the man with the airplane appeared on the cliff above us. In that same way, I awoke on that hill after running and found I could watch the anger and pain and joy and know they were there without being consumed by them.

That brought me comfort and a sense of being in control of my life for a long time. The rages stopped overwhelming me and became instead companions that I acknowledged and felt sorry for. When they came, I waited, knowing that with time, they would subside. With the rage and the anger and the heat and the noise all separated from me, my emotions became more manageable. But their absence also created room for me to be aware of a sense of longing that wouldn't go away, longing for how our lives might have been if my dad hadn't been taken from us. How things would be different if he had come back from the war or had listened to my mom and hidden in the quiet of our forest and hadn't gone at all.

Chapter Thirteen

OAKLAND

Mom's loneliness got worse. Some days, she felt closer to my dad's memory, and I would hear her talking to him as she did the chores they used to do together. Other times, she would be quiet and sad. When I asked her if there was anything I could do, she would smile at me and say that she was missing him especially much right then.

One morning, we were gathering mushrooms in the forest in companionable silence when she turned to me and said, "You know Van, I thought I would feel better by now."

I kept my head down, searching. "Yeah. I'm getting better, but I don't know if that sharp pain when I think of him will ever go away."

"It feels like it's getting worse for me." She looked up at the trees and stood for a moment in silence. "Tom and Cindy and Ed are great. This place is amazing. But it was our spot, Norman's and mine. It's not easy living here, and he's not here to be my partner in it."

I hadn't thought about the possibility of living any-where else. "What else could we do?"

"I don't know. I feel like I'm growing moss here from the lack of sunlight, though. I'll hold on and see if it gets better. I love it here too, but it's wearing on me."

One day, she told me she couldn't hang on any longer. I was twelve when we moved to Oakland to live with her friends Katheryn and Walter in their small house on 44th Street, a row of small houses in the flat part of the city be-tween the low brown hills and the bay. Oakland was sunni-er. The breezes blew from the west, but the fog stayed on the other side of the water most days, stuck in the hills of San Francisco. The sun burned the moss off us, and it felt good.

Any twelve-year-old boy moving to a new city and en-rolling in a new school would be nervous, but I had never been in a classroom and hadn't spent much time around kids. I was used to talking with grownups and having them treat me as if I had an opinion that counted.

Back in Big Sur, Cindy, our neighbor, was the most talkative of the adults, and even with her, there were long periods without words. When I showed up on baking days to wait for a broken cookie to be passed my way, Cindy and I would talk as I washed bowls while waiting for a pan to come out of the oven, but there were tasks other than talking that needed our attention, and long silences were comfort-able for both of us. But the kids in school talked all the time.

One boy, Bart, picked on me from the day I arrived. He wasn't the biggest kid in class, but he was the most grown-up. When the kids wondered how sex happened, Bart told them. When one boy said he had found an unopened can of beer and had drunk some of it, Bart said that his dad let him have beer all the time.

Bart found ways to torment me almost continuously, and I took it from him because it never was obvious that he was doing it on purpose. He would hit me on the head as he walked past my seat. It seemed like an accident, but it kept happening. One time it would be a thoughtless elbow knocking into me, and the next it would be a book that slipped out of his hands the moment he passed me.

One day, he brought his antagonism out in the open. As I came around a corner in the hallway, a foot shot out and tripped me. I caught myself and didn't fall, but I turned and saw Bart in a group of three boys standing with their hands on their hips. "Hey hick," Bart sneered, "They didn't teach you to walk where you came from?"

This was new, and it was something I could work with. I stepped up to him, stared at him straight in the eye, and said, "What's the deal?" His buddies crowded closer behind him in support.

"I don't like you, hick." He shoved me with two hands in the chest.

One game that Ed and I played in in his front yard was a shoving game. We would get our feet set and try to push each other with one hand to make the other person take a step. Since Ed was bigger, we came up with handicaps like Ed standing on one foot or Ed starting out off-balance. I'd have to take advantage of his being uncentered and decide by glancing at him how to push him off-center. I knew how to play this game. I had been playing it for a long time with someone who was a lot bigger and stronger than Bart.

I took one step backward when Bart pushed me, caught my balance, bent my knees, straightened my back, and, using one hand like Ed and I used to do, shoved Bart. The strength of my legs traveled through my arm and into Bart's chest. His hands flew up as he stumbled backward, tripped on his own feet, and fell on his back. He jumped up, yelling, "You'll pay for that!"

I watched him coming. He seemed to reach behind him to grab an object out of the air but was just winding up his fist for a huge punch. It flew on an arc toward my head. I ducked it. Then, I punched Bart hard in the middle of the chest with my right hand. It seemed natural because I had been working on this in Ed's yard for months, and Bart moved in slow motion compared to the speed I was used to. My punch stopped Bart. He backed up, not sure what had happened. I waited, my hands by my sides, trying to keep any emotion off my face. He worked his face into a grimace as he came toward me. First, he swung a left, then a right—big looping punches. I blocked the left with my forearm and stepped to the side as the right came past my head. I punched him again in the chest with a right hook, putting my weight behind it. I felt that one in my knuckles and all the way up to my elbow. Bart's sneer dissolved into a slack, open-mouthed stare as he fought to breathe in. He scowled down at his chest. I saw the awareness come to him that I could just as easily have hit him in the face.

I remembered what Ed had told me about winning and losing. "Give the other guy a way out. Let him save face, even when you're winning." So, I held up my hands and backed up. "Wait. Wait," I said. "We better quit this. If you connect with one of those punches, you'll take my head off."

He glared at me for a second, smiled, and turned to his buddies. "He's right. I wouldn't want the hayseed to be dumber than he already is. Let's get out of here." He seemed to have a grudging respect for me after that, and the accidental shoving and knocking stopped. We went to the same high school later, and though I'm not sure we ever talked during those years, the regard was there. We would nod to each other when we passed in the hallways, two tough guys acknowledging each other.

I found that schoolwork wasn't too hard for me, and I was ahead of my grade level with the work that Mom and Dad had made me do. I tried not to stand out while also getting good grades. There was a kid in class who loved to answer all the questions the teacher asked, and I saw that the other kids looked down on him. So, I waited until three or four kids answered before I spoke up and didn't volunteer too often. I was trying to keep my head down until I figured out how the system worked.

Still, I didn't understand the other kids. They talked about fads and radio shows and movies that were only words to me. They had been hanging around with each other for most of their lives and used slang that was like a foreign language. There were unwritten rules they took for granted—like who hung out with who at lunch—that I hadn't figured out. So, I stayed quiet most of the time. I decided to not say anything rather than say something the kids would ridicule.

I was lonelier among the kids in school than I had been when I was by myself in the hills. Being on your own when nobody else is around bolsters your sense of self. Being alone in a crowd, doubt pecks at your inner strength like seagulls with a piece of bread.

One day, I noticed a bunch of boys heading out to the lawn carrying a football. I followed, curious about what they were doing. A small boy next to me said there weren't many rules, but usually one guy ran with the ball as long as he could until he got tackled. Then someone else would grab the ball and start running. There were no goals and no points scored. The mass of kids ran from one end of the huge lawn area to the other, pushing and yelling and falling down until the bell rang for the end of lunch and they all trooped into class sweaty and worn out.

I ran around with the crowd for a while, staying outside of the swarming school of fish that collapsed on itself every so often then flowed away across the lawn with a new person at the head. Then I got too close to the front, and the guy with the ball tossed it back to me. I was so surprised I almost stopped. But I had seen what would happen if the pack caught me, so I sped up. With my first burst of speed, I got some separation from the group, and glancing back, I realized that nobody was keeping up with me. After a while, I tossed the ball back to one kid who was behind me, and I joined the swarm again. Staying in front of a mass of them was easy.

I had found my niche. I was used to catching fleeting objects and working with my hands. I saw patterns in the action on the field the same as I had learned to watch birds and squirrels to know where an animal was in the forest or notice where grass had been disturbed to see where it had gone. It didn't take long to learn whatever game was being played. Sports gave me a place to be quiet and learn social skills while being accepted into the group. Nobody cared that I didn't talk much if I played well.

When baseball season came around, I discovered I was good at it. As with Bart's punches, the ball came at me slower than I expected. It was easy to tell where it was going compared to the wood chips that flitted through the air without pattern and required me to wait until the last second before I committed to a swing. I hit the ball well, and I threw it with speed and accuracy, as I had done with rocks when I knocked over cans or tried to throw farther than Ed. Maybe Ed knew what he was doing, or maybe he was only trying to wear me out. Either way, his games gave me the skills to slip without too much trouble into the strange world of kids my age. I was just beginning to understand the gifts Ed had given me in his quiet way.

Walter and Katherine's house was small, but they didn't have children, so I had my own room and Mom had one too. There was a simple generosity that emanated from them. It was never like they were helping us or giving us charity. The rooms were there, and it was natural that we would stay in them for a while—for as long as we wanted, it seemed to me, although we didn't test that premise.

The picture in my mind of that time is of Mom and Katherine sitting in the corner of the kitchen by the window with the sun coming in, empty coffee cups on the small aluminum and linoleum table. When I came into the room, they would turn and smile at me, and both of my mothers would ask if I wanted a bite to eat. Then one would get up while the other watched, contented.

Mom seemed to be revived by moving to Oakland. Katherine, who was like a sister, gave her someone to talk to. Mom didn't have to bear the responsibility for all that happened to us. Walter made repairs and did projects around the house. Katherine and Mom worked side-by-side in the kitchen. And the sun. There was always the sun in Oakland. It took me years to get over my surprise at waking up to yellow light in the morning instead of gray. I never tired of warming up on the porch in the morning for a moment before continuing my day. I hadn't realized how many days I had passed in our canyon without ever being warm.

We started to build a life in Oakland. And it went well—until the next plane crash, that is.

Chapter Fourteen

THE BAKERY

After we had been in Oakland less than a year, I came home from school one day to find Katherine and Mom sitting at the kitchen table. They were writing on papers spread out around them and seemed surprised that I was home so soon, like time had gotten away from them. Mom looked at Katherine, and she looked at Mom, and their smiles were about to burst their faces. "Guess what we found!" Katherine said.

I took a breath to answer, but she jumped up and hugged me, then continued. "We were walking on the street where the grocery market is, and I peeked in the window of the store across the way that's been empty since the war." She stood behind Mom and put her hands on her shoulders. "Guess what was inside!"

This time, I was determined to get a word in, so I said quickly, "Mannequins with straw hats on them."

She looked at me strangely, like I wasn't supposed to answer, then shouted, "A bakery! There's an oven and cooling racks and a counter. We asked around and found out that the older couple who had run that bakery just up and quit when the rationing started during the war." She sat down, then got back up immediately. "Your mom was thinking about renting it."

Mom's voice was a little calmer, but I could tell she was excited too. "So, I'm thinking that I could make the sourdough recipes I learned from Tom and Cindy."

"You've been improving them the whole time you've lived here," Katherine added. "You're always reading books on pastry, and your dough is chewy and flaky at the same time. I keep telling you that it's better than anything I've ever tasted."

Mom turned to me, squinting. "Do you think I should?"

I thought it was a great idea. She had been working in an office as a typist, but she didn't love it. She loved baking, and she was happiest when she was the one who decided what she should do next. "Mom, Katherine's right. You make the best bread I've ever had. Better than Cindy, even. And your cookies are amazing. They're not like anything you can get around here. So, yeah. I think people will eat them up and pay to do it." She groaned at my pun. "I can help, in between school and sports."

And I did. Mom bought the equipment from the owners for what seemed like almost nothing. The rent wasn't bad, but the place needed care, and we had to figure out how to use the ovens and the mixers. We started by cleaning everything inside and out, then we painted the front of the shop lemon yellow. Katherine found some photographs of kids to hang in the customer area. One was eating a slice of buttered bread while sitting on a wooden front porch step, and another held a fruit pastry and sat on a bench with a dog gazing up at them. They were cute, but not cutesy.

We gave away a lot of baked goods during the time she was testing her recipes in larger batches with the new ovens. When a batch was done, we would taste it, wait, and then sample it again after it cooled fully. Then we would search for someone to give it to, sometimes stopping people walking by on the street with a pan of cookies or muffins in our hands. Though we didn't know it, that was the best advertising we could have done. Everyone in the neighborhood was aware we were getting ready, and they came by to try a sample and ask when we would be open for business. At first, we hadn't thought that far ahead. But people kept asking, so we set a date: June 15, 1949. On that day, we could bake three things. One was a round sourdough loaf with a crack on top made with a razor blade right before the bread was put into the oven. Another was a sourdough chocolate chip cookie, patterned after the tollhouse cookies that were invented in the late 1930s and had become popular. The sourdough gave the cookies a tang that offset the sweetness of the chocolate. And we made one pastry, a round Danish with fruit in the middle—whatever fruit was in season. In the early spring, they were filled with strawberries. Cherries took over in May, apricots in June, and blackberries and peaches in summer. In the fall, we used apples and pears.

Once again, we stumbled on a perfect business strategy. By making only a few items, we made them very well. People craved them and came back. We didn't have much left over at the end of the day. The neighborhood had been without a local bakery for most of the war, so people came early to make sure they got their favorites before we ran out.

We started keeping baker's hours. Mom and I woke up well before dawn and walked together through the quiet streets to the bakery where I would work for a couple of hours before I had to go to school. We were closed on Sundays and Mondays. Sundays were the days we did the paperwork and chores we hadn't had time for during the week. I got to sleep in both those days, and waking up when the light of day nudged me instead of to the jarring sound of the alarm clock was its own kind of luxury. We were working together on a project that was important for both of us, and I was proud of what we had accomplished.

After we'd settled down, Mom and I moved into our own small house in the same neighborhood as Katherine and Walter. The three of them went on day trips and to exhibits together. I tagged along, sometimes bringing a friend. Some of those trips were to visit our old neighbors in the redwoods. They were like mini vacations away from the noise and speed of the city. We slowed down and remembered what had drawn Dad and Mom to that life. Ed and I would find some time to throw rocks and talk a little. We went for hikes with our old friends. The smell of the decaying earth under our feet reminded our bodies to breathe deeper and match the rhythms of the woods. Shafts of light slicing through the redwoods and illuminating greenery and tree trunks made us gaze up at the cathedral of trees rising around us.

It was comfortable to spend time with our friends, but we found that by the end of a weekend, we were ready to get back to what we were doing in the city. Gradually, our visits down the coast became less frequent as life in Oakland became fuller.

One Saturday in June after my junior year in high school, I was closing up the bakery for the weekend. I had propped open the door with a brick to let the heat out. As I mopped the front floor, I saw out of the corner of my eye the shape of a man walking in. "I think we have a loaf of bread left and a couple of cinnamon rolls," I said over my shoulder.

He came over to the counter. "I'm not interested in the bread." His voice was low and desperate. "Open the cash register and give me all the money. I have a gun."

I put the mop into the bucket and wiped my hands on my jeans as I turned to face him. He was skinny. That was the first thing I noticed. And his eyes were deep set, like he hadn't slept in a while. But he didn't look like a crook. I'm not sure what I mean by that. How would I have known what a crook looked like? He wasn't wearing a mask like robbers are supposed to, like I expected when I turned around. But more than that, he seemed beaten down rather than scary. His shoulders slumped like he was a man out of options, not a criminal.

I don't know where I got the courage, but I said to him, "I can get the money for you out of the cash register, but you look too honest to be a robber. I have a better idea. Why don't we say that you came in asking for food, and I gave you what we had left in the case and threw in twenty dollars?" I was shaking, but I forced myself to stand squarely to him.

His brow furrowed. "I would need a hundred. My kid's sick."

I let out the breath I had been holding. "That's just about all we have, but if you're asking and I'm giving, I think I could manage that."

He seemed relieved, too. "I could get by with eighty and the bread."

My fingers were still trembling as I opened the register, took out almost all the cash we had in there, and put the rest of our inventory in a brown paper bag. After I handed it to him, he peered inside it hungrily. He looked up at me like he might apologize. "I don't have a gun, by the way."

I nodded. "I thought that might be the case," I said, keeping up my outward veneer of toughness. Inside, I felt a little calmer. "Come back in and let me know how your kid's doing. My name's Van."

He stood straighter, like a weight had been lifted off him. "I'm Carl. Thank you. I thought I had run out of options. I'll be back." He walked out of the shop without turning around. I breathed a sigh of relief and told myself I had seen the last of him. When I told Mom about Carl, she asked, "How did you know he wasn't violent?"

"I'm not sure. I guess I just knew. This is weird to say, but even though he was trying to rob us and telling me he had a gun, he seemed like a gentle soul."

The next week, Carl came back. He had taken his daughter to the hospital, and she was getting better, but he was still out of work. He asked me if there was anything for him to do in our shop. Mom was behind me, putting loaves on the cooling racks. From where she stood, she said, "I need someone for hard physical labor and awful hours at low pay. How does that sound?" He started the next day.

Mom quickly ran out of physical labor for him because he worked efficiently, did his job well, and asked for more. So, she began showing him how to do other tasks, like preparing the cinnamon sugar mixture and cooking the fruit filling for the pastries. He kept coming back, saying he was done, and wondering what else there was to do. He was putting on weight, too.

Then, she showed him how to work the dough with his hands. When Mom kneaded or shaped the dough, it flowed and rolled with her hands, not against them. There was a rhythm and rightness to their dance, and the dough was in step with her. But when Carl touched the dough, the dough led the dance. The dough seemed to have a memory of where it was supposed to be, and his hands were along for the ride. The expression on his face when he finished his first batch was like a child who had just tasted their first marshmallow. "I think you should change your last name to Baker," I said. He beamed. He had found his calling. He had been lifted by the dough up into the light. Then he had been presented to the gods of grain and yeast and been pronounced special. No, not merely special: chosen.

Carl never did hard physical labor for low pay in our shop again. The bad hours remained, although he said he never had to use an alarm clock. He told us he popped awake at three in the morning because the dough was waiting for him.

❧

During my senior year, Mom started having stomach pains. She only mentioned them a couple of times, but I caught her standing off to the side by herself more and more often, like she was thinking of an ingredient she had forgotten. When the pains got worse, doctors told her to stop eating rich food and try cutting out bread and butter. But the soreness persisted. Katherine talked her into going back to the doctor, and this time, he sent her to consult with a specialist over at the medical clinic on Stanford Campus.

Two weeks later, on an overcast February morning, I drove her across the Dumbarton Bridge. As we approached it, we saw the steel trusses that looked like they were floating on the bay. It went on for miles, staying just barely above water level.

When we were about halfway across the steel gray water, we saw a small plane. It had taken off from Palo Alto Airport and climbed toward us across the bay. Then it made a sharp left turn above us and headed back in the direction it came from. We watched it circle to our right and head back toward the airport, losing altitude the whole time. As we approached the end of the bridge, it crossed so low in front of us that I didn't have to lean forward to see it. The propellers weren't turning, and I had to remind myself to keep an eye on the road. My stomach lurched as I watched it head for the marshlands at the edge of the bay. It wasn't going to make it. This would be my third plane crash.

When the plane was almost touching the ground, the left wing struck a pole sticking out of the marsh. The wing ripped off the plane about one-third of the way from the tip. I managed to pull over to the side of the road and stop the car. As I opened the door, I saw a figure get out of the plane. I relaxed for a moment as I watched him walking normally. There wasn't a way to reach him across the marshy wetlands from where we were, so we just stayed in the pullout until we saw fire trucks coming from the airport. Then we got back on the road to our appointment in Palo Alto. We heard afterward that someone had accidentally fueled the plane with incompatible aviation fuel, causing engine failure so soon after takeoff. The pilot was fine.

My mother wasn't, however. After the tests, the doctor told her she had pancreatic cancer. He didn't mince words. He said that most people didn't live six months after their diagnosis, and there wasn't much they could do.

She died three-and-a-half months later, the last day of May, Memorial Day.

After the diagnosis, I had started working longer hours at the bakery, but I couldn't keep up once Mom stopped working. Caring for her took time, too, so we needed someone to be in charge of the bakery. I got Carl to take over more of Mom's duties, and he did well. Just before she died, I asked him what he thought about becoming a half-owner of the bakery. I told him I couldn't work in the bakery anymore and explained that he should pay himself what a head baker would make, and after all the expenses, he could split the profits with me. He agreed to do it, and

I left the store that day. I didn't go back to the bakery until the passing of time had brought experiences and people I loved to fill in the void where Mom had been.

Before Mom died, I made her a couple of promises. One was that I would take her ashes to the cemetery in Iowa and bury her there next to her parents. The other was that I would go visit Dad's parents in Chicago and get to know them. She said that they were the only family I had left, and it was right that I go find them. She gave me the thin silver watch that Dad's grandmother had given her when they got engaged and asked me to take it to Dad's mother. It said "Hamilton" on the face and had square-cut diamonds around the dial and on the band. It looked expensive. She never had it appraised, but she said whenever she wore it, people who should know commented on it.

After she died, I stayed in our house until high school was done. I had done the bare minimum there since Mom had received her diagnosis, but I graduated anyway. I think I got some consideration from my teachers in my grades because I know I didn't do enough to earn them.

I had begun to fear plane crashes. Surely the fact that they occurred before major tragedies in my life was a random coincidence. My rational mind told me they weren't connected. But my heart rate jumped at the thought of seeing another one and living through the loss that would follow. My body's reactions made them seem that they were linked. Like how hearing the song, the Nat King Cole one, "Too Young," that was playing on the radio when I got my first grown-up kiss, brings a sudden picture to my mind of the inside of the car I had borrowed for the date. When I hear that song, I can feel my arm sticking to the vinyl seat after I put it around her. Her perfume, sweet with vanilla and something citrus, maybe lemon, fills my nose. I'm there again with the softness of her lips and the surprise when her tongue touched mine. She said, "I love this song," right before we kissed. Did the song cause the kiss? It feels like it did.

The only explanation I could figure out was that plane crashes happened when I let myself be too happy, and then fate took that happiness away. That day on the beach was such an idyllic first memory, but after the plane crashed on the rocks, Peppy disappeared. My mom and dad found a place of their own in the redwoods. Then the war and a plane crash took it away. Mom had been so courageous in opening the bakery and had kept with it through the stress and hard work. She had friends and a business, and we had made a life that fit us. We saw the plane crash in Palo Alto, and then she was gone. Every time we fought and scratched and found a bit of happiness, it felt like fate noticed, and stuck out its finger and flicked us off our hill of contentment, like you would flick a crumb off your knee.

The part of me I had found on the sunny mountaintop gazing out at the ocean in Big Sur—the part that watched my emotions without being my emotions—hadn't left me. It had helped me control the rage and anger that had taken over my body after Dad died. But this time there was no place that the sadness didn't go, so there was nowhere for me to stand aside from it or above it and watch it. The hole in my life caused by Mom's death spread in all directions until it encompassed all of me and all of my world. All I had was that hole, that emptiness, that longing, that lack of anything that mattered.

Later, I would call it numbness or loneliness or missing, or shock, but at that moment, it was a void that was as big as all that I could imagine and spread backward and forward in time as far as time would go.

The day after I graduated, I handed the keys to the landlord, stopped by Katherine and Walter's house to say goodbye, and left Oakland with only a backpack. In it were, among other things, my mother's ashes and a diamond-and-silver watch. My plan was to hitchhike up the coast. Maybe I would get lost up there. Possibly, if I made myself small and kept my happiness pared down too, I could hide from another plane crash and fate's flicking finger.

Chapter Fifteen

LOGGING

Outside of Eureka, up near the Oregon border, the truck driver pulled off the highway. "I'll have to let you out here. If I'm seen with a rider in my rig, I'll get in trouble. It's not too far, and you can walk the rest of the way into town." I thanked him for the lift and gathered my pack, staring out the window at the mist hanging in the air. I was just beginning to be able to see trees and creeks in the soft gray pre-dawn light. As I opened the door, he asked, "You have any money with you?"

"Not much," I replied, wondering what he wanted.

"Good answer. If you have any, keep it out of sight. Make sure you have a little available in your pockets if you need it. Stash the rest in the bottom of your shoes under the inner sole or somewhere hard to get to. People can smell cash, and even the honest ones want a piece."

I thanked him again and climbed down from the cab of the semi onto wet pavement. The gray sky was so low I thought I could reach up and touch it. In Big Sur, the land gave way grudgingly to the sea, and the mountains rose up in defiance of its force. Here, the two seemed to have made an uneasy truce, although chunks of rock rising from the waves told of past battles. The redwoods, too, were more at ease. Instead of defending their damp creek beds between dry hills as they did further south, they spread out, knowing they were the rulers of this soaked land.

I hiked on the shoulder of the road heading toward town until I smelled bacon cooking. At first, I thought I must be smelling it because I was hungry, like a craving, then there it was again. I stopped and scanned the surrounding landscape, searching for its source. To my left was a salt marsh that stretched almost a mile before it met the gray-blue waters of the bay. It was low tide, and I could see the mud between the grasses with rivulets branching and re-branching between them. To the right was a small meadow with a creek that cut through the grass and reeds, and pine trees rising dark behind it. A bridge took the highway over the stream, and I leaned over the edge and peered into the dimness below it. I saw two men huddled around a fire. "That smells good from up here," I said. "Is there any coffee you might share?"

The younger one looked up and said, "We can spare a cup. Come on down."

The older guy with the bushy beard and beaten-up leather hat watched me as I picked my way down the wet rocks to where they were. "I hope you like it strong," he said when I got close. He was missing a tooth on the right side and the gap showed when he talked. "It's cowboy coffee, and it's thick enough to float a horseshoe." He smiled, and I got a good view of that missing tooth. "I think that's a quote from a Louis L'Amour book, but since he's not around, we'll say it's mine."

As I had come down the slope, I had seen a third man sitting by himself up behind them under the bridge. When I told them my name, he giggled and said from the shadows, "Van. Moving Van. Vandals breaking windows."

"He's pretty harmless," the young guy said. He was about my age with black eyebrows that almost met in the middle. "I'm Al." He glanced up at the guy on the slope and said, "Almonds. Aladdin and the magic carpet." Then he waited.

"Fettuccini Alfredo, Ali Baba," came the reply from above us.

The guy with the missing tooth poured coffee from a smoke-blackened aluminum pot into my cup and whispered without sound, "You can call me Bob."

The voice behind us stayed quiet. We sipped our coffee in silence for a couple of seconds. Then, the voice above us said, "Bobsled."

"Where you headed?" Under his eyebrows, Al's eyes looked friendly.

"I'm just passing through. Thought I might explore some of the coast up here. Got to get a job soon, though. I'm running low on cash." I said that mainly because of what the truck driver had told me.

Al leaned in. "I heard that they're hiring for work up in the timber, logging. I'm thinking of heading into town and rummaging around to see if that's true. Want to come?"

I pulled a loaf of sourdough and a knife out of my pack. "I might tag along with you and see what they're offering."

I didn't have much of a plan. I was just wandering. The thing about wandering is sometimes you get somewhere. I liked Al, and that was as good a reason as any to go with him to look for a job.

I sawed off a few pieces of bread and offered them around. Then I sliced some cheese off my hunk and passed those out. They gave me the last piece of bacon that had been sitting in the pan, and we all dipped the edges of our bread in the grease for flavor.

Later that day, Al and I went together to the office of the hiring manager for the timber company. On the wall was a framed photograph of loggers who had stopped their work to pose for the picture. They had cut a wedge out of an enormous redwood tree to get it to fall in the direction they wanted it to. Two men were lying in the wedge-shaped cutout while two others stood beside the tree with axes in their hands. The width of the tree was more than the two men lying end to end, plus a couple feet. "Are those kinds of trees still out there?" Al asked the manager.

He didn't turn around to look at the photo. "They are, but most of what we cut now is second growth. It's easier to handle." He pointed with his chin at another photograph on the side wall that showed families standing outside a small town of wooden cabins surrounded by trees. "We don't live up in shacks in the forest anymore, either. Everyone drives to work in their own trucks up logging roads, and we take the logs out on the same roads in bigger trucks." He explained how they used to make the loggers' tiny houses just big enough so they could load them on railroad cars and carry them to the next area where they were working. He smiled to himself. "A man would bring his whole family to live up in the forest with him back then. It was a community. Sometimes, if we're a long ways out, we'll camp for a night or two, but most of the time these days, we come back home."

He paused for a moment, took stock of us, and continued. "I can't tell who's going to make it and who isn't, so I hire guys like you and send them out there. Then I let the trees and the work sort you out. The toughest looking kids give up the first day, and doughy boys like you..." He pointed at Al with his coffee cup. "Doughy boys like you turn into my best men. So, I put you out there and see how you turn out."

He leaned forward across his desk and stared straight at us with a serious expression. "There is one lesson I want to make sure you leave my office saying to yourself over and over. Here it is: Do everything the way we teach you. Don't take shortcuts or think you have a better way to do something. This is dangerous work, and accidents happen despite everything we do to keep safe. Never let yourself think that you'll let your guard down or do it the easy way just this once. That's when you'll get your hand crushed, or your saw will kick back into you, and it'll cripple you for life."

I know that was meant to scare us, but hard, dangerous work sounded good to me right then.

Once we got paired up with more experienced guys, the tone of the advice changed. We were told once how to do the job safely, and after that, all attention turned to getting it done efficiently. It was up to us to keep our fingers and toes and not break an ankle on the slippery logs.

Al and I were limbers. That meant we sawed the limbs off the trees that were cut down by the more experienced men, called fellers. The fellers had to make the tree fall so that it missed the other trees. Otherwise, the trees could be damaged by the falling tree. Or, worse, the falling tree would get hung up and create a dangerous situation—a suspended tree that might come crashing down at any moment. So, they cut them down with precision, lining them up in the same direction. We could pull them to the road without getting tangled in other trees. It was as if a great wind had rushed up the hillside and had blown them over in one breath.

It was hard and dangerous work. We clambered over trees, cutting off limbs with chainsaws that would cut through bone as easily as wood. Especially hazardous was the possibility of kickback—when the tip of the saw would catch on the tree and fling the bar of the saw with its rotating chain and sharp biting teeth back at us. It almost never happened, but that was what made it perilous. It was always a surprise.

It was wet in those forests too. Redwood trees grow where there's constant rain or fog to bring moisture to their shallow spreading roots, so everywhere we stepped was slippery. The ground turned to mud as machines drove over it and dragged trees to staging areas, and we worked on drenched tree trunks in muddy boots with stiff, icy hands.

I liked the hard work, though, and the danger too, in an odd way. It was like I was growing up by testing my limits. One of the older guys said to me once, "When I was your age, I was crawling through mud and brush and swearing at the weather too, but there were people shooting at me." That might have been the appeal. Young men need to find dangerous and demanding and uncomfortable challenges, and since I didn't have a war to go to, I substituted logging. Maybe the peril and the need for concentration were the truckloads of dirt filling in my void from the edges. Possibly, I wanted physical pain so that I felt something. Or it could have been that just like running up hills in the sun, breaking stuff felt good, and we were destroying things on a grand scale.

Chapter Sixteen

THE BEAR

The flames of the campfire were still bright and hot and hadn't burned down enough yet to cook with, but it felt like I had been talking a long time. I was surprised when Josh said, "But what about you and Mom?"

I was just about to tell him how we met when Russ rode into camp. He was dusty and looked like he had spent all day on the trail. "Hi you guys! I thought that might be you when I saw the fire from up on the trail. Nice camp you have here. You have water?"

I was glad to see him, but I felt a pang of possessiveness about the mine we had found. "We had to dig a bit, but there's a nice seep down below in that flat spot on the creek over there."

"Great, be back in a minute." Russ rode his horse over to the creek, and we watched from beside the fire as he filled his water containers before he let the horse drink.

Josh raised his eyebrows toward me. I made a downward motion with my hands, then whispered, "We have all the time we need. Let's go with whatever happens tonight."

Once his horse was out grazing, Russ came back to the campfire. "I don't think I'll set up a tent tonight. It's so clear and warm, and I'm heading out early in the morning." He unrolled a groundsheet on the edge of the clearing and put his sleeping bag on top of it, then he came over to the fire with a sack of food and his bottle of whiskey. "I can't drink much tonight if I want to be on the trail early. I'm headed further south to check out what I can find down there. I might stop in at that mission, then go down to the west. I still haven't been to the old mine where we hung out that summer." Despite his words, he poured his cup almost full. "What have you guys been up to?"

I told him we had been exploring further down the valley, looking for a waterfall we had heard about. Josh stared at me like I was supposed to do some talking, so I did. "Well Russ, we're also out here on a treasure hunt. My dad had an old map that he thought showed something down near the coast, but he never could find it. When we looked at it again just before we headed out here, we put some of the pieces together we hadn't before. We're not optimistic about finding anything, but it keeps us busy."

Russ nodded. "Yeah, Stevie thought there was something out here. My stepfather got his hands on Stevie's notes after Stevie died."

That settled it. I took a deep breath. "We need to talk about that too, Russ." I moved to a log on the same side of the fire as him. "A plane crashed in the meadow above our house five or six days ago. The pilot didn't survive. Could that have been your stepfather?"

He raised his eyebrows and opened his mouth. He looked away for a moment, then he turned back to me.

"That was probably him." He wiped the corner of his eye, then looked at me. "It's funny how you can hate an old bastard and want him dead a hundred times. You can plan how he would die. You can fantasize about it, then when you find out it finally happened, you cry about it. Go figure." He opened his mouth like he was thinking of telling me something, then closed it again. Finally, he asked, "Did you see him before he died? Did he say anything?"

"He gave us a toolbox with papers in it. We have the papers with us." Josh stood up to get them, then handed them to Russ.

Russ looked them over and said, "These are Stevie's treasure hunting notes." His eyes narrowed, but he seemed more interested than wary. "Is that why you're out here?"

I shrugged. "It got us thinking, but they're almost illegible. They did make me go and look at my dad's map again, though. I wouldn't have thought about it if your stepdad hadn't said the box had treasure in it."

We told him more about the plane crash, leaving out the details about his stepdad coughing blood. He thanked us for the papers and for trying to save his stepdad.

I nodded at Josh, then said, "You want to come with us on our search? We're bushwhacking up and down these valleys in the manzanita looking for the X on the map."

He was quiet for a moment, then shook his head. "I don't think so." Then he changed the subject. He started talking about a guy in Monterey who keeps bees and tends the hives without wearing a protective suit or even a net hat. "He uses one of those smoke canisters, then he gently guides them around with his hands. His bare hands. He says he almost never gets stung. And the honey drips off the honeycomb, and it's almost too sweet." He trailed off and gazed into the fire. The silence was fine for a while, then it started to seem like we needed to say something into the quiet.

Josh told the story about the yellow jackets. He started slowly, but by the end he was dancing around the fire imitating me, yelling, "Bees! Bees! Oh no, they're flying away with me!" That made Russ laugh and seemed to pull him out of his reverie. He offered the whiskey around one more time. Then he turned to Josh and asked him if there were any beautiful Amazon women around.

Josh nodded and after a second, he added, "If only we could turn stories into reality, huh?" I saw in that moment what Josh had been doing his whole life: pretending to be someone he wasn't. And he would continue to have to make the decision of who to trust and who to lie to. And somehow, although he had told Jenny and Nate and me, I still hadn't earned his trust. I stared into the fire and swallowed hard.

Russ thought for a minute, then said, "Sometimes they're a little too real. You remember when I told you about the guy in the bar and the bear? I didn't tell you the part that keeps bothering me." He pushed his hair back. "I protected both my mom and Stevie as best I was able from my stepdad, but when he had been drinking, he got his licks in. He beat up my mom especially, and he did it when I wasn't around to get between them."

He reached over and put a new branch on the fire, watching it smoke until flames caught. "One time, near the end of high school, I came home late. I thought everyone was asleep, so I opened the front door without making a sound. I knew how to do that. I turned the key in the lock and turned the knob at the same time, so it slid open without a click, then I pushed down on the door a bit to keep the hinges from squeaking. I was turned toward the door closing it behind me carefully when I heard a strange noise from upstairs."

He tilted his head as if he was listening to the sound again. "It was a mewling sound. At first, I thought a kitten had gotten into the house. But as I got to the bottom of the stairs, I saw him at the top, with his back to me. He had my mom in the corner at the top of the stairs—she had made that noise. He was growling half sentences, almost under his breath at her. He was hitting her open-handed, left, then right, then left again. After the first bit I heard, she wasn't making a sound. She was just taking it."

His voice had gotten gravelly while he was telling the last part. He was growling like his stepdad had in the scene he was telling, then he took a breath and started talking faster. "I ran up the stairs and grabbed him by his shirt collar and yanked him backward. He hadn't even heard me behind him. I watched him tumble down the stairs, bouncing on his back and grabbing at the stair rail then falling over again. He crashed headfirst into the corner of the landing and stopped there with his head at a strange angle. I thought I had broken his neck. But he got up and stomped out of the house."

He looked at Josh, then at me, across the fire. He took another sip of whiskey and continued. "After that, he left for a lot of years, and he left his Stevie with my mom. I was relieved but also sort of disappointed when he stood up and was okay."

He pointed at me with his cup. "I don't know how, but that guy in the bar in La Paz knew about me and my stepdad. He wasn't talking about a bear when he was telling me that story. He was talking about my stepdad. That part about the bear bouncing down the cliff and landing against the tree sounded too familiar. And then when my stepdad came back, it was like he was following me somehow, stalking me. I kept thinking about what the guy in the bar said about the only way to be free of him. Sometimes, you have to do what you think is right, consequences be damned.

"After Stevie died, I didn't hear from my stepdad at all. I was happy he didn't come around, but it pissed me off that he didn't seem to care that his son had died. But then, last week, he showed up on my doorstep. He said he wanted to see Stevie's belongings, so I showed him the boxes in Stevie's old room. He searched through them, obviously after something. Then he found a metal box in one of the cardboard boxes I had taped and stacked. He said he had gotten a letter from Stevie saying that there was an old mine in these mountains with treasure in it and that Stevie wanted him to have it. Stevie told him in his letter where he thought it was and told him all the details were in the box. He wouldn't let me see what was inside the box. He said he was going to take his plane and fly over the area, surveying it, then land on an airstrip he knew of by a cattle ranch—Uncle Murray's place, I think. Uncle Murray and Frank moved further into the hills after they gave up the mine."

I looked over at Josh as Russ was talking. He was as enthralled as I was. The parts of the puzzle were starting to come together. "As my stepdad was standing on the front porch about to leave, he turned away from me, then turned partway back and said, 'I forgot. I owe you something.' Then he swung that box from his hip and hit me on the side of the head. Knocked me out cold." Russ pulled back his hair and showed us the stitches still on his temple. His hair was still short where the doctor had shaved around it. "I woke up in a pool of blood and had to drive myself to the hospital. That's what's got me. The old bear I threw down the stairs got me in the same place with his claws as the bear in the snow got that guy on the beach in Mexico."

He leaned in toward us, lowered his voice, and said, "I snuck into the airport and topped up his fuel tanks with diesel fuel. I figured he wouldn't get over thirty miles like that. I imagined him somewhere in the brush back in one of these canyons trying to figure a way out." He took a deep breath and let it out. "As much as I hated him, I didn't imagine him dead."

I stared into the fire. "Damn, that's tough." Outwardly, I was calm, but I wanted to get up and get away from him. I wanted to pack up and ride out of there that minute. He had just told us he killed his stepfather. He had done it in a typically Russ fashion: Doing something without thinking about it and having the outcome way exceed his intentions. But the fact still remained that he was the cause of the crash. I stood up and walked around the campsite for a minute. As I walked, I talked myself out of my initial impulse to run. Russ was dangerous, but he wasn't malicious. We would be okay. I took a deep breath and sat back down. Josh kicked at a rock near the fire, then stirred the fire with a stick.

Russ rubbed both his ears at the same time, then rubbed his face with his hands, then looked up. "I wish I could change so many things. I feel bad about what happened in the desert. I shouldn't have talked Stevie into going there first. I shouldn't have left him alone out there. I don't know yet how I feel about the old man. But it's done." He looked into the darkness, as if he could see something out there, but there was nothing to see.

"But I know I don't want to go with you guys on your treasure hunt. I'm going to have to spend some time figuring all of this out by myself. That's the truth of it. You'll always be unsatisfied until you make peace with what you can't change. After that, you can decide how you feel about the rest of it."

We stared for a while into the fire, its flame small against the moonless darkness of the night. I could see stars, even though the brightness of the flames made my eyes less sensitive. I thought about pulling my sleeping bag outside and sleeping under the stars like Russ was planning to, but I decided against it.

I thought about what Russ had said about regrets. I decided to tell the story that I had thought of the first night but didn't want to share at the time. "A guy I was working with told me a story when I was cutting timber in Northern California. Most of the time, I did the hard and heavy work they would give to a new young guy on the crew, but one day, they assigned me to go out and mark trees with one of the older guys. Mel was his name. For Melford. We spent the day walking through a redwood forest marking the trees that were going to be cut down and planning where the staging area would be. That type of thing.

"It was quiet in the forest, and we kept it that way. Mel didn't talk much, and neither did I, until lunchtime. After we had eaten, he leaned back and started telling me about how he had been in a fire on the ship he was on during the war. He said he thought it might help me understand some things. I guess I looked like I needed some wisdom. I suppose I did."

I reached for the whiskey and poured some in my cup. "Mel was on a destroyer off Okinawa, supporting the landing force there, and the Japanese were sending kamikaze pilots at them. They were able to shoot down most of the planes before they got close because they saw them coming straight at them, and they knew what their intentions were. One of them got through, but at the last moment, they hit the pilot, and he must have been knocked backward in the cockpit because the plane pulled up and it only hit the deck of their ship instead of down by the waterline where it was headed. But it hit right where Mel was stationed, and it burst into flames, trapping him between it and a corner of a steel bulkhead behind him. The fire was fierce, and he was sure he was done for. Fire crews were running from all over the ship, but he wasn't sure anybody even knew he was there, and he had no way through the wall of heat that surrounded him. One of the fire crew waded into the flames from the side, asbestos suit on, spraying foam from a hose in his hands, putting himself in terrible danger to save his life. That firefighter cleared a path for him to get out."

I paused and took a sip of whiskey. "I thought Mel must have been on the same ship as my dad because that's what they told us happened to him. When I asked him the name of this ship, it wasn't the same one. Still, my nose started running as he told the story, thinking about my dad and how I had only known him when I was so small."

Josh was staring at me like he was seeing someone he hadn't met before. I smiled at him and continued. "Mel told me he found the firefighter afterward, and he told Mel that when he saw a man trapped behind that wall of fire, he was thinking of his kids, and thinking that the guy there about to die in the flames must have kids too. He said he wanted them to have their dad come home. Here's where I started crying, in the cool and damp of the redwood forest, sitting on a log. Mel said he told the firefighter that if he hadn't made it out of there, he would have wanted someone like him to be there to guide them and help them grow up in his place." I could feel tears coming into my eyes as I told the story, and I looked up at the sky for a moment. When I looked back down, Russ and Josh were waiting for me to finish. Russ nodded at me to encourage me.

"The weird thing was, I was bawling out there in the forest with snot coming out of my nose, and Mel, this rough old logger, just sat there and watched me. Mel didn't say anything else, and I wasn't embarrassed at all. I felt as if someone had lifted a tremendous weight off me because it was like I had been told the story of my dad's heroism and how he was thinking of me at the end." I stared into the fire for a bit. I hadn't thought about all of this in a long time, and the story seemed to be taking on new meaning as I was retelling it.

"When Mel talked about someone being there to guide his kids in his absence, I thought of Ed, the guy who lived in the cabin below us. I don't think you met him,

Russ." He shook his head, and I continued. "He helped me figure things out after my dad died. I thought of how he had been such a quiet, powerful presence in my life, before we moved to Oakland. I took him for granted like kids do, thinking he was always there and would always be there. When I moved back to Oakland before classes started at junior college, I traveled down south to see him and thank him for being there for me, but he was gone. The Forest Service was trying to get people out of that canyon because we were all squatters in those days. I asked around, but nobody knew where Ed had gone. I wish I could have thanked him for watching out for me and for teaching me how to find that quiet space that you reach when you're making something with your hands."

Russ had been listening across the fire with his mouth open. When I finished, he stayed like that, thinking for a moment. Then he cleared his throat and said, "Ed knew what he was doing. He knew what he meant to you as a kid without a dad."

I swallowed and squinted. "I hope so. It would have been nice to be able to thank him, though. A lot of times in life you don't get to see the reverberations of what you do in the lives of the people you affect. It comes as a surprise when they tell you how much it meant to them because it had seemed to you like such a small kindness at the time."

The fire burned down. Russ drained his cup and put it away. "Well, I've gotta turn in early. I want to get started at daybreak and head further south." A few moments later we heard him flop onto his sleeping bag with a grunt.

Chapter Seventeen

GOLD

The next morning, Russ packed up and left, shouting, "No bear following me now. I'm a free man!" as he rode away.

Before he left, while Josh was off in the trees for a moment, I had told Russ about the deer we had seen. "Frank and his dad were around our house a lot when my stepdad was there," he said. "Frank's dad, Murray, is my mom's brother. He and my stepdad got to be buddies. I didn't know Frank was still doing that stuff." He sniffed, like he had just caught a whiff of a bad smell. "I'll keep my eye out for them. Damn, Frank was a weird guy."

Josh and I sat side by side on a log, finishing up the cold breakfast of cheese, bread, and salami we had pulled from our stores. As we chewed, we watched Russ climb up to the ridge at the end of the valley. "That's some serious stuff," Josh said.

I shook my head. "Russ is a complicated guy, isn't he? I mean, he killed his stepfather. He didn't mean to, but that's the way it turned out."

Josh had been putting some of the gear away, and he stopped with his hand in the bag. "And I'm not sure what exactly happened with his stepbrother. It's strange. I like Russ, but at the same time, I'm kind of afraid of him."

I poured the last of the coffee on the fire and watched the steam rise. "I know. Even back when I hung out with him in Eureka when we were young, I never knew exactly what he was going to do next. He got some notions in his head."

As Russ disappeared over the top of the valley, Josh said, "Let's go. We've got treasure to find."

We quickly packed and started hiking back up to the spot just before daybreak. Once we got there, we banged on the rocks around the opening of the mine with a stick to get any rattlesnakes to show themselves. None did. With daylight, we could see that the ceiling was low. We would have to crawl to get inside even though we had widened the opening. I stepped forward. "I'll go in first. One of us has to stay outside in case something goes wrong." Josh nodded as I put on my headlamp and gloves and crawled in.

The small rocks on the floor of the cave were sharp under my knees. Dust rose as I moved, and I almost sneezed. I rolled on my back and looked at the ceiling. The light from the entrance made shadows in the indentations, and the beam from my headlight filled them in as it played across the rock. I thought about how I've always been at home in places like this. I love rolling on the mechanic's dolly under a truck or car on a hot day to start a repair, the coolness in the shade with the bulk of the car looming over me. My breath slows in these places and a meditative mood always overtakes me. Despite the apprehension I felt about the danger I was crawling into, I felt relaxed.

On the walls, I saw marks made by digging tools and hollows where rocks had been pulled out. I knocked on one of the pine branches that had been used to shore up the ceiling, and it sounded hollow, insubstantial. I crawled further into the tunnel. The floor was crushed rock that had been left behind as the larger pieces were carried outside.

Almost right away, the tunnel turned left. As it curved, it blocked out the light streaming in the entrance. The only illumination was my headlight, yellow and dim after the brightness of the morning light outside. Beyond the curve, the tunnel stopped at a pile of rocks and rubble. At first, I thought that was as far as the excavation extended, then I realized the ceiling had caved in there. I peered through gaps in the rubble and saw that the tunnel continued on the far side. I could also see where the ceiling had let loose. A large chunk of rock and dirt had fallen down, blocking the way forward. I started to turn around to go back out and tell Josh when I heard a rattle behind me. My mind screamed *Rattlesnake!*—then I realized it was only the sound of a pebble falling down the wall from the ceiling.

As I turned around, my back scraped the ceiling of the tunnel. My right hand touched something thin and hard in the soft dirt at the edge of the tunnel. Rebar. *Rebar? Someone's been here lately. When was rebar invented? Who brought rebar all the way out here?"* I picked it up and found that it was much heavier than I expected. Maybe it wasn't rebar. I'd have to drag it out into the light to see. I held it in my hand, pushing it ahead as I crawled. When I reached the opening of the mine, I passed it out to Josh and pulled myself out of the hole on my elbows.

After I pulled my feet around to sit outside the mine, I stood up to brush the dust and pebbles off my clothes and hair, then I looked over at Josh, who was examining the rebar. "Dad. This is important. Come over here." The foot-long piece of metal was flat on one side and curved on the other. It wasn't rebar. Maybe it was a piece of lead someone a long time ago used to make bullets. Josh spit on it and rubbed on the flat side near one end and held it out to me. A dull gold color showed through.

I noticed I was breathing heavily, like I had run up a hill. It wasn't from exertion. My hands were shaking as he handed it to me. "We found it!" He was whispering, but his voice was hoarse. "Dad, this is gold. It's so heavy for its size. This strap must weigh five pounds."

I scraped at the crusted dirt. "It's rounded on one side." I brought it up closer to my face. "You can see the joint of a plant imprinted there. They must have poured the gold into a bamboo-like reed as a mold. I've read about the Spanish doing that with silver when they first started mining in Mexico, but not here." I grabbed him and hugged him. "Wow! Gold! I didn't think we'd find anything. I kept telling myself we were just on a camping trip."

We were both grinning like fools. Josh just kept shaking his head and repeating, "This is so cool." I slapped him on the back, then he slapped my back, then we hugged again. He pulled away from me and stuck his head in the entrance of the mine and let out a huge whoop. Then he came back and danced around me, almost falling off the side of the hill.

We leaned against the rocks outside the mine, passing the strap of gold back and forth, drinking in all the details of it. I was trying to believe that we had actually found gold out here deep in the mountains of Big Sur.

Josh jumped to his feet. "I'm going in." He grabbed his headlamp and gloves.

I put my hand on his shoulder. "Wait. The tunnel curves to the left just a little way in. Right after that is a cave-in, but the tunnel goes further back. You can see past it a bit. I found the bar as I was turning around at the cave-in, buried in the loose rocks at the edge. It's not a stable tunnel. Don't pull any rocks out. For now, just dig along the edges in the loose gravel there." He nodded. We were working as a team. That felt good.

He disappeared into the cave, and I sat on a rock at the entrance, bent over, holding the strap of gold in my hands. The sun warmed my left cheek. A ground squirrel chattered on the hillside above. An airplane left two white trails of vapor across the unbroken blue sky above. The excitement that had made me breathe so heavily only a moment before settled into contentment. We had found the treasure. We had found gold. Spanish gold, from the looks of it. Old. Pre-California old. Pre-United States old. Even if this was the only piece, it was worth a lot of money. I heard Josh yell, "Got one!" from deep inside the hill.

I'm doing it, I thought to myself. *I'm breaking the cycle. The plane crash is bringing good this time because I'm making it happen.*

Josh came back out, coughing and spitting dust, with two more straps in his hands. "It's dusty in there and digging into the soft dirt stirs it up. I almost couldn't see because of it." He handed the bars to me. "These were along the left edge too, parallel to the tunnel, like they were laid in a line."

They were different. Their shape was squarer. It looked like the mold the molten gold was poured into had been gouged out of a chunk of wood with a chisel, and the marks of the tool that was used to make the mold were left in the gold. There was an insignia near one end, like someone had pushed a metal stamp into the still-soft metal as it was cooling. These bars were made at a different, probably later, time. Regardless of how old they were, they were worth a lot. We could figure that out later. Right now, we needed to keep moving and get as many out as possible. As Russ and I learned all those years ago, these places are unstable.

Over the next few hours, we took turns going into the mine, wearing tee-shirts tied around our faces and trying not to stir up too much dust while still searching thoroughly. By mid-morning, we were convinced we had found all that was hidden in the part of the cave we could reach in front of the blockage. We had found ten bars.

I crawled in for one last look. I had purposely ignored the cave-in all morning and had instructed Josh to as well. But this time, I crawled closer to it, excavating near the walls of the tunnel where the rest of the bars had been. I found the end of another bar, but it was under a rock that was part of the blockage and was wedged in tight. I tried to wiggle it free, then paused. "Van," I said to myself under my breath, "Van, stop. You said you weren't going to mess with this." I rested on my side with the sharp stones cutting into my hipbone. Then I closed my eyes. With a grunt, I heaved myself back to my knees. I knew I could get it.

With care, I cleared the debris around the flat rock that was trapping the bar, then slowly wiggled the rock toward me. The dust had settled some in the tunnel, but now new dust was falling from the cave-in and from the ceiling above it. I swore under my breath. "Let it go, Van. Crawl out without it." But it was right there in front of me.

How far should I push things? I knew I was tempting fate by disturbing the cave-in to get the last bar. But that was the point, right? That's what I had decided to do. I wasn't hiding from fate anymore. I was making it do my bidding. I was fighting to create the outcome I wanted, and it was working. Then another voice in my head said, *Fighting too hard can be worse than not fighting at all.* I could feel my breathing become short and quick. I didn't know which voice to listen to—the one that expressed my newfound resolve not to hide, or the one that sounded so reasonable. I consciously slowed my breath, closed my eyes, and counted to ten. Then I opened my eyes. I would keep fighting.

Grunting, I tugged on the rock a little more. The bar seemed looser. I pulled one more time, and the rock fell out of the pile onto the floor of the tunnel. I reached for the bar, and it came out of the rubble without a fight. A chunk of rock slid down and landed where the bar had been. I swore again and turned toward the entrance.

I emerged with the last bar. "Wow! I can't believe we really found a treasure," Josh said, as we took off our clothes and beat them on the rocks of the hillside and watched the dust billow out of them. Then we put them back on and washed our faces with water from our water bottles. Finally, we put the straps of gold in the daypack. Josh heaved it onto his back, and together we hiked down the hill to the campsite.

Everything had changed. We had to reexamine how we looked, how we acted, and what we would do and say if we encountered someone. Josh worried that we looked like raccoons with dirt all over our faces and cleaner spots around our eyes. I thought the weight of the daypack was suspicious. We discussed what alibi we would use if someone asked what we were doing up that canyon that led to nowhere. Back in camp, we went immediately to the water hole, filled our bottles, and washed our faces and hands better.

"Let's bury them here," I said. Josh nodded and found a spot under a bush uphill from the creek. We dug a hole there, put the gold bars into it, and put a rock on top of it. Then we went back to the tent and ate lunch.

"We've got enough," Josh said. "Fifty pounds of gold— that's a hundred thousand dollars! It's more money than we could save in years."

I shook my head. "There's more in there. There might be a lot more. Those pieces weren't made at the same time, and they didn't come from around here." I was speaking slowly, putting this together as I was talking. "The Spanish were mining gold in Mexico and Colorado. Why wouldn't they mine gold in California too? They had learned how in Mexico and wouldn't have missed the signs of gold in the Sierras." I could feel the skin tightening around my eyes like it did when I was stressed. "Look, Josh. This is an opportunity. I'm starting to see that life gives you a couple of opportunities where if you work hard and gut it out, you can make a lot of money, and not so much the rest of the time." At that moment, not going after more seemed like quitting in the middle. It was too close to what I had done with Mike and the trucking company. Having called myself a coward so many times for not going on, the word still rang in my ears. I couldn't live with that again. "I'm going to take the chance with this one, but I want to be the one putting myself in danger, not you. Okay?"

"All right. You do the dangerous work."

Chapter Eighteen

SNAKES

I could tell that Josh was conflicted about going back into the mine. "There haven't been any problems so far," he said. He was looking worried for the first time on the trip. "Maybe we can get more gold. But it's going to be more dangerous when we try to clear the cave-in." But my determination convinced him we should try. So, after lunch, we hiked back up to the mine site. Along the way, we gathered branches thicker than two inches in diameter to use as shoring for the ceiling. When we got there, I crawled in until I reached the cave-in and jammed the branches against the ceiling and under existing cross beams. I wouldn't let Josh come in further than the turn in the tunnel.

When I had done all I could to reinforce the ceiling, I started pulling pieces of rocks off the pile and stacking them along the wall on the right side of the mine, opposite where we had found all the bars. As the afternoon wore on, Josh came further into the cave, piling rocks or dragging sacks of dirt out toward the entrance. I noticed but didn't comment. How far was too far?

We didn't need to fully clear the cave-in; we just needed to clear it enough on the left side that someone could crawl through. Josh argued he should go through because he would fit in a smaller hole, but I was adamant. The ceiling above the slide creaked as we moved rocks. I could feel the tension building in my shoulders. "Stay a little further back. I'm worried about the sounds the cave is making."

Josh said, "Why don't we jam some of the rocks into the right side of the cave-in? That way we won't have to carry them all the way out. Might shore up the ceiling too."

I looked over at him. He really was a smart kid. "Good thinking. That'll be so much easier." We started building up a wall in front of the cave-in to support the ceiling where we were removing the rocks from.

When the opening was large enough for me to slither through, I put my head through the hole. I looked straight down the tunnel to see how much further the mine continued. I saw another cave-in about twenty-five feet beyond where I was. I checked above to see how secure it was. It seemed good. I was optimistic about our prospects. Then I turned to look to the right and came face-to-face with a desiccated skull.

I almost screamed. I managed to stop myself, but I still made a choking sound and flailed a bit before I collapsed, limp, with a relieved grunt. It wasn't just the skull; it was a full body dressed in gray homespun clothes. A rock so big I couldn't have reached around it had trapped the skeleton's lower body.

Josh crawled to me and tapped my leg. "What? What is it? Are you okay? What did you find?"

I backed out of the hole and crawled toward the entrance of the mine. Josh followed. When we got outside in the daylight, I said, "You're supposed to be further out in the cave. I don't trust that ceiling." Then I told him about the skeleton. "He wouldn't have lasted long with the rocks on top of him like that. We won't either." I tried to shake some of the dust off of me. "The clothes he was wearing were homemade, from a long time ago. It might be the guy who was hiding the gold up here." I was still panting. "That would explain why the gold was still there."

I reached into my daypack and pulled out a bag of nuts and raisins. I poured some into my mouth and handed the bag to Josh. My heart rate was finally starting to slow down. "Okay, I'm just making this up here. But, what if during the mission period, the Spanish were mining in the Sierras and sending shipments of these gold straps back to Spain along the mission trail? If one of the people at the mission stole a little from each shipment, he might have hidden it here. Then one day he disappeared, and there would be no explanation where he had gone, but he never came back."

Josh nodded. "It makes sense. Does it look safe on the other side?"

"The ceiling looks solid, but I'm going to be very careful. My headlamp is getting dimmer. We should have brought extra batteries with us."

I took a big drink of water, passed the container to Josh, and crawled back into the entrance of the cave. "I'm going through the hole in the cave-in. Stay on this side of it."

Josh moved back for me to pass into the mine. He put his hand on my shoulder as I got close, and I stopped.

"Dad, get out of there if it doesn't feel right. We have enough now. I'll be right on the other side of the slide if you need help."

I nodded and started crawling. "I'll be careful."

When I got to the blockage, I wiggled into the hole and nodded at the skeleton as I passed it. I kept crawling to the far end of the tunnel where the next cave-in blocked the tunnel completely, planning to work toward the entrance. I touched the rock of the far cave-in as I turned back toward the entrance, my headlamp lighting up the fractured sandstone on the ceiling.

As I turned, my right hand closed on a bar in the loose rock by the blockage. This was going to be easy. *There's one right on top,* I thought. Then the bar wiggled in my hand.

I didn't know where I had grabbed the snake, and I couldn't see before it bit me. I expected the fangs to puncture my arm, so I slammed my hand and the snake into the wall of the tunnel. I let out a guttural scream and twisted my hand back and forth like a terrier with a rat in its mouth, trying to crush the snake into the rock. I felt more weight on one end, so I whipped that end toward the wall over and over. I didn't know if I had the tail or the head, but I couldn't let go. I kept slamming the snake again and again against the side of the tunnel. The snake stopped wiggling, but I still didn't let go. I held it at arm's length, gasping in horror as I tried to see through the dust in the yellow light of the headlamp. After a moment, I saw that I had ahold of it toward the tail, and my panicked swings had knocked it out. With a grunt, I reached up and gripped it below the head, then found a rock and brought it down on the snake's skull. I rolled onto my back in the dirt, breathing hard, sweat congealing on my skin and the adrenaline jitters dissipating in my body. My hands were shaking as my breathing slowed.

Josh's headlamp shined through the hole in the slide. "Dad. Dad. DAD! What's happening?"

I sat up and rubbed my knuckles through the gloves. "Snake," I shouted back. "I grabbed it without seeing it and had to thrash it against the wall." I took a deep breath and tried to slow my pulse.

"Are you okay? I've never heard you make sounds like that."

"I'm okay. Slammed my knuckles, though. They're going to hurt later." I looked toward the hole in the slide, but I couldn't see him. "It's good I had gloves on. I think I used up one of my nine lives. Go back to the cave entrance. It's dangerous in here. I'm going back to work."

I looked back toward the cave-in behind me, took a deep breath, and swore. "Josh, just so you know, more rattlesnakes are coming through the rocks back here at the end of the tunnel. I'm going to try to stay ahead of them." I saw one snake on the right side of the cave-in at the back of the mine. It was out of the rocks and on the floor of the mine. Another was poking its head out of a hole between the rocks.

I started digging along the side of the tunnel. I found a bar almost right away. I tossed it toward the opening next to the skeleton and dug for another. I was kicking up so much dust that I couldn't see at all. I felt a second one, pulled it out of the dirt, and threw it toward the hole in the cave-in. Then a third. They were lined up almost end-to-end, about four inches deep. Sometimes there were three or four of them sitting on the harder rock of the floor below the debris.

"Rattlesnakes aren't mean," I said to myself as I dug. "They don't want to bite you. Stay calm, you can do it." I tried to look back to see if the snakes were following me but couldn't see past my own feet through the dust I was stirring up. "They're not coming after me. They're staying by the rocks back there." I said this almost like a mantra. I could feel fate bending to my will.

My mind kept bracing for the bite, and I kept feeling phantom bites on my ankles—pains out of nowhere, sharp and deadly, but not real. Dig, pull, toss, dig, pull, toss. I was having a hard time breathing. Grit was in my eyes, causing tears to flow down my face. I started laughing, thinking about what I must look like: grunting and talking to myself, snakes slithering toward me from behind, frantically digging along the edge of an abandoned mine, tears running down my cheeks, a skeleton leering at me in front, and gold straps piling up near the hole in the cave-in ahead.

My imagination was fighting with my logical mind. *They're biting you. Feel the pain in your ankles?*

Then I was sure the skeleton was behind me, hitting any snakes that tried to come close with a stick he brandished. He seemed real, though I knew he couldn't be. I started thinking that the snake had bitten me when I had grabbed it, and the poison was just reaching my brain. But the skeleton was my protector. He was behind me, jumping side to side, talking to the snakes, threatening any that tried to get nearby.

Then the real skeleton was there in front of me, and I remembered that the ceiling of the mine might fall down at any time. I dug faster for the last of the gold, called for

Josh, and started handing bars out to him through the hole. Finally, I shouted, "That's all!"

"We have a lot, Dad." Josh's voice was hoarse as he shouted back at me. "A whole pile of them. Get the hell out of there!" I still didn't know where the snakes were behind me, but I stopped for a second before I climbed through the hole. I touched the skeleton's cheekbone with my finger, and said, "Thank you, my friend." Then I put my head out into the clearer air.

It took a few trips to get the gold out from the cave-in to the entrance of the cave. When we were done, we collapsed onto the hillside. Sprawled on the rocks and dirt in the sunlight, I let the immensity of what we had done wash over me. "I'm glad we're done with that. We did it, but we took some terrible chances."

Josh sat up, then rolled onto his hands and knees. He frantically patted his butt a couple times. "Shit. I have to go back in."

My adrenaline surged again. "No, you don't."

He stood up and brushed off his jeans. He gazed out at the valley below, then picked up a pebble and tossed it down into the bushes. "I do. When I was waiting for you, my wallet was digging into my side, so I pulled it out and set it on a rock by the slide. I forgot to pick it up."

For a while that morning, as we worked together, watching each other's backs, I had forgotten he was a teenager. In a moment, I was his dad again. "You're kidding. Why did you do that?"

He dropped back into his role of the kid again too. "I don't know why I did it. I just did." He scowled at me. "I can go right in and come straight back out."

"I can't believe you did that." I took a deep breath and let it out, then said, "Go. Don't touch a thing." He turned to go back into the tunnel. "Kids," I muttered. Then, I sat back against the hillside and closed my eyes, letting my fingers explore the contours of one of the gold bars. We had done it. We had fought fate and won. We had found the treasure on Bobby's map, and now we could go back down to our camp and wash off and get something to eat. I looked forward to cooking a good meal that night and to starting back home the next morning when it would be cooler.

A great sense of relief settled over my body. I thought about how finishing something scary and dangerous brought the same release from the anxiety as quitting Mike's business had. I wondered if that feeling would have come to me in business had I held on a little longer. But at that moment, there was also the satisfaction that we got through the gauntlet, and we did it together.

My thoughts strayed toward logistics. It would take a couple of trips to get the bars down to our camp, and we would have to hide them there. We would have to wrap the gold up in rags so it didn't appear so densely heavy in our pack saddles. It would have to look like regular pack saddles. If we put a couple of bags of those fossils that Josh was setting to the side on top of the gold, we would have a good story in case anyone asked. If we took the shorter route back, away from the coast, we could make it in two days. Then, when we got home, we would have a celebration. I would have to figure out where to sell the gold, but that would work itself out. It would be a shame to melt down the bars, but if we didn't, there would be questions about where they came from. There could be collectors that would buy them without asking too many questions. What if we said we found them on our land and paid the taxes? That way we wouldn't have to worry about sneaking around.

A rumbling came from the hillside and shook me out of my daydream. I didn't hear it as much as sense it through my back. At first, I thought it was an earthquake and flashed back to Russ and me in the mine above his uncle's house. It wasn't the same though. The earth wasn't shaking. The sound was coming from the mine. As I realized this, air came whooshing out of the hole, followed by dust. A sickness overwhelmed me as I realized what it was. I jumped up, ran to the opening, and stuck my head in. "Josh! Josh! Are you all right?"

Nothing. No response. My whole body went weak and wanted to collapse. I shouldn't have let him go in. The wallet wasn't worth my son. The gold was a fool's errand. What idiots we were to take this chance for money. *That's what I get for letting myself be happy for a moment.* I thought about the vapor trails of the plane I had seen earlier and wondered if it had crashed too. Again, I yelled—louder, with panic in my voice. "Josh?" I fumbled for my gloves and headlamp as I crawled into the hole. I thought for a moment that I should just kill myself right there.

"Dad." A wave of relief flowed over me at the sound of his voice. I closed my eyes and said a prayer of thanks. I don't think of myself as a religious person, but right at that moment, I knew that whatever power there was in the universe had handed me my son back from the edge of the void. The sickness that had taken over my body was replaced by an overwhelming desire to lie beside the hole and cry for the son that had been taken away and given back to me all in a moment. "Dad, I'm trapped." His voice was calm, almost serene.

"What is it?" I pulled on my headlamp and gloves and grabbed the short-handled shovel before crawling through the entrance. "How bad is it?"

"I'm okay, but my legs are under the cave-in."

I turned on my headlight and crawled into the mine through the dust, not able to see anything in front of me. I thought about turning off the headlamp because it was so useless, but I didn't. Just past the first turn, I touched his hair; he was lying with his head toward the entrance of the mine. "Is that you?"

I heard him chuckle in the dark dustiness. "It's either me or you just put your hand on something scary and hairy."

I was glad to hear him making a joke. It made me feel that he thought things were going to be okay. I reached out until I felt his hair again, put my fingers on his face, then leaned in and kissed his forehead. My son. "I'm going to feel along you until I reach a rock or something." I didn't find any rocks or rubble until I reached his legs. He was lying on his back, and there was a mound of debris on top of both his legs. I felt a large rock near the top of the pile. "I'm going to roll a big rock off you. Put your hands over your face." I grabbed a flat rock about the size of a couch cushion and pulled it towards me, trying to control its slide so it fell away from him. I could feel further down his leg after that.

"I can wiggle that one. The left one is stuck deeper."

Carefully, I moved rocks and scraped debris off of his right leg. It came free pretty quickly, and, as soon as it did, I could see him bend it and give it a shake. "It's okay. I think the right one is fine." The left leg was further in the mound of rocks. The dust was starting to settle out of the air, and I could see vague shapes with the help of the headlamp. A huge chunk of the ceiling had come down. One of the slabs of rock must have weighed two thousand pounds. It was canted at an angle with the base of it at Josh's left foot and the top wedged into the ceiling.

I couldn't help myself. I imagined his foot crushed under that rock, and I thought about having to leave him in the cave to get help. My mind started to spiral into all the possibilities. I had to tell myself to stop it. "What are you talking to yourself about?" Josh said.

I guess he knew me better than I thought. "I'm just telling myself to focus. I was getting distracted. I'm fine now."

I kept scraping and digging with my hands. The shovel was useless because his leg was right there. As I got closer to the slab that was over his foot, I started digging more frantically and had to tell myself to slow down. When I was able to feel his ankle and dimly see both the ankle and the huge rock for the first time, I must have let out a whoosh of breath because Josh asked me what was happening. "I'm at your foot. Give me a second." I cleared more debris and was able to feel a space above his ankle. The top of my head was tingling in anticipation. I felt to the side, and there was a rock beside his ankle, supporting the slab. "Don't move. I need a moment."

The smaller rock had kept the large one from crushing his foot. He might be okay. I closed my eyes for a second and breathed slowly. Then I opened my eyes and cleared some more small rocks from around his foot. Below the big slab, the gap between the rocks was just large enough for his ankle to fit through. "Okay, Josh, try to pull your foot out a little."

After a pause, he said, "I can move it, but it's scraping."

"Let's get it out of there without pushing on the rest of the slide." I crawled up near Josh's shoulders, cradled his head and shoulders in my lap with my arms under his armpits, braced my feet on the floor, and pushed with my legs. Josh shifted a little. "Did that work?"

"I think so. It scraped a lot, but it's not bad. I might lose my shoe. Do it again."

"We're not leaving your shoe in there." I was clear about that. The other cave-in buried Russ' shoes, and this one wasn't getting Josh's. Besides, he only had one pair with him.

Down at his foot, I pulled more pieces of rock out of the space next to and under it. I was worried about removing too much in case it caused the smaller rock to shift, allowing the big slab to come down on his leg. When he said that his ankle felt freer, I went up to his shoulders again, and we pulled together. We both grunted a few times, then he yelled, "I'm out!"

I took a deep breath. I would think when we were out of the mine. "Let's get out of here!"

We crawled quickly back toward the entrance of the mine. "Can you move everything?"

"I think so. I think I'm bleeding some, but I'm okay."

"Did you get your wallet?"

He snorted. "Not that it matters now, but yes." His sarcasm was oddly comforting.

When we got outside, Josh told me that he had gone in and found the wallet quickly. But, as he turned around to leave, he kicked one of the old shorings, and it gave way. "I thought I was going to be like the skeleton. I had a vision of my face all dried up with my leg trapped in there."

"We have been so lucky." I wiped my face with my shirt. "That slide could have trapped you on the far side of it, like the skeleton. I would have been digging for you until my fingers were bloody, hoping but not knowing if you were alive under the rocks." A cold shiver went through me, and I closed my eyes until it passed. We were taking too many chances. Gold wasn't worth Josh's foot, let alone his life.

I reminded myself that I had started this trip thinking the map was a dead end and that the goal was to have some harmless fun in the backcountry. It had turned into something much bigger and much more dangerous. We didn't need to take any more chances.

I had certainly been fighting fate, and it had turned out well. I felt a sense of contentment, and for the first time in a long while, I didn't think of something bad in my life to keep fate from seeing my happiness.

Chapter Nineteen

THE MELLO

A s we sat around the campfire that night, Josh said we should tell Russ about the gold.

I wasn't so sure. "I like Russ, but he's the reason his stepfather's plane crashed. The guy might have deserved it. Maybe he was the wife-beating, child-beating son of a bitch that Russ says he was, but that doesn't change the fact that he's dead."

I looked over at Josh, who was sipping freeze-dried soup out of his cup. He shrugged. "You may have a point."

"And what about Stevie? Did Russ take him out to the desert and leave him? Did you notice his story changed a little from one night to the next?" I took a spoonful of my soup. "The first night he told us the story, Stevie convinced him to go out in the desert, but last night, he talked Stevie into going to the desert before coming up here." I moved closer to Josh to get out of the smoke from the fire. "I only knew him for a couple of weeks when I was a kid. We don't know what he might do if he knew we had the gold."

Josh stood up to get another piece of bread, then sat back down. "I agree that we have a claim on the gold. I mean, we had the map. We found the mine, and we made it through the cave-in and the snakes and did all the work to clear it out." He rubbed his ankle for a second before continuing. "I'm glad we told him about his stepdad. And we should think about sharing part of the gold with him."

I didn't answer for a moment. He was growing into a thoughtful, kind person that I was proud of. "Let's get the gold out of here before we go sharing it. It's like they say about mountain climbing. You think you've done the bulk of the work when you get to the summit, but the dangerous part is coming back down the mountain."

He sat back against the log and put his hands out toward the fire. "You know, you still haven't told me about how you met Mom."

"Let me think about where to start." I stared into the trees by our campsite, remembering.

I must have gotten lost in my thoughts for a while because Josh leaned in and said, "I was sort of hoping you would tell me about her tonight."

I jumped. I'd been back in the cool of the coast, not by the campfire. "I'm getting there."

"Look at you." Josh whacked me on the shoulder. "You had a funny smile on your face just then, like you were seeing a vision. Mom must have been hot when you met her."

I smiled again.

Al and I had settled into life in Eureka. We rented a two-bedroom apartment, bought pickup trucks, and found the bars we liked to hang out in on our nights off. After we had been working together for a while, we taught a batch of new guys to be limbers. We graduated to manning the chains and the bigger saws and to making a little more money. I didn't have many more plans than that and didn't really want more than that.

I stumbled out of my room on a Saturday morning a few weeks after Russ had stopped coming to the poker games. Al was sitting at the table in the kitchen, appearing surprisingly chipper after the amount of beer he had drunk the night before. He always told me that beer didn't give him a hangover because he peed the hangover out all night long. There might have been something to that. He nodded to the coffeepot and said, "New York steak and eggs. Over medium eggs with hash browns. And maybe a side of pancakes." I poured my coffee and looked at him over the cup as I wondered if it was worth burning my tongue to get that first sip right away. I waited for him to continue because he would let me know what he was talking about in a second. He always did. "That café downtown. The Mello. We can get breakfast there, and I have a craving."

As we sat down in our booth a half-hour later, Al said, "That dark-haired waitress is beautiful. I hope she's ours." I didn't want to stare, so I didn't turn around. When she arrived at our table, coffeepot in hand, I looked up at her. He was right. She was tall and had long black hair pulled back in a ponytail. Her face was tanned despite the fog that hid the sun on that part of the coast most days of the summer. Her blue eyes were so dark they were almost black.

As she flipped my mug over, I smiled. "I know you. You're Jennifer Wharton. You were at Oakland Tech. Two years ahead of me, I think."

She stepped back and squinted at me. "I recognize you. I saw you around school, but I don't know your name. You played baseball."

"I'm Van Weathers, and this is my friend Al. What are you doing waitressing? You were always one of the smart kids." As soon as I said that I regretted it.

She arched an eyebrow at me. "I'm going to college up here, and this pays the bills. Those brains help when it comes time to add up your check. Let me get your food started."

As Jennifer left to put the order in, I poured cream into my coffee and shook my head. "That didn't start well. I came right out and insulted her and waitresses all at once."

"Yeah. A bit rocky there." Al seemed to be enjoying himself at my expense.

I glanced over my shoulder at her as she clipped the ticket on the rotating rack by the kitchen, then I turned back to Al. "She was hard to miss in high school. Gorgeous like that, and smart. She never hung out much with a crowd. People thought she was stuck-up, but I think she must have just been studying a lot. I would have thought she was at some Ivy League college or something."

I kept watching her out of the corner of my eye as Al and I ate breakfast, but she was too busy to spend any time at our table. She never seemed to move fast, but whatever her customer needed next appeared without them asking for it. She knew all the regulars, and they clearly liked her. I could see becoming a regular at this place.

I drove by myself to the Mello Diner early the next morning before it got busy. I asked to be seated in Jennifer's section. As she poured my coffee, I asked her if she had family in town. She put the coffeepot down on the table and wiped her hands. "I'm living with my mom and dad. We moved up here after high school."

"Didn't you guys have a bunch of restaurants?"

"Yeah, we did. This is the last one left, though. My dad had a stroke, and we lost them all." She glanced over her shoulder, but all the tables seemed to be fine for the moment. Then she turned back to me. "What are you doing up here?"

"My mom got cancer and died my last year of high school, and we had to sell half the bakery. My dad died in the war, so I didn't have any family anymore. I just left. It seemed like I had to burn it all down and start over fresh."

She nodded. "I know what you mean. I almost wish this place had gone with all the others. It would have been easier for everyone if we had burned it down." She looked behind her again, and this time she must have seen someone that needed attention. "As it is, here I am." She smiled and walked off.

When she came back with my eggs and hash browns, I asked what she was studying in school.

"Accounting. I've always liked the orderliness of numbers, and accounting is nothing if not orderly. It's like a puzzle where you can put all the pieces together into a whole if you're patient enough." She shrugged. "You're logging?"

I tilted my head at her. "I am dressed the part, aren't I?"

"That and, if you throw an axe in this town, you'll probably hit a logger."

I glanced at her, and she looked back down at me with a kind of amused smile on the edges of her lips. Her eyes were laughing too, like she had a secret. We didn't say anything for a moment; we just looked at each other. "I imagine guys are asking you out all the time, you being so pretty and all."

She blushed a little. It just made her prettier. "Well, not all the time, but I never say yes."

"Boyfriend?"

"No, just reducing the noise." Her face became more serious. "If I never say yes, word gets around, and people stop asking." She raised her chin a little. "When the right guy shows up, I'll let him know."

I thought I better find out what that meant. "If I came back next weekend, would you have time to talk a little?"

She let a small smile show through, like I had asked the right question. "After lunch, about one-thirty, it gets slower around here."

"A late lunch sounds good to me."

She refilled my coffee cup before moving to the next table to take their order. I stared out the window to hide my silly grin.

The next weekend, the lunch crowd was thick, so we just snuck a few words in while she was working. After they cleared out, she sat down across from me in my booth with a glass of Coke. "How does that sit with you, cutting down entire forests?"

Well, here we go, I thought. *She's not messing around with small talk.* "It's strange. Some of the older guys tell stories about the giant trees back in the days when they carried the logs out on railroads. They talk about the beauty and wildness of it all and how quiet it was when they walked through it. At the same time, they're proud of the size of the trees they cut down. It's like they don't see a conflict between loving the forest and destroying it."

She sipped her Coke, set it down, and looked at me for a moment. "How about you?"

I took a deep breath. Conflicting emotions had been rolling around in my head for a while, but I hadn't put them into words or even contemplated them seriously. When I looked for an answer to her question in the café, though, I found that I had made sense of them without consciously deciding. "I haven't been doing it long. At first, it was exciting. There was so much to learn and a lot of danger. You have to be alert all the time, especially when you're a beginner. I didn't think about it much. It was something I was doing, just like all the rest of the guys." I reached over and grabbed the mustard bottle so I would have something to do with my hands. "I found myself seeing what they loved about logging. We show up early in the morning to a beautiful section of untouched forest and stand for a second, soaking in the grandeur of it. Those moments in the morning can make you forget what we leave behind. It's a wasteland when we're done with it. It's getting to me, but it's a living."

She leaned back a little. "Why do you keep on doing it?"

I thought about that for a moment too. "When my dad died, and I was still a kid, I used to run in the forest until I couldn't stand up. I had to do that to get all the rage and sadness that was inside me out. When I was so tired that thoughts wouldn't form anymore, I would fall asleep out in the middle of nowhere. I'd wake up still sad, but somehow the fire in me would burn lower than before." I had been rolling the mustard bottle between my fingers, and it fell over with a clatter. We both jumped. I picked it up and set it on the table between us and looked at her. Her gaze was steady. She was listening with a concentration I wasn't used to. "Logging is kind of like that. It wears me out every day, and I can't think about very much except what's in front of me. If I'm not focusing on the tree and the chainsaw and where I'm going, that's when I can get hurt." I sat back, and she reached forward and picked up the mustard bottle. "I haven't put it into words before. It was just a bunch of feelings that I hadn't sorted out until just now. But talking to you made me put it in order." I took a deep breath. "I'm disgusted at what we're leaving behind. That bad taste is becoming larger than the benefit I'm getting from the hard work. We start out with a tract of forest, green and alive, and we leave behind broken brush and stumps and churned-up earth." I stopped and thought about what I had said. I meant it. I knew the next step was doing something about it.

We talked for another fifteen minutes or so, but I could see her watching the other waitresses cleaning up and she seemed uncomfortable not helping. "I should let you get back to work."

She stood up. "Yeah, I suppose I should."

I got up to leave, then paused. "Jennifer, can I come back tomorrow?"

She studied me for a moment, like she was considering, then she smiled. "I'd like that. And I'd like it if you called me Jenny."

Chapter Twenty

EXPLORING

The next Saturday, we met at her house after she got off her shift. We drove up the coast with her sitting beside me on the bench seat of my dark blue 1950 Ford pickup. It was a beautiful day without wind or fog, and the sea reflected the turquoise of the sky. The road wound inland through meadows with grazing cows and then back to the ocean. Jagged gray rock spires, broken off from the mainland, jutted out of the waves. We stopped at all the tourist attractions along the highway. We tasted jam made from local blackberries and huckleberries at one small stand. We growled at the full-size steel and concrete dinosaurs that bared their teeth at us from among the trees and ferns at a place called Prehistoric Times.

At some point, I turned to her and asked, "Why were you willing to go out with me when you don't usually go on dates?"

She looked out the window, then back at me. "I knew your name when you came in. I was just messing with you a little. Then when you made that comment about wait-resses and why was I there, I thought I needed to let you dangle for a while."

I nudged her. "Paying me back for being an idiot, huh?"

"Yeah. You two were like puppies in that booth. You were chewing on each other's ears and knocking water glasses off the table with your tails. Cute, but not worth worrying about."

The road was straight, so I snuck another glance over at her. "When did I get worth thinking about?"

"Oh, I started worrying when you showed up by your-self the next morning. I thought, *Here we go. He's serious.* You're my type too. You're kind of rough on the edges. But there's a stillness about you, like you're walking in the forest. You don't fidget." Later she told me she liked my sadness too. She said it felt like vulnerability, like depth of feeling and experience.

We stopped in a market and bought cheese, salami, French bread, and beer in cans. Then, we drove to the gray sand beach below the windswept town now resting in the calm quiet of the unexpected respite from the wind. We sat on an old blanket with our backs against a log that was half-buried in the sand. We watched waves crash on the rocks for a while, then I asked, "When did your dad have his stroke?"

"In the fall of fifty-two. So, a bit more than two years ago now."

"What was it like for you?"

She picked up a handful of sand and let it fall out through her fingers. "We were scared. My dad was in the hospital, and people kept calling or showing up at the door telling us we owed them money."

"Did you tell them your dad was sick?"

She shook her head. "One time a guy came up our driveway, and he wanted to know when he would be paid. I started crying when I told him I didn't know. When I told him my dad was sick and might die, tears were running down into my mouth. He got embarrassed and left. Both Mom and I got good at crying after that. But it wasn't an act. We really didn't know if he would survive."

I knew that feeling. But I didn't say anything; I just wanted to let her talk. "That must have been terrible."

"Yeah." She picked up another handful of sand. "He was in the hospital for a long time, and I had no idea what to do. My mom wasn't taking charge, so I started trying to figure it out. I got some information out of her, but my dad had mostly kept her out of his business dealings. Except that she's who made him keep the original Mello, the one up here. She had him keep it out of the corporation and in her name—as insurance.

"I picked up pieces of the story from him and parts from the people calling for money." She stopped playing with the sand and looked up at me. "That's when it started to come together. He had kept borrowing money to open other diners in other cities. He wasn't making money, but he was sure that expansion was the answer that would unlock profits. At one point he had eleven diners. Eleven! Crazy, huh?" I nodded.

"We had always had money and lived in a big house. I guess I was a pampered princess who never had to worry about a thing—until, all of a sudden, I did. It got easier when he got out of the hospital, but he was in bed all the time, so I kept doing everything for the business. I didn't get any of the thrills of building the business up, but I got to be in charge as it fell apart around me. I was the one shutting down the corporation and paying enough of the bills so people would be satisfied. Still, every one of them came out short."

"So, this is the only Mello left?"

"Only this one. We're getting by, but Dad never has worked again." She pursed her lips, then pushed them together in a line. "I know this is mean, but I wonder sometimes how much of him not being able to work is physical and how much is that he's beaten down and doesn't have any more fight in him."

She didn't say anything for a minute. Then she said, "Mom couldn't help much either. She was dealing with her own problems. During that time, I think I cried every night before going to sleep from the exhaustion and from feeling so alone taking care of everybody."

The beer and the sun and the sound of the waves made us drowsy, and she put her head in my lap and closed her eyes. "I see a nap coming on, but I need one too." I pushed the sand under the blanket into a pillow for our heads, then slid my legs around to spoon her from behind. We fell asleep with the sun on our backs and our heads in the shade of the log.

Over the next few weeks, we saw each other for short snippets. One evening, I came by her house, and after meeting her parents, we strolled around the neighborhood. We walked and talked for a couple minutes, then stopped at a tree with her back against the rough bark and kissed while laughing at our neediness. It started to rain, and we ran back to get my truck. We drove until the heater warmed up the cab, then parked on a lonely street and made out some more. When we slowed our kissing and pulled away from each other a little, Jenny nibbled on my ear and whispered, "It's inevitable. It's building and we can't hold it in forever."

"I know. It makes me wonder why we don't just give in now, but there's something intoxicating about this rampaging, overwhelming feeling. It's so alive. And we're talking almost as much as we're kissing." I ran my fingers through the hair behind her ear. "I'm getting to know you inside with an urgency that's like lust. I want to understand all of you. I want your body, but I want your brains too, and your... you. I want all of you."

She giggled. "It sounds like a horror movie." In a vampire voice, she said, "I want to eat your brains." I laughed too, and we went back to kissing some more.

We both knew we were in the middle of something we hadn't found before, and I knew I wanted to experience it slowly. She seemed to agree.

I've always had a connection to something greater than myself, and that connection is strongest when I'm in nature. I felt that in Jenny, too. She had an appreciation for the grandness: the stars on a moonless night pulling you deeper and deeper into forever, or the ocean's endless horizon reminding you that all you can see and all you can imagine are only a small part of all that is.

And we both appreciated the details. When I showed her a leaf I had picked up off the ground, I knew that we would stand together in appreciation of the veins becoming smaller and more numerous until they disappeared. I knew that they would take us into contemplation of the intricacy and pattern that reached into depths we would never fathom.

But when we were kissing like that, there was a need within my body to push even closer to hers. She would put the arch of her foot on top of mine or I would caress the back of her neck while still holding her tight, and for a moment, I would think we had quelled the need. Then it would start again, that urge to squeeze her to me so hard that our skin and bones and blood would meld into one glorious being, sharing one body.

On the couch in my apartment, she said, "I think we should."

I pulled back and looked at her. "Now?"

"I can't wait any longer."

"I think we should too. But we both have to agree. You say it first."

"Okay. Here we go." She scrunched up her face, like it was hard for her to get the words out. "I think..." She paused and rubbed her chin. "We should... get pepperoni!"

I punched the air. "That is exactly what I was thinking! Get your coat. We're going out for pizza."

We both knew how the game was going to end, but we were having fun making the anticipation last.

Later that week, we were drinking beer and waiting for our sandwiches in a café a few miles up Highway 101 in Arcata. She had been talking about how the sound of a mockingbird in the middle of the night is restful, not annoying. "It should keep you awake. I mean, it's a bird making racket all night long, and it's not even a pretty song, but it puts me right back to sleep when I hear it."

She stopped in the middle of her thought and looked at me like she was seeing me for the first time. "I know you." She blinked and shook her head. "I know you."

I didn't answer right away. I nodded slowly and smiled. "I know you too."

What we were waiting for wasn't clear until that moment, but we didn't wait much longer after that.

At work, I scrambled over the wet bark of trees that had been standing tall just the day before. Now they weren't trees but logs, and I was cutting them into sections that would fit on the trucks or attaching chains to them so other men could drag them to the loading area. It was the same thing I had been doing for over a year.

But there was a difference inside. The void—the one I had been feeling ever since my mother had died—wasn't as big. The numbness that I had to fight with hard physical labor was filling in. It hadn't gone away, but there was something larger than it. Every moment, visions of Jenny washed over my conscious mind. Inside, where I was used to finding a pit of loss, there was solid ground. The nothingness that had seemed so overwhelming before was itself overwhelmed by the physical need that permeated my body.

But, as usual, once I found a little ground to stand on, I worried about it being taken away. It had become a reflex to deny that I was happy or to find an unhappy thought to dwell on. I thought that by doing this, I could rub out the footprints of contentment. Then fate wouldn't know they were there. This was how I hid.

I stopped telling the story to Josh for a moment. I had been lost in my memories of those days in Eureka for a while and had almost forgotten there were a few things he shouldn't hear. So, I stood up to get some more wood for the fire. Then I skipped over the whole trip I took to Chicago to visit my grandparents, and what a disaster that turned out to be, and the plane crash that happened while I was there—the fourth one. I hadn't told anyone some parts of that. I skipped right to when I got back from my trip and proposed to Jenny.

Chapter Twenty-One

TAHOE

When I got back to Eureka from Chicago, I drove straight to Jenny's house. She answered the door, then she let out a yelp, and almost jumped into my arms. "Were you only gone a week? It seemed like a month." She lowered her voice. "I felt like an addict when my supply was cut off." I waved to her parents who were sitting at the dining room table, then pulled the door shut so we could make out in peace on the porch. After a couple minutes, I went inside and said hi to them, and Jenny told them she was going to ride over to my place with me. We almost didn't make it into the bedroom.

Afterward, we breathed into each other's faces, noses touching. Her hair tickled my forehead. I kissed her cheek and whispered in her ear what I had been thinking for the entire trip back across the country. "We should get married."

She pulled her face back away from mine far enough that we weren't cross-eyed. She examined my eyes and my mouth to see if I was serious. "Is that a proposal?"

"Yes. Well, you're not a person I would spring that on, so, yes, it's a proposal, but it's also telling you how I feel and asking how you feel about it." I pushed her hair back off her face. "I missed you so much while I was gone. I've known all along how amazing you are, but being gone from you brought home to me how much of what I imagine my future to be has you right in the center of everything."

The serious look on her face dissolved. She kissed me and said, "Yes, I think we should get married." She put her palm on the side of my chin. "I love you, and I missed you too. You're in all my visions of the future, too." She took a deep breath and smiled. "So, if that was a proposal, I say yes."

Then she looked away, over the top of the curtains and out at the leaves of the tree moving in the wind. When she looked back at me, she sighed, and the serious look was back. "Well, I guess we almost got it in the right order."

"What do you mean?"

She took a deep breath, let it out, and said, "I'm pregnant."

Later that afternoon, we drove over to her parents' house. We told them that I had proposed to her, and that she had agreed to get married. When we said we didn't want to wait, they asked if she was pregnant. We were ready, though; we had practiced answering that question. I had stood above Jenny with my hands on my hips, trying to act like her dad. "Are you pregnant?"

She looked at me straight in the eyes, trying not to seem shifty. "Not that we know of."

I sat down next to her. "Nope! That's a liar's answer. Try it again. What would you say if you weren't pregnant?"

She thought for a moment. "I'd tell them to quit being such parents."

"Try saying no first, too." I put on my serious parent face again. "Are you pregnant?"

She raised the pitch of her voice, so she sounded like a teenager. "No. God, you guys. How about some congratulations? We're in love."

I clapped. "Good! I like that. That sounds natural. It puts them on the defensive. Let's try another one." I pretended I had a pipe in my mouth. I blew out some smoke and squinted through it. 'So, Van and Jennifer, this seems awfully quick. Anything you want to share with us?'"

She started laughing. "You look just like him. Am I marrying my dad?"

I struck an imaginary match on the table, used it to light my pipe, and puffed a couple of times before I said, in her dad's voice, "You could do far worse, my dear. Far worse."

We were both laughing then, but she made downward motions with her hands. "Wait. We have to get this right." She took a few deep breaths. "Seriously, now!" Then she giggled again. She scrunched up her lips to make her face look serious. "I would start by telling them how you proposed. I would put my hands beside my cheek like a maiden, and flutter my eyelashes, and say, 'It was so romantic. He said everything he imagined his future to be has me right in the center of it.'"

I couldn't help laughing at her expressions. "Without the theatrics, that's a pretty good answer. I would say that you told me if I shaved more often, you might consider it."

"Nice touch. A bit of a joke to throw them off."

I put the pipe back in my mouth and took it out again. "But son, why do you want to get married so soon?"

"He called you 'son'! He must think you're okay."

I rolled my eyes at her. "Well, sir, we are in love, and we know there's an order these things are supposed to be done in. We don't think we can wait too much longer. We want to do what's right."

She pointed at me. "Good answer. They'll be stumbling over themselves to help us stay pure, and it'll throw them off the pregnancy trail."

I looked sideways at her. "You know that the first thing we're doing as a partnership is figuring out how to lie to your parents, don't you?" I thought it was the right thing to do, but it felt strange.

She thought for a second. I almost thought she would say we shouldn't, but she brightened up and said, "Perfectly acceptable given the circumstances. Sometimes our team will need to do dirty work, and we're in it together."

We were co-conspirators. That's exactly why I knew I needed to spend my life with her. "You're still going to change all the diapers, though, aren't you?" She tried to grab my head and ruffle up my hair, and somehow, we ended up on the bed again.

Her parents still weren't thrilled. We had only known each other for a couple of months. But when we told them we were set in our thinking, they gave us their blessings.

Everyone knew that Las Vegas was where you got married without much waiting, and the quickest route there was through Reno. While we were looking for a lunch spot on Virginia Street in Reno, Jenny pointed at what looked a little like a little white church with green trim. A neon outline of a bell at the top of the building completed the design. The sign said, "Park Wedding Chapel."

We left the car in front and walked inside. The couple who owned the chapel directed us across the street to the county courthouse to get our license. Less than an hour later, we were back. They had a room behind the altar where we changed into our nice clothes, which weren't that nice in my case anyway, and they married us. We had to wait for a while because an older couple got in front of us when we were across the street. She was seventy-two, and he was seventy-three. They told us they had known each other since high school but had been married to other people all that time. They had found each other again after both their spouses had died and didn't want to waste any more time.

Before we went in to watch their ceremony, I whispered to Jenny, "They seem more eager to be married than we are."

She stood on tiptoe and whispered into my ear, "They have a lot more years stored up."

I ran my hand over the curved smoothness of her dress. "I wonder if they're still horny at that age?"

She nibbled on my neck as she whispered, "They're acting like they are. This whole getting married thing is doing it for me."

"I know. I'm buzzing. We're getting married! It doesn't feel real. But at the same time, it feels just right."

She put her hand on my cheek, and we looked at each other for a second. "It does feel just right." She patted her stomach. "Even without our little reason for getting married, I have no doubts."

I felt a tear forming in the corner of my eye. "Me neither."

We got married when our turn came, but it felt like we had whispered our vows to each other in the alcove of the chapel while waiting for someone else to get married.

Since we had saved so much time and money by not going to Vegas and were so close to Lake Tahoe, we drove up into the mountains and found a rustic wood-sided motel with cottages facing out towards the mountains across the blue water. We spent the next couple of days there and found a bakery down the street that sold fantastic pies with lemony apples inside and sprinkles of sugar on the top crust. They were our breakfast each morning, and sometimes our lunch too.

One afternoon, we were on the soft and lumpy bed in the cabin under the covers. The breeze coming off the lake was cool, and it brought the odor of sun-warmed pine needles through the screen door. Through the window, we had a view of the lake between the trees becoming rough with the rising wind.

Jenny turned to me and asked, "Did the trip accomplish any part of what you wanted it to?" With all that had been going on, we hadn't talked much about it. She knew it hadn't gone well, but there were still details she hadn't heard.

"I buried my mom next to her parents. That was good. But I was also trying to find my family."

She rolled up onto her forearms so she could look me in the eye. "And family disappointed you."

"They weren't who I thought they would be. I think my mom knew that." I told her everything—what they were wearing, what the house looked like, the things they said about my parents, especially my mom. I felt my stomach cramp up as I spoke. I looked up at the ceiling, at the knots in the pine boards, then back at her. "In my imagination, they would be like my memories of my dad. He was warm and slow and always had time for me. I don't have a lot of memories of him, but the ones I have don't mesh with who I found in Chicago." She put her hand on my knee, and I continued. "The way they acted, it was like they weren't my relatives at all." I rolled up onto my side and ran my arm down Jenny's chest, then onto her stomach. "I don't have any family left in this world except you and the guppy growing inside you. I'm glad you guys are here, but still, it's lonely."

She wiped a tear off my cheek with the back of her knuckle. "Yeah. But we're here, and we're family. You and me and Guppy." She took my face in her hands. "We're family, and we have people who care about us, and who we care about. Mom and Dad, and Al. You're close to Walter and Katherine and Ed, and I want to meet them." She kissed me slowly. "I'm starting to believe that family is who cares about you, not who you're related to."

The next morning, we hiked up a trail beside a creek that came steeply down the mountainside. We crossed and recrossed the creek as the trail wound up through meadows of mule's ears with their yellow daisy-like flowers and fuzzy leaves.

The sun was still warm when we reached a small alpine lake rimmed by aspens. Its surface reflected the surrounding mountains. We left our clothes on the bank and tiptoed into the snowmelt water, staying in for as long as we could stand it. Then we chased away the chill by lounging like lizards on the sun-warmed salt and pepper-speckled granite boulders.

"I'm so happy right here. I never want to leave," Jenny said drowsily, without opening her eyes.

I made a humming sound of agreement. But I didn't say anything. I was happy. Too happy. And that scared me. So, I started thinking about how I didn't have grandparents, how I had lost them along with my parents. A familiar twinge of sadness shot through me inside, and I felt safer. It was like I had pulled a camouflage net over my head so fate couldn't see me happy and take it away from me again. A breeze blew over the lake, cooling us down, and we knew we would have to leave soon. It was only the first tentative whisper of the afternoon breeze, so it stopped again. The strength of the sun won out for a while longer before we had to put on our boots again.

I wondered if everyone had to manage their emotions this way.

Jenny's parents never found out she was pregnant. A week after we got back from Tahoe, she lost the baby in the bathroom of our apartment.

I had been sure it was going to be a girl, and I mourned her when she was gone. In my mind, she was already a child, and I knew her. I had already played with her and laughed with her. But the plane crash in Chicago had taken her from me. It left a ragged, raw wound inside of me, but a part of me was relieved that fate hadn't taken Jenny.

Chapter Twenty-Two

THE WATERFALL

The next morning, Josh and I packed up early, distributing the gold straps into the four pack saddles on the two horses. We wrapped the gold in our extra clothing and gear to add bulk, but the panniers still looked suspicious, like there was too much weight in too little space. We even put Josh's sacks of fossils on top of everything in case we had to open one of the packs.

We were tired and scraped-up when we hit the trail at first light. Despite the scrubbing we had given ourselves the day before, grooves of dirt showed dark in the cracks of our skin, especially on our hands and around our fingernails. Josh was limping a little from the pounding and scratching his legs had been through. Still, we were both in a good mood and anticipating the ride.

We climbed out of the valley to the ridge where the trail was. At the top, we saw Russ coming up from the south. I really didn't want to see him with our packs full of gold, but we waited for him at the top of the trail.

He said he had gone out to the mission and camped in the hills near there and was going to make a loop toward the coast. "I forgot to tell you the other night. Don't go through the valley with the hippies. They might be a little mad right now."

I thought, *Uh oh, Russ did something again.* But I just said, "What happened? Did they tell you to turn around too?"

He snorted. "Oh, it was worse than that." He put his knee over the saddle horn, pulled a flask out of his saddlebag and unscrewed the lid, smiling to himself. "I was moving pretty slow that morning after we camped together by the stream. I might have had a little too much to drink the night before, so I lazed around fishing a bit and lying in the sun. Later on, I started out on the trail you guys went on. When I saw you had headed up the creek, I rode up there too. I saw your tracks going up then coming back down. I wondered about it until I got up to the meadow. You had turned around when you met the hippies with guns. They told me to go away too. I did."

He looked at Josh, then at me, his eyes crinkling at the corners. I knew his story had a surprise coming. "I rode right back to our perfect campground and hung around the rest of the day. I waited until it was almost dark and rode back up that creek again. They were drinking and smoking weed and climbed into their tent not too soon after it got dark. I waited until I heard two sets of snores, then I picked up the madrone staff I had cut while I was hanging around down below. It was about six-feet-long and an inch-and-a-half in diameter, and you know madrone is hard wood, heavy for its size.

"I snuck up to their camp and cut the lines keeping their tent upright, and it fell in on them. Then, I started poking and whacking at whatever bump showed up in that collapsed tent. When I heard a zipper opening, it was time to quit. I knew they had those rifles with them, so I took off down the creek. I snuck back down to my horse and rode for half the night to make sure they couldn't catch me. So, they're not going to want company for a while."

Josh and I exchanged glances. He said, "Damn. You beat those two guys up with a stick?"

"Yes, I did." Russ crossed his arms across his chest. "They deserved every bit of it."

I realized my mouth was hanging open. I closed it. I knew Russ did some crazy stuff without thinking about it, but this was straight-up premeditated violence. Somehow it scared me more than him killing his stepdad without meaning to. My gaze wandered from his feet to his face, like I was seeing him for the first time. Acting casual, I nodded my head and said, "Pretty ballsy. They had guns, and they were probably growing pot back in that canyon. I don't think we're going that way anyway, but it's nice to know."

He looked out across the valley to the west, then pointed with his chin at the saddlebags. "You find something you liked up there in the valley?"

Josh looked at me, then pulled a clamshell fossil and a smaller snail out of his pocket and held them out to Russ. "These are so cool, and there are a lot of them out there. We spent a lot of time wandering around gathering these."

Russ glanced at the shells, but didn't seem very interested, which was the response Josh and I had hoped for. I was impressed with the coolness Josh showed. Russ turned his horse toward the ocean. "I'll see you guys around. You live up above Carmel Valley?"

I nodded. "Yeah. Pretty far up, though. Maybe we'll see you in Monterey."

"I'll call. You're in the phone book, right?"

"Yeah. We're in the book. See you."

Russ went up the ridge toward the ocean and his uncle's old mine, and Josh and I went north toward the valley.

The trail we took back toward home wound up to Serra Peak again, then turned north. Instead of heading west toward the Valley of the Condors and the ocean, we took the dryer route, dropping after a while into Esselen Meadow, a high valley of oaks among short brown grass and dry stream beds with water-worn boulders suggesting that the creeks ran full sometimes. The surrounding hills were rocky, with sparse covering of manzanita and sage. We knew there was water ahead, but as we climbed the switchbacks out of the valley, I wondered aloud if we should have left a little more room for water in the packs.

We had passed our first test on the way home. Russ had bought the story about the fossils and moved on. I was worried about him, though. He just kept showing up. We settled in for the long ride through lonely country.

In the next valley, we rode through Cedar Creek Campground with its water spigots, so we drank and re-filled our water supply. The horses were grateful for the water, but we took them away from it before they had drunk their fill, not wanting them to over-drink. We let them graze in the meadow for a while, then started up the canyon. One tent was set up at the far side of the campground, but we didn't see any people.

We wound our way up the valley on a trail beside Tassajara Creek, a rocky stream that had a steady flow of water despite the lateness of the year. Sycamores shaded part of the canyon and gave way to maples and oaks as we climbed higher. At a wide spot in the trail near a creek crossing, two college-age women with backpacks and hiking sticks waited in the shade for the horses to pass. Josh smiled at them as we went by and asked if they had hiked up from the campground below. They said they had.

"Do you know how far it is to the waterfall?" the taller one asked. "We're thinking of camping there."

Both of the girls had trusting, open faces. The taller one had brown hair, long legs, and an athletic build, and the shorter one had bobbed blonde hair and a sweet smile. We got down off the horses to let them drink. "It's still a couple of miles up, if it's the one I'm thinking of," Josh answered. He looked less tired than he had just a minute before. "Where are you two from?"

The shorter one replied, "We both go to UC Santa Barbara. We haven't seen each other all summer, so we planned this hiking trip. It wasn't supposed to be this hot, even in August, though."

Josh nodded and smiled. "Crazy, isn't it? Most of the time when you're camping, you're glad to warm up in the sun in the morning, but we've been sitting in the shade even while we're eating breakfast."

"Are you in college?" the shorter one asked.

Josh looked a little embarrassed. "No, I'm about to be a senior in high school. I'm not even sure I want to go to college right away. Is it very different from high school?"

"Night and day," said the shorter one, "If we see you up at the waterfall, we'll tell you about it."

"Or you could walk with us," the tall one added. "I'm Julie, and this is Kim."

"I'm Josh, and this is my dad, Van." He looked at me like he was about to ask to borrow the car to take them to prom. "Would you be okay taking all the horses, Dad?"

I looked back at the three of them standing together. I saw why Josh wanted to walk with them. "Sure, I can take all the horses and wait for you at the falls."

Now, I know you can't control all the thoughts that pop into your head, and I knew when it came up it that it wasn't right, but as soon as he asked me to take the horses, I thought that maybe those two pretty girls would be what he needed. Then I had to remind myself I had known him since he was a kid. This wasn't a new thing. The only new part was that we were acknowledging it.

Josh tied his horse to the back of the packhorses, and I rode on ahead. As soon as Josh started talking with them, it seemed like he forgot that we had packs full of gold with us. His gold was hiking and talking with kids his age. We weren't going too much further that day though, so I didn't feel the need to rush things.

I waited for them near the waterfall. The horses and I enjoyed the shade. They showed up around a half-hour later, and Josh looked animated and alive. After we left the two girls, we headed up the Tassajara Trail, riding silently north towards where we'd intended to camp. After about ten minutes, Josh spoke. "Dad, it was so different from high school with them. Girls my age keep trying to be someone they aren't. Julie and Kim just seemed normal."

I nodded, and said, "That must have been refreshing."

His voice got more excited. "Yeah. And they seemed to like me how I am. I didn't have to act differently with them.

"What did you guys talk about?" I looked back at him quickly to show that I was interested.

"I asked them what it was like at college. They told me it was so different from high school—which both of them said they didn't really like. They said people at college wanted to be there, and they had worked to get there, so they studied. I mean, they said they partied too, but in between, they studied. Julie said the best thing was that college gave her the chance to start fresh, without anyone knowing how awkward she had been in high school."

We rode for a couple more minutes, then he said, "Dad. You know what the best part was? It was when they told me that they were a couple."

I stopped and looked at him. "Those two?"

"Yes. Then we really had some good discussions. There's a whole gay community at college. They support each other. We connected. That hike went way too fast, but they said they would show me around if I wanted to visit Santa Barbara."

I felt like he was letting me see glimpses of his thoughts without the filters and blockades that had been there earlier in the week. But we were both holding back something. I told myself it would get clearer as time passed.

We rode up the rest of the trail to the top, each of us lost in our thoughts. Telling Josh the night before about how Jenny and I met and the trip to Reno to get married brought me back to what had happened between the two parts of the story. The trip to Chicago to meet my grandparents, and the fourth plane crash had been a huge turning point in my thinking. I wasn't going to share those details with him, but they kept coming into my mind.

Chapter Twenty-Three

ROAD TRIP

Jenny and I were parked down the street from her mom and dad's house in Eureka. "I wrote to my grandparents in Chicago," I said into the silence of my truck. We had opened the windows a crack, so we didn't steam them up with our breath, and the wind from the ocean brought a fresh oyster-seaweed scent through the cab. "They said they'd be okay with me coming to visit. I've never met them. I want to surprise them with my great-grandma's watch."

Jenny snuggled into me on the bench seat so that her head rested on my shoulder, and she put her foot up on the passenger door. "You never visited when you were a kid?"

"No. We were living hand-to-mouth in that little cabin, and I don't think it was in our budget."

Sitting side by side like that, with both of us looking out at the mist in the trees, it was like we were talking into the space of the truck more than to each other. The sentences came slowly when there were enough words, like water drops building up then falling off the end of a branch. After a moment, she asked, "They didn't come to your dad's funeral?"

"We didn't have a funeral. They didn't send his body home. I think they buried him at sea. We didn't go to Chicago afterward either." She waited for me to continue. "I was a kid, so I didn't think about it much. My mom and I retreated into our own ways of dealing with what had happened, and we kept on living our lives. Besides, it was wartime, and people weren't traveling much."

She took my hand in hers and rubbed my palm for a moment. "What makes you want to go now, besides delivering the watch?"

"They're all the family I have." I kissed behind her ear, my nose in her hair, breathing in her honey butter smell, my lips touching the softness of her skin there at the top of her neck. "My mom's parents are gone. My mom and dad are gone. I have a craving for family. I should understand where I came from and who my ancestors are. If I meet my dad's parents, maybe I'll know my dad better, and I might understand myself more."

"I get it." She reached back and moved her hair to the side, then tilted her head so I could more easily kiss her neck. "The memories I have of my grandma teaching me to crochet or my grandpa and me kicking a pinecone on the way home from a walk...those are part of what makes me who I am now. Not knowing those people must feel like a missing part of you."

"Yeah, there's a hole where my parents used to be. It's gotten smaller with time, but it doesn't go away. Maybe my grandparents will help fill in the hole a bit."

Later that month, near the end of July, I took some time off work to go to Chicago. Jenny couldn't leave the Mello. "Besides," she'd said, "this feels like a journey you need to go on by yourself. I'll be here when you get back."

I drove through Reno and Salt Lake City and into the Rockies. Mid-morning of the third day, after I had been driving alone with my thoughts for a while, I pulled off the highway into the gravel parking lot of a low, glass-fronted diner in a small town at 7000 feet of elevation. It didn't seem like I was very high up, except that the gathering clouds getting darker as I traveled were closer than you would expect.

I parked in front and saw the reflection of my truck in the restaurant's window. It looked like all the others parked there, dusty and dry. I peered through the window at the people inside. I figured I would stand out because I wasn't wearing a cowboy hat. I thought about getting one to have a souvenir of the trip but then decided that those things are better bought with some thought or they just end up on the top shelf of the closet. I reached for the handle to open the door of the truck and saw a kid about my age standing in the parking lot. He seemed like he was waiting for me to get out of the truck, so I did.

"Hey," he said, when I had my feet on the ground. "I saw you're headed east. I wonder if I can catch a ride with you when you get done eating."

His name was Pete. He was my age, but he seemed unsure of what he was doing, and that made him seem young. "Have you eaten?"

He shrugged and looked down. "I ate earlier."

He probably hadn't, with that kind of answer. "I'll take you with me when I go. Let me buy you breakfast or lunch first, whatever it is people eat at this time of the day, so we're on the same schedule." He ate like he hadn't had food in a while. Then we got in the truck and headed east. We hadn't talked much during breakfast. It would have been hard to squeeze many words past the food that was going into him. I did get from him that he was headed to Nebraska, which meant we would be driving together for most of the day. Once we got settled in for the ride, I looked over at him. "You headed home?"

"Well, it's home, but it's not where I live. I grew up there. My dad still lives there." Pete was silent for a while. "My mom died. About a month ago. I haven't been back yet. She wasn't sick or anything. I would have thought my dad would die first, with all his smoking, but no."

I didn't know what to say, so I said what people always say. "I'm sorry for your loss."

"It was a heart thing. Came on suddenly." He looked out the window for a bit. Then, he asked me what I did in California, and I told him about the quiet green dampness of the forests in the morning before we cut them down. He took a deep breath and let it out. "I don't know why for certain I'm going back. My mom isn't there anymore, and I haven't gotten along with my dad for a long time." We both watched a man on a horse as we went past. He was moving a herd of brown and white cows through a metal gate, waving his hat to keep them moving. "I already missed the funeral." Pete messed with the brim of his hat for a bit, turning it around in a circle in his hands. "There doesn't seem to be any reason to go there now. I'm not looking forward to being in the same house with my dad again."

We talked about girlfriends. He said he was hanging out with a blonde girl named Sally who was a bit wild but was a lot of fun. I told him about Jenny—how I knew her a little from high school, how we had run into each other way up in Northern California where neither of us had any reason to be, and how it had become so obvious so fast to both of us that we were meant to be together.

I turned on the radio and tried to find a station, but there didn't seem to be much out there in the middle of the foothills that were smoothing out into prairies. Pete shook his head and swallowed hard, then he started talking again. "It got to the point before I left where all my dad did was tell me what I was doing wrong. That's why I haven't been there in a couple of years. My dad would start telling me how I was screwing up, and my mom would tell him to give me a chance, then he would start telling her how her son was wasting his life away, forgetting that I was his son too. Then the fight would be on. One day, I just left. I should have at least visited."

I was silent for a moment before I turned to him. "It's hard to know what's right when you're in the middle of living it." I found a station on the radio. It wasn't coming in strong, but he tried to sing along with a song he knew.

When the song ended, he said, "It wasn't always like that. My dad used to take me hunting, and I would help him when he was fixing things around the house." He stopped talking again and seemed to be thinking. I adjusted the wind wing, so we got a bit more breeze through the cab. He cracked his wind wing a little to let the air flow across. Then he looked over at me and said, "I know what you're going to say. It might be me who changed, not my dad." He scratched his head. "I know I wasn't the perfect son. What kid is? But I wasn't as bad as my dad kept saying. There were a couple of years there where I couldn't do anything right as far as he was concerned."

I said something stupid like, "It's hard to believe parents were young once, isn't it?"

He didn't seem to hear me. "What would we even talk about? I'm going back there, and my mom won't be there. I don't know if we have anything to say to each other."

I didn't have the answer to that, so I shared a story about my mom with him. I thought maybe it would help him. I told him about how when she was sick, I kept asking her what I could do for her, and she would never let me do anything. She kept telling me to go out and live my life, but of course I couldn't go out and be a normal teenager with my mom dying at home. Her friend Katherine took care of so much, but it left nothing for me to do. I spent a lot of time at the bakery trying to keep that going, but I wanted to do something for my mom.

She loved to read, and she would have a book open anytime she wasn't sleeping. I was doing my homework in the chair in the corner of her room one day when she sighed and put the book down on the covers. "I want to keep going, but it's getting hard to focus my eyes," she said. I asked her if she wanted me to read to her a little. That became what I could do for her.

When I think about it, my heart seizes up because we spent so many hours when I was a kid in our little house in the redwoods with me sitting on her lap with a book.

For almost a month that spring, I read to her until she fell asleep. When she woke up, she would turn to me and say, "Where were we?" and I would start again.

Right before she died, the cancer had become too painful, and the morphine made it so she couldn't keep up with a story anymore. But she liked the sound of my voice, so I kept going. At one point, she opened her eyes and said, "You know, it's more the companionship than anything."

"I wish I could do more," I told her. But I didn't know what.

She said, "You're doing the world for me just by being here, by showing up. It doesn't matter what you say or do."

I suppose I was telling the story as much to myself as to him, not expecting him to gain much from it, but when I dropped him off in front of his dad's house in Cozad, Nebraska, Pete grabbed his bag out of the bed of the truck, then came back to the door he had left open. He leaned into the cab, holding on to the window frame. I saw that he had that cottonmouth thick saliva you get when you're about to cry, but you're trying not to. "I'm going to show up," he said. "I'm going to show up and see what happens after that." I watched him until he walked up to the front door of the house and opened it without knocking.

I was going to show up in Chicago too. I was hoping for family to fill in some for the family I had lost. At the time, I hadn't considered that Ed and Al and Jenny were already showing up for me.

Chapter Twenty-Four

CHICAGO

Late the next day, I stopped at a motel a couple hundred miles from Chicago. I called my grandparents from a pay phone outside the office to let them know I'd be arriving the next afternoon.

They met me at the door of their wide brick house in a neighborhood of low, prosperous-looking houses surrounded by manicured grass and leafy trees. They were dressed like they were going to church. He was in a suit and tie, and she was in a solid-colored dress with a collar and a belt. They stood behind the screen door, just looking at me. When it became clear that they weren't going to talk first, I said, "I'm Van."

My grandfather pushed open the screen door and said, "I'm Calvin, and this is Maeve. Pleased to meet you." I put out my hand, then pulled it back when he didn't respond. After a pause, he did, and I shook his hard dry hand.

They showed me into their front room. The curtains were drawn, so it was in semi-darkness. The coolness should have felt good after the heat of the day. Instead, the room felt like it reflected their attitudes toward me. I sat on the edge of the embroidered chair with carved wooden arms under my elbows and sipped my glass of tap water without ice.

Calvin finally spoke. "Norman was always going off on his own without thinking about what the consequences would be." He looked angry as he said it. Like he would pound on the side table at any moment. "It seemed like he never thought about what might happen past the very next moment. Lord knows we tried. We gave him all the benefits we never had, and he never seemed to notice." His face dissolved into sadness, and for a moment I felt sorry for him. "Then he took off to the other side of the country without so much as a backward glance." As he finished his sentence, his stone face came back up. "That girl, from the reservation. She put those ideas in his head."

Maeve leaned forward and added, "He was a good kid for most of his life growing up, but he stopped listening to us as he got older. Then he met Ruth, and it seemed like they decided between them to discard everything we had to say and all we held as important. We warned him that her people thought differently, but hormones took over. You know Ruth dragged him away to California and the native life in the forest there as soon as she could, don't you?"

My fantasy of a warm grandmother giving me cookies and hugs was fading. I forced myself to smile at her. "I didn't know that. I knew my mom was raised on a reservation, but I thought she went to school here in Chicago."

"She did. That's where they met. We even told Norman that we were okay with him dating her. We just pointed out the possible problems." Calvin peered over his glasses at me. "So, what are you out here for?"

"Family." As I said that, I was doubting if I would find it there. "I lost both my mom and dad, and it's like I'm missing an important part of me. I thought I would meet you all. I'm out in the world on my own without much of a base." I took a breath. I didn't want to say what I had been practicing as I drove across the country. It didn't seem to fit. But I had to say it. "At least, if I have family behind me, I know where I came from."

Maeve frowned. "You know we don't have extra money."

This was getting worse by the moment. How could they think I was asking for money? "No, that's not why I'm here. Sure, I'm poor, but I'm a kid, so that's expected." Maybe I needed to try a little harder. "Would you tell me a little about what my dad was like when he was little?"

Maeve shrugged. "He was just a normal kid until he got to be older. That was when he started to get ideas in his head."

The questions that I had been storing up in my head the whole trip across country came spilling out one after the other: "What did he do when he was a kid? What do you mean by 'normal?' What did he enjoy doing when he was young?"

Calvin rubbed his nose as he thought. "He was obedient. He got his schoolwork done and did what we told him to. I almost never had to use the belt on him. He ate what we put in front of him and did his chores as he was supposed to."

I looked around at the living room walls. "Do you have some photographs of the family from when he was little?"

Calvin shook his head. "We weren't much on taking pictures. We have the ones they took in church that time." He got up and walked over to a credenza and opened a drawer. As he handed me a pile of old photographs, he said, "There should be some pictures of your dad in there." When he sat back down in his chair across from me, both feet were on the floor, hands were on his knees. I felt like he was waiting for me to be done. There weren't any typical photos of a kid playing on a bike or opening a present at Christmas. All the pictures were posed, stiff. *I wonder if Dad was adopted? How did he come from this?*

After a while, I asked to use the bathroom, and they directed me down a hallway. When I came back into the front room, Calvin stood up and said, "This has been nice meeting you, but it's getting toward our afternoon rest time. We don't do well if we miss it. Let me show you to the door." I reached into my pocket and touched the watch Mom had given me to pass on. I left it in my pocket.

Standing in the hallway with the door open in front of me, I asked them if Bobby's parents still lived nearby. I told them that he had visited us when I was a kid, and I wanted to see if I could find him. Calvin scowled. "Bobby never came back from California. He didn't write his parents, either. Broke their hearts. His parents are both gone now. There's nothing more to tell." An image of a small animal staked out in the forest popped into my head, and I wondered if Bobby had run into the sick guy after he left us. Calvin reached for the edge of the door behind me and closed it quietly when I was outside.

I trudged down the concrete steps toward my truck, staring at the ground, the gray fog of sadness closing in to twist the tightness around my eyes with its icy fingers. What my grandparents said made me doubt what I remembered of my parents. But I grabbed my own memories back and told myself they were real. My dad was warm and slow and caring, and my mom was thoughtful and inclusive. I knew my parents. They didn't.

I had driven a long way trying to find family to help replace what I had lost, and their bitterness had tried to take away the scraps of memories I still had. I stood there holding my truck's door handle, feeling very alone. I couldn't bring myself to open the door right away and get in. I had been stupid for placing so much hope with the two of them. And I had a long trip ahead of me to think about what a waste of time it was.

"Are you related to them?" a voice asked from the next driveway over. I looked up to see a girl about my age leaning against a newish Cadillac sedan, smoking. She held the cigarette between her thumb and forefinger like a cowboy and blew the smoke slowly out of her mouth. She had on jeans and a loose-fitting cotton shirt. I wondered if she thought about the rivets on her pockets scratching the paint on the car as I noticed how tight the jeans were.

I was still standing with my hand on the handle of the truck door. "They're my grandparents, but this is the first time I've met them. It might be the last time, too, from the looks of it."

She dropped the cigarette on the ground and stepped on it, then bent over, picked it up, and walked towards the garage. "They've never been what you would call welcoming people," she said over her shoulder as she tossed the butt in a garbage can. "They turn off their lights on

Halloween, and they yelled at us when we were kids if we played too close to their flowers." She turned back toward me. "Hey, I'm bored. Want to take me somewhere?"

Jenny's face flashed through my mind, but I pushed it back out. I needed something fun after that disaster. "Yeah. What did you have in mind?"

"Well, I know they didn't feed you. They're not feeding type of people. So, first we find food. After that, we get on with the adventure." She flashed a smile, then turned and ran toward the house. "I'll be back in a second!" The screen door slammed behind her. When she came back out, she had a large bag slung over her shoulder and a small one in her hand. She tossed the big bag in the bed of the truck and climbed into the cab. "Let's go forget about the old fogies." She rolled down the window, pushed in the cigarette lighter, and turned to me with her hand out. "I'm Lisa." I shook her hand and felt my shoulders relax a bit. She adjusted the dial on the radio to a station playing popular music and turned up the volume. With the radio playing and the windows open, we didn't talk much.

I glanced over at her a couple of times as I drove. She was good-looking in a tough kind of way, without any makeup. She had high cheekbones and had pulled her blonde-brown hair into a ponytail. She lounged in the corner of the cab with one foot on the seat like she was the princess of the truck and I was her hired driver. "Turn in here." She pointed at Curly's hamburger shack. It was a run-down brick building with smoke coming out of a steel vent on the roof and picnic tables scattered around it. "These are the best hamburgers you'll ever have. They're grilled, and they're sloppy, and they only come one way, but that way is good." I pulled into a spot in front. "Order me a cheeseburger with fries, and I'll get us beers across the street."

I had ordered the food and was sitting at one of the tables when she jogged back with four green bottles of beer, already opened, between her fingers. She sat on the bench next to me and bumped my shoulder. Then she held her bottle up to clink with mine and drank half of hers in one long swig. I drank half of mine, too.

I went to pick up our food. When I came back, she pointed at the license plate on the front of my truck. "You're from California?"

I nodded. "Northern California, up on the coast."

"When you headed back?"

I shrugged. "I guess soon. I didn't find what I thought I might find here, and I have a job to get back to there."

"Well, we'll have to make the time you have here memorable." She poured catchup from the bottle onto the wax paper beside the fries. "Do you want to see the most impressive thing Chicago has to offer?"

I started to tell her I already saw that when I met her but stopped myself. I wanted to keep things light. "Sure. I'm at your mercy today. Wherever you take me will be amazing, I'm sure."

Lisa took a bite of her hamburger, wiped catchup off the side of her mouth with a napkin, and said, "It's called The Bobs. It's a big old wooden roller coaster out at Riverview Amusement Park. It's creaky, and it's rough, and it's rocking, and it's the best roller coaster in the world. I can't count how many times I've ridden on it, and I still love it every time." She raised an eyebrow at me. "Now I have to warn you. We're not going for a day at the amusement park." She was acting stern, like a drill sergeant, but she ruined the fierceness with an impish smile. "We're there for The Bobs. Three rides. If you need to, you can get some cotton candy between them, but there'll be no merry-go-rounds or sharpshooting today. We have a job to do, and we're going to do it right. Understood?"

I smiled and saluted her. "Yes, sir!"

When we got there, so many rides looked interesting—spinning cars on tilting platforms, boats that came rocketing down a water slide into a pool of water, even one called Flying Cars. I made a game of asking her if we could go on each ride we passed, and she made a game out of scolding me for asking. I stopped her as we walked by the ride where people floated down from a tall tower on a parachute. I put both of my hands on her shoulders. "I really want to go on that ride."

She put her hands on my shoulders, and we stood there for a second, close, staring at each other. "If you're a good boy, we might have time for one extra ride." Then she turned me around and patted me on the butt to get me moving.

A minute later, we were standing in front of a bright white Grecian temple with fluted columns and an ornate roofline. The wooden support structure of a roller coaster stood behind it. She took my hand. "This is The Bobs. Prepare to enter the house of worship."

When we were locked into the ride and waiting for it to start, she leaned over and said, "Kiss for good luck," and we pressed our lips together in a friendly way. She put her hand on my knee, and we started up the first hill. I'd ridden the Giant Dipper at the Santa Cruz Boardwalk many times, and still, there was always a thrill of anticipation as it climbed the first hill, clacking slowly toward the top and almost stopping before it flew down and around all the curves. As the car at The Bobs lurched into motion, I felt a huge grin spread across my face. We rode with our hands up in the air and jostled against each other the whole time. When we were about to start the second ride, I was the one who leaned toward her and said, "Kiss for good luck." We took a little more time with that kiss.

After we rode The Bobs three times without stopping for cotton candy, we left. I drove us past mansions on the lake shore as Lisa gave me directions to a park. "We can watch the sunset from there if we hurry. It should be good tonight with the low clouds out over the lake."

When we got there, she grabbed the big bag, took my hand, and led me down the beach to a grassy spot near the water. She pulled out a jar of apple juice, a bottle of vodka, and two glasses. "It's all I could find inside the house," she said as she set them on the grass. "Help me spread out this blanket."

We watched the red and orange fingers of light spread across the bottoms of the clouds. We sipped the apple juice and vodka, which was surprisingly good, as the sunset lit up more and more of the sky. It was as if the clouds across the lake were on fire, dark on top and glowing with popsicle colors underneath. Each moment, the pattern changed as the sun dropped lower and illuminated more of the clouds. When it was dark, she leaned against me and kissed me. I kissed her back, her face silhouetted against the darkness of the sky, thinking how this would make it clear to fate that I wasn't so happy back in California after all.

I was stewing in a wild mix of emotions. Sad about and disappointed in my grandparents. Missing my parents. Worried that fate would take Jenny away and trying to find a way to deny that happiness and hide from fate. Still needing this excitement with Lisa to happen to make me feel better now. It didn't make sense, and I didn't try to parse it. I just did it.

She had rolled on top of me and put her hand under my shirt to touch my nipple when a flash, like lightning, lit up the sky over the water to the north. We scanned the clouds over the lake, but there were no more flashes, and a low booming sound followed it a few seconds later. "Must be a storm coming." I put my hand in the pocket of her jeans and pulled her against me.

She kissed me again and said, "If we don't get our clothes off soon, they're going to get wet."

My shirt was off, and her bra was undone when I saw a flashlight on the beach near the parking lot. It was bobbing, like the person holding it was running toward us. We got our clothes back in order by the time the man approached. He shined the beam at the ground to keep it out of our eyes and asked, "Did you guys see anything?"

I lifted my head up and squinted at him. "What's up? What was there to see?"

"There was a plane crash. It was coming into Midway Airport, and it crashed out on the water. Did you see it?"

My mind screamed, *plane crash*. I saw Jenny in that plane blowing up and going into the water. It couldn't be, but it seemed so real. I touched the edge of what it would feel like to lose her, then, scared, pulled myself back to the blanket by the lake. I croaked out some kind of a reply.

More flashlights appeared along the beach as people gathered, talking about getting in boats to go out and search for survivors. "We should go back," I said to Lisa. On the drive to her house, we were quiet. When I came around to open her door for her in her driveway, she said, "My parents aren't home. You could come in."

I had noticed that the Cadillac was gone from the driveway when we had pulled in, and I looked over at the space where it had been that afternoon. I shook my head. "I'd better be heading back. Thank you. You made me forget my grandparents for most of today, and that was worth a lot." As she got out, she stood up on her toes and gave me a soft, knowing kiss on the lips. Then she touched me on the cheek and walked away. I headed out of town and found a motel.

The next morning, as I drove along a straight stretch of road with cornfields on either side and the gold of the rising sun in the rearview mirror, I thought about the people in that plane. I thought about their families waking up this morning knowing they wouldn't see their loved ones again. After that, I didn't think for a while, and just drove, holding on to what it feels like when people are there and then they're gone.

Then I thought about the plane crash—my fourth one. This crash had kept me from making a foolish mistake. I left my grandparents' house so lonely and feeling so deserted that I had convinced myself I deserved an adventure with Lisa in her tight jeans. We both had known all day where it was going to end up. It was going there when the plane crashed. And, it would have ruined what I was sure was the truest good I had found.

I had to admit that part of me had wanted to blow it all up so it wouldn't be taken away from me. The plane crash had kept me from that, but I knew the pattern by now. Life got good. I found or built a place of contentment, but I didn't hide it well enough. Fate saw that I was happy and sent a plane crash to taunt me. Then it swooped in and took it away.

Chapter Twenty-Five

GRAVEDIGGER

The road from Chicago to California passed through Iowa, and a bit to the north of it was Sloan, Iowa and the cemetery where Mom's parents were buried. The Tupperware container holding Mom's ashes that I had been carrying with me since I left Oakland was in a brown paper grocery bag on the floor of the truck. It had migrated from my backpack as I carried it hitchhiking to the top shelf of my closet in the apartment I shared with Al. I had put it on top of my suitcase as I packed for this trip so I wouldn't forget it, and when I was loading the truck for the trip, I stuck it behind the seat for a while.

I met the guy in charge of the cemetery at the funeral home downtown. I had called ahead, and he had said I could bring her ashes to be buried beside the graves of her mom and dad. I hadn't told him I wanted to dig her grave. In his office, I reached into the paper bag and held up the jar-shaped container. "I brought my own posthole digger. I bought it in the hardware store before I came here."

He leaned back in his leather chair, grabbed his nose between his thumb and the knuckle of his forefinger, and stared at me for a moment. "I've never had anyone want to dig a grave." Then he sighed. "I can't see what it would hurt."

"It just feels like something I need to do."

He reached behind him for a sheet of paper and set it on his desk. He leaned forward and pointed with the same knuckle. "Here's where they would be. You'll have to search a bit. Dig between the two headstones and a little in front. You won't hit anything there. Go as deep as the posthole digger will reach."

After he gave me directions to the cemetery, I thanked him and got back in my car. I drove through town with the windows open, breathing in the smell of rain on hot asphalt, dry and damp at the same time, from the squall that had passed while I was inside. I drove past pickup trucks parked on gravel driveways and a low, yellow-brick Baptist church with a sign advertising Sunday school in plastic letters. Out near the railroad tracks, I passed a line of grain silos that rose gray and solid above me. The road continued out of town alongside the tracks until I turned across them onto a gravel road between green walls of corn made dusty by the cars driving by. The cemetery was a square patch of grass, about an acre in size, surrounded by tall green stalks like a garden wall.

I parked and walked out through the damp grass. The smell of corn was all around me. It didn't smell like grass as I had thought it would. It smelled like ears of fresh corn, waiting to be eaten. I wandered in and out of headstones until I found my mom's parents' graves. I stood and gazed around at the flat-mown grass and the headstones and the corn all around me, six feet tall and blank green. My perspective shifted for a moment, and I felt like I was in a hole dug in the middle of the field, like a grave. Then it shifted back, and I was on level ground. There was no sound but the buzz of cicadas. A breeze came up, and the corn rustled, scraping like a broom sweeping concrete, and the cicadas quieted or were drowned out by the sound.

I laid the canvas tarp on the grass. The first bite of soil I lifted with the blades of the posthole digger was soft and dark, and it crumbled apart. Worms wriggled in it when I knocked the handles together to drop the dirt on the tarp. Three feet down, it was the same, but without the worms. When my wrists hit the grass and the hole was as deep as I could make it, the soil still seemed like it would grow anything.

Along with the tarp, the funeral director had given me a steel rod about six feet-long. It was shaped like a nail that a giant would use to build his house. He called it a "toothpick," and he told me to use the head of it to tamp down the dirt as I put it back in. I couldn't figure out how to lower the ashes into the hole with care, so I lined the container up with the hole I had dug and dropped it in. I used the toothpick to make sure it was all the way to the bottom of the hole.

I stood over the hole for a minute thinking about what to say. I took a deep breath, and the words flowed out. "You were a good mom. I felt safe. Things were right then, the three of us together in our cabin. I think even a kid can know that." I blinked, and a tear fell out. "And after Dad was gone, you and I took care of each other. Yeah, you took care of me more than I took care of you, but we did help each other. I appreciate that. We became a team. I miss you. I miss so many things about you." I was crying, but I didn't wipe the tears away. I just let them roll down my cheeks and fall into the hole on her ashes. "I miss you most now, with Jenny. I wish you could have met her. You would have liked her. You two would have liked each other. You would have laughed with her."

I asked myself if there was anything I wanted to tell her that I hadn't said when she was alive, and the only thing that came to mind was, "I'm sorry I didn't follow your directions. You must have known what Dad's parents were like, but you had hope." I dropped her diamond watch in the hole with her ashes. "I love you, Mom." Then, I put the first scoop of dirt on top.

Before I left Eureka, I had bought a granite stone, like a steppingstone, and had it engraved with her name and the dates of her life. After I had filled and tamped and filled and tamped and all the dirt was back in the hole, I cut a square out of the grass and fitted the stone into it. Then I turned into the wind, breathed in the corn on the wind, and walked back to the truck.

Chapter Twenty-Six

DRY LIGHTNING

Josh and I continued up Tassajara Creek to Pine Ridge as the afternoon heat waned. From the top, we could see down Tassajara Canyon and into Clear Creek Canyon, the one that headed toward the ocean. It was a greener, wetter valley. We decided to camp there that night. We had both been lost in our thoughts. I'd been thinking about Dad's parents—about how they thought they'd been approving of Mom when it was clear that they were still holding doubts about her. This made me see in a different light how I had handled Josh's news. I knew what I needed to do.

The spot we chose to camp was down Clear Creek a ways. We found a flat area in a grove of pine trees beside the creek. The murmur of the water on the rocks reached our camp. A slight breeze wafted up the canyon, and the tops of the pine trees swayed in the wind. The air became more humid and cooled a little, and a high mist made the blue of the sky look fuzzy and out of focus.

Josh had just taken the saddle off his horse when I put my hand on his shoulder. "I have something I need to say."

He set the saddle on a rock and turned back to me.

I took a deep breath. "I've loved you since you were born, and I will always love you. You're my son and you always will be."

I paused for a second, because I wanted to make sure I got the second part correct. "And when you bring someone you love into our lives, that person will be my son too. Loved and cherished, just like you and Nate."

He stared at me for a moment, then he frowned, and I thought I had blown it again. Then I saw a tear in the corner of his eye, and he said, "Thank you." He wrapped his arms around me, and we hugged. There. Unconditional acceptance. That was what had been missing. I felt lighter, and it seemed like he did too.

As we were putting up our tent, we heard thunder in the distance. Over the next hour, a dark cloud bank rolled in from the west. The air was humid but there wasn't any rain. The clouds were powerful and roiling, with lightning knifing out of them. As the thunder grew louder, the horses started to stamp and toss their heads. We moved them to a low area and stood by them, talking in quiet voices, telling them it was okay. We counted the time from the flash of lightning until the thunder. Fifteen seconds became ten, then five. As the storm was advancing, they calmed after each blast to the sound of our voices and our touch.

Then, the flash and boom of lightning and thunder came at the same time. The pressure pushed the air out of my lungs. A metallic smell, like burning wires, seared my nostrils. The horses jumped, wild-eyed, and looked for somewhere to run. I felt the ropes being pulled out of my hands and leaned into their necks, hoping to calm them with my touch while holding on with all my strength. They stayed with us.

We stood by them, waiting for the next blast. They were still dancing, anticipating another, but they weren't pulling as much. Then the next flash came. We counted. One, two, three, four, five. When it arrived, the thunder seemed small compared to the one that was on top of us, and the horses jumped, but not with terror. The flashes and thunder came further apart until the thunder was only a distant rumble following unseen lightning.

"There must be fires from that," Josh said, once the storm had passed. "It's so dry out here, and there was no rain at all." We walked all around, trying to get different views of the hills above us to determine where the flames might be. When we didn't see any, we made a small camp-fire and went to sleep early.

We awoke before dawn, worried about the whiffs of smoke we had smelled throughout the night. It had been a nervous sleep. Both of us had woken during the night at different times and scanned the surrounding hills for signs of fire. We packed our camp without wasted motion and headed back up to Pine Ridge. From the top, in the pre-dawn darkness, we saw red light glowing on the hills in five or six places around us. "Just what we thought," I said. "There had to be fires from that lightning. At least it looks like there aren't any on our path home. But we'll have to go right between those two to the north."

"But down the valley to the south is where Julie and Kim are," Josh said. I could hear the worry in his voice. "That fire at the bottom of Tassajara Canyon is below them. It's blocking the way down to the trailhead, and it's coming up the valley. They can't get out the way they came. They'll need to climb up to the ridge." He started talking more quickly. "We could go get them and take them to the top and out the long way—around the ridgeline and down to the parking lot. They can't do that walking. We need to take them on the horses."

I wanted to tell him they would be okay by themselves, but I wasn't sure. If we went to them, we could be sure they would be out of danger. But I really didn't want to leave the gold. I wanted to get out of those mountains and back to safety. I tried to think of another alternative and couldn't find one. At the same time, I was impressed that Josh was showing concern for other people—even with hundreds of thousands of dollars on the pack horses—and I wanted to honor that. And he was right. They could find themselves in a lot of danger, and we could help. "Okay. If we leave the gold here, we can use the pack horses to take them the extra distance."

I looked around for a good place to cache the gold. A hundred yards below us, the trail crossed a rocky slide area, right before it wound into a copse of pine trees. I pointed at it. "We can hide it under some rocks there." Josh nodded, and we rode down toward it. I had a bit of déjà vu as I shifted flat pieces of sandstone to make a hole for the leather bags. "It feels like we're clearing out the mine entrance again. But this time, we're leaving the treasure behind." I was making light of it, but it was hard to let all that gold out of my control.

After the mine collapsed, I had told myself we were taking too many chances, that the gold wasn't worth it. As we had ridden, I felt the tug and importance of the gold building up in me. But, as I buried the bars, I realized that this was the right thing to do. Leaving it behind now felt like a test of my statement that lives were more important than gold.

We covered the bags well. Then we triangulated on the peaks around us and the trees close to us to cement the location in our minds. From twenty feet away, we turned to stare at the rocks again, memorizing everything we could. We backed further away and looked again. We wanted to make sure we could find the important pile of rocks in all the other piles of rocks in this open field of stone and in a different light than the semi-darkness of pre-dawn.

"We've got this, Dad. We know the spot." I looked at my son, who was showing so much confidence. "No one's going to dig here. We're doing the right thing."

Since we were on our horses and the pack horses had no cargo, we were able to make good time down Tassajara Canyon toward the waterfall where we had last seen Julie and Kim. After about an hour, we saw them heading towards us. They had their packs on their backs and were hiking quickly uphill away from the smoke below. When they saw us, they waved their arms above their heads, and their faces broke into huge smiles.

As they got nearer, Josh waved at them. "We saw the fire below you. It's blocking the trail down the valley." He pointed at the surrounding hills. "We can take you the long way on the horses around the circle of Eagle Ridge Trail there, back to your car."

Julie dropped her pack beside us. She was breathing hard. "Oh, my gosh, are we glad to see you. We were almost running up the canyon, and we didn't know if there was a way out up here."

We let them ride our horses because they had saddles, and we rode the pack horses bareback. We didn't waste any time getting going. When we got to the top of Eagle Ridge, we saw the fires in the Tassajara Canyon below and those on either side of us moving like a slow curtain north with the gentle breeze. "We'll be riding between two walls of fire when we go back out," I said. I was worried, but the wind seemed to be pushing the two fires straight north. We could get between them.

Two hours later, we got to the Santa Lucia Campground. I dismounted and tied my horse loosely to a tree. "This seems like a good spot. From here, it's only another two or three miles—maybe an hour or so—to your car. You should be fine from here."

"How can we ever thank you?" Julie said.

Josh smiled. "Well, I'll just have to take you up on that offer for a tour of UCSB next month."

They all hugged, then the two girls waved at me and heaved their packs on their backs. As we watched them head down the trail, we let the horses drink. I turned to Josh. "I have to say, I'm worried about those fires on both sides of our path home. What if they grow together? We could be trapped."

He nodded. "Yeah, we lost a few hours doing that, I know. But I'm glad we did it."

I nodded. I wondered how glad we'd be later. "We'll be able to see more when we get back up on the ridge. Let's get moving."

We rode further down the valley and up a dry arroyo which intersected with Clear Creek Canyon, where we had left our saddlebags. We tried not to push the horses too hard going uphill, knowing we would need them later, but our worry about the fires kept us moving with purpose. Near the top, the canyon widened out.

I kept scanning the grove of pine trees on the left for people. We were going back to dig up saddlebags of gold, and anyone who saw us would wonder what we were doing. I didn't see anyone, but that didn't make me less nervous. When we were just below the cache, I told Josh to wait for a moment. We sat on our horses as if we were giving them a breather after climbing the hill and looked around carefully. After a couple of moments, I said, "Okay, Josh, go ahead and start uncovering the packs. Let's do this." I moved our horses above the cache so they shielded us from the path then went to help him with the rocks. We had only lifted a couple of the flat stones off the saddlebags when two men rode out of the pines to our left. "People on horses coming out of the trees," I whispered to Josh as I stepped up closer to my horse. The men got close to us before Josh could move, so he stood where he was.

I turned my head around to look at them. There were two of them, and they were both rough-looking. The older one was about 60 and skinny in that way people get when they've worked hard all their lives—skinny but stronger than they seem. He probably hadn't shaved in this decade, and his patchy gray beard was yellow around his mouth. The younger one was maybe in his forties, and he looked mean. Not big-and-tough mean, but stab-you-in-the-back-without-any-guilt mean. His face was composed of sharp planes, and his mouth hardly moved when he talked. "What you guys got there?"

"Fossils and shells." Josh sounded remarkably calm. "We had to go back down the canyon to bring a couple college students out around that fire. So, we left our packs full of them here and carried the students out on the pack horses."

"We're going to get the packs and head right back down the valley," I said. "Where you guys headed? Going down the valley away from the fires?"

Josh looked at me, and I nodded to him, and he went back to moving rocks. I watched Josh for a moment, hoping the two men would continue past. Out of the corner of my eye, I caught a glimpse of a black object in the young guy's hand. I turned to look. In the moment my attention had been on Josh, he had drawn a gun. He was about ten feet from Josh and pointing a short, black revolver about three feet to Josh's right. Josh threw away the rock he had just picked up and stood up.

"I think you found Stevie's treasure." The young guy jabbed with the gun toward Josh. "That's our treasure." He had a big knife in a sheath on his belt. There was a brown stain on his jeans below the sheath, like he had wiped the knife there before putting it back in its holder.

I looked at the older guy. He was just sitting on his horse, watching. He wasn't smiling or frowning. The younger one was doing all the talking. "We've been watching you and Russ wandering around up here. When we saw you with him up on the ridge, those saddlebags seemed awfully heavy for a bunch of rocks."

Russ? He knows Russ? I kept looking at his face. There was something off in the way he stared at Josh. Like he wanted to hurt him. Hatred. That's what I saw there. But how could he hate him if he didn't know him? My pulse was racing.

The young guy pointed at Josh with his chin. "What did you find? Gold?" The words came out as a snarl.

Josh put his hands up in the air. "Fossils. Fossils and extra water in the packs."

"I think you found gold." He waved the gun towards the packs. "Uncover it. I'll wait here." His attention was on Josh like a hawk watching a mouse.

"How do you know Russ and Stevie?" I asked. He didn't answer. Instead, he looked over at me, like he was seeing me for the first time. Then his attention went back to Josh.

The old guy spoke up. "We've known Russ since he was a kid." His voice was slow and measured. "Him and Corey and Stevie's dad. He was supposed to fly out to meet us out at our ranch, but he didn't show up. Russ met us down below. He's going to help us carry this gold out. Our gold." What he said about Russ bothered me. I guess I had been hopeful about him. But it sounded like he was saying Russ had schemed with them to get the gold.

Josh hadn't moved. He kept his hands up. I was beside my horse but wouldn't be able reach my rifle quickly enough. They were going to take our gold, and there was nothing we could do about it. I looked at the young guy. He knew Russ and Corey. There was only one possibility. "Are you Frank?"

He stared at me for a moment, trying to figure out who I was. The gun drifted further to the right, away from Josh. His eyes narrowed. "Who are you?" Under the intensity of his gaze, my palms started sweating. I had thought I might defuse the situation with conversation, but his stare was unyielding. He seemed like he might shoot me just for fun. My heart was racing in my chest. I took a deep breath to calm it down and told him that I had grown up down in the redwoods. "I used to play with Russ that summer when he and Corey were at the mine. I never met you. I almost did the day of the earthquake, but you guys had gone to check on the mine and I missed you."

My hand was on the saddle, and I thought if I could get his attention completely away from us for a second, I might be able to get the rifle out. It would be close. But then what? Would I shoot him? Would he shoot me or Josh if I wasn't fast enough? I didn't think I could get away with it. My thoughts moved from saving the gold to saving us. They might not let us go even after they took the gold.

The gun jumped out of Frank's hand. A split second later, I heard a rifle shot, and I knew a bullet had hit the gun. Frank fell off his horse, awkwardly. He crumpled and writhed on the ground, swearing and holding his hand. I don't think either Josh or I had any idea what had happened, but we saw our chance. Josh ran to the pistol and picked it up. I pulled the rifle from my saddle and chambered a round. The old guy didn't do anything. I didn't know if he had a weapon, but I couldn't see one. He just sat on his horse, his hands on the saddle horn.

A couple seconds later, Russ emerged from the trees to the right, about a hundred yards away. He led his horse into the open, holding his rifle. Josh moved Frank's horse over with ours and checked for another gun. I kept my rifle on the old guy.

"It's broken," Frank wailed when Russ got close. "Damn you, Russ. You broke my hand." Frank kept his string of profanity going as Russ got off his horse, strode over to him, and kneaded his fingers roughly between his hands.

"I don't think it's broken," Russ said, "It's bruised, though. It's going to hurt for a while. Stand up." He turned to the old guy. "Uncle Murray, you have a gun on you?"

Murray's expression didn't change. He still showed no emotion at all. "I do, Russ, and I'm not going to give it to you."

The corner of Russ's mouth turned up just a little. "Would you please move further down the hill, then? I think you two should get out of the way of these fires." Russ patted Frank's pockets and ankles, searching for a hidden gun.

I motioned with the rifle for Frank to go to his horse. "You can head down that valley we came up. You should be safe, and there's people down there to help you get out." I was surprised at how calm I was as I said it. "Keep going though. If I see you again, I'll shoot you, and I probably will hit a part of you that's meatier than your hand."

Frank climbed back on his horse and rode a couple of steps away from us. He turned and looked at me. "You wouldn't shoot me over treasure, would you?"

I stared hard at him for a second. "It's only fossils in those packs. You were holding a gun on my son. I would shoot you for that." I wasn't feeling as tough as I sounded.

When they had gone a few yards down the canyon, I yelled after them. "Frank, hold up a minute." Frank turned his horse. "A year or two before the earthquake, did you meet a guy named Bobby up near the mine?"

I could still feel the hatred burning in his eyes. "I've met people trespassing on our property lots of times over the years. Most of them just turn around and go back where they came from."

"Bobby? A guy with a leather prospector's hat and a black mustache?"

"It's dangerous back there. Lots can happen to people traipsing around searching for treasure." He turned away again, and Russ and I watched them go. Josh rolled more stones off the packs.

I exhaled deeply and wiped my brow. My emotions had been jumping all around, and now I felt relieved, but my hands were starting to shake. They had been pointing a gun at us. Russ had shot it out of Frank's hand, just like in the movies. It seemed like we were safe, at least for a few minutes—assuming we were safe from Russ, which I still wasn't sure about. I looked up at him. He was smiling like he had just won a huge poker hand. "You came at exactly the right time." I shook my head. "Damn nice shooting. Who taught you to shoot like that?" I smiled.

He smiled back. "I had a good teacher."

I nodded. Reverberations from an earlier time rippling through our lives. "Frank said you were with them. Why did you shoot the gun out of his hand?"

He looked up at the smoke above us, then back at Josh and then me. I thought he might reach into his pack for a swig of whiskey, but he didn't. "After I went out to visit the old mine site, I headed up this way. I saw them down below. I hadn't seen them in a long time, but I wasn't surprised because of what you had said about the deer." He winced at the memory. "They said they had been watching us. When they saw you this morning on the ridge with the girls and no packsaddles, they figured you must have stashed what you were carrying somewhere. They assumed you found the gold, and they told me they wanted to wait around for you to come back and take it from you. They wanted me to help them." He rubbed his face and took a breath. "I admit, I thought about it."

I wondered if he was still thinking about it. "But you didn't. Why? They're your relatives."

He frowned and stared at the ground, then looked up at me. "All my life, I've been doing things that had both bad and good in them. Mixed up, you know, so it's hard to figure out what's right. It hit me while I was with them that this was a clear choice. Was I going to be on the side of the bad guys or the good guys?" He half-smiled. "I chose the good guys." He took a big drink from his canteen and put it back on his saddle. "I told them I would wait below because you guys would suspect something if I came up with them. After they left, I moseyed up the valley in that brush over there. I was waiting to see what happened when they showed up."

I reached out my hand, and he took it. "Well, damn, I'm glad you chose us."

He seemed pleased, like he had come over a hill after a long journey and seen home in the distance. Then he looked over at Josh and the packs on the ground by him. "Did you guys find something?"

"Yeah." My eyes grew wide as I spoke. Between moving the girls and the fires and having a gun pulled on Josh, I had forgotten just how big a deal the treasure was. "We found some old gold from the Spanish mission time. My dad's friend Bobby had an old map. They thought it was showing the ocean and mountain peaks, but when we looked at it differently after the plane crash, we saw that it matched up with the missions and the ridge to the west of where we camped by the seep. Stevie's scribbles had initials for the missions, and that might have sparked something in my thinking." I looked over at the smoke rising above the ridgeline. "Let's get out of here. We can talk on the way."

Russ nodded. "Which way, you think?"

I shrugged. "I'm torn. I'm sure we can make it between the fires, and that's the fastest way home. Downhill is the safest way, though."

"Well, I wouldn't be too sure it's the safest way. Frank and Murray are down there. You know Frank's got a loose wire, but Murray's the more dangerous one. He's quietly dangerous, and they're both mad as hell right now. I wouldn't put it past them to wait in ambush for you. I would think about going through the hills."

"You want to come with us?"

"I didn't say it's the safest way for me." He pointed to the saddlebags. "Show me what you found, then we'll split up. Frank and Murray will forgive me. The fires scare me more than those two do. I want to get out of here and take a shower. But I want to lay eyes on that gold first."

We dusted off the saddlebags, and Josh shoved the fossils out of the way. Then he reached in and pulled out one of the straps wrapped in cloth. Russ took a deep breath. "Wow. Gold! You guys really did find gold. I know you said it, but look at it! That almost makes me want to chance the fires with you." He stared up at the smoke and narrowed his eyes. "Nah, I'm still going the safe way. See you back home." He got on his horse and started down the same trail Frank and Murray took. He had only gone a few feet when he turned around. "Van?" His expression had changed from one of resolve to one of uncertainty. "You know what I said about the diesel fuel and wishing the old man was dead? Can we keep that between us?"

I nodded slowly. "I don't see why not. I don't remember much of what you said anyway. The whiskey blurs those things."

He nodded and smiled, then turned his horse downhill. I gave Josh a quick hug around the shoulders before I picked up a pack to put it back on the horses. I stopped in the middle of buckling the strap to look at Josh as he worked on the other pack horse. He seemed older, somehow, like he had lived a year in this week.

Josh looked up and saw me gazing at him. "I'm glad Russ turned out to be a good guy."

"Yeah. I like him. He always seems like he's trying to do what's right, and not quite getting it. But he seemed relieved with his choice this time." I was happy too, with my new decision to fight fate. Despite the difficulties, things seemed to be working out. I don't know, maybe I should have fought more after the fifth plane crash. Things might have been different if I had. Here's what happened.

Chapter Twenty-Seven

ANXIETY

The fifth plane crash wasn't even a plane crash, but it goes with the others in my mind because of the losses it marks and the regret I have for what I let slip away.

Jenny, Nate, Josh and I had lived in the hills for seven years when Jenny's cousin, Mike, and I started a trucking company together. The company he was working for couldn't get their products shipped reliably across the state. There was a need for a good hauler, and we had our first customer lined up: his old company. We worked well together. He knew logistics, and he knew how to run a business, and I knew the trucks.

Every night, I would worry, and every morning, I would wake up scared and tense, imagining what would go wrong. Things did go wrong. We lost contracts we thought we were going to get. Trucks broke, and drivers quit. It didn't seem to bother Mike, but for me, every time something happened, it was like someone had punched me. I felt it in my body. People would ask me if I was sick. I looked sick. We were losing money too.

By the winter of 1967, I wasn't sure I could keep going. Jenny and I talked about the stress, and I cried in front of her. That wasn't what I had wanted to do, but it was like the tears were being squeezed out of me by the pressure. I felt bad for letting her see how worried I was and for making her more worried than she already was. "You know you can quit and go back to your old job."

I shook my head. "I couldn't. I've put us through so much stress—for what, just to quit? It would be cowardly."

She nodded. "It would feel awful. It would still be okay. We would go on."

In the newspaper that February morning, I read they were going to do a test of the Apollo capsule, a kind of dress rehearsal for the next manned flight. I remember wondering how those guys handled the stress. The photo showed the three astronauts in their space suits, holding their helmets under their arms. They appeared well-rested and relaxed. I got up from the kitchen table and stared at myself in the mirror in the bathroom. I looked thin. Drawn out. Sickly.

That afternoon, the guy who owned the tow truck business next door came over. He was almost crying he was so distraught. "They burned," he said, collapsing on the plastic chair in our office. "The astronauts burned to death. It's on my TV."

I couldn't believe it. I had been envious of those guys just that morning. I turned away for a moment while the impact of the news washed over me. "Can I come watch on your TV?" He just nodded and turned to go back to his shop. The news was on all the channels. It was horrible, but I kept watching, hoping something new would come up. The thought that crept into my mind was that at least they didn't have to endure the stress and worry anymore. When I noticed that thought, I knew the time had come to do something.

I told Jenny that night. "I know I'm being a coward, but I can't take it anymore."

She had tears in her eyes as she said, "It's okay. We'll be okay."

I started crying too. "Those guys died. All I'm doing is starting a business. I want to quit it. I have to." I felt immediate relief.

I used the word "coward" to describe myself until Jenny told me to stop it. Then, I just stopped saying it out loud. She was making pretty good money, and we were fine. I could be the dad I wanted to be when I stopped worrying so much and working so much. Mike was understanding. He told me he would pay me back the money I had put in, and, as soon as he made some money, he even paid me a wage for six months.

Within a few years, Mike had built a hugely successful business. I could have been part of it with him, but I had stopped before it really got a chance to start.

Why had I been so anxious? Was it that I was afraid of failing? For years, I had done a good job of hiding from fate by keeping my happiness small. Every time I started feeling good, I found a way to deny it. It seemed to be working. There hadn't been a plane crash in years, and I hadn't lost anyone I loved. Perhaps I was afraid that doing something would attract the attention of fate—like dropping an arm over the edge of the bed out of the safety of the covers, where a monster might see it and bite it. Really, what I was afraid of was success. That made sense. Quitting was the right thing to do; there was no reason to draw the eye of fate my way.

I got my old job back, and I could rest again, like an old dog sleeping in front of the hearth. By that point, my strategy had worked for ten years, and I trusted it would keep doing so.

Chapter Twenty-Eight

DIABLO WIND

Before we started off again, Josh and I stood together to look around at the smoke from the fires. The blaze down Tassajara Canyon was growing. It was burning up the slopes toward the ridges where we rode with Julie and Kim earlier in the day. But that was behind us.

Ahead of us was the rough country we needed to pass through to get home. The two lightning fires that had seemed so small earlier had grown and were flowing north with the wind. They were on both sides of us, moving ahead of where we wanted to go. Massive plumes of dirty smoke rose into the sky. "The fires are getting bigger." Could we really move faster than them? "They're growing together, but we're heading right for the valley below the peak between them." I paused and decided that was the way to go. I spoke decisively as I continued. "We can go between them as long as the wind holds."

Josh seemed unconvinced. "Why don't we just go down the valley with Russ? It's the shortest way out, and with the fires, nobody would notice us. We can handle Frank and Murray. We handled them before."

I thought for a moment, then affirmed my decision with an emphatic nod. "It's more than just them. Sure, they're dangerous, but there's something about a pack full of gold that doesn't look right. It's too heavy for its size and draws attention. We know there will be other people down there, not just those guys. Believe me. We're better off going over the hills where nobody will see us." I flashed back to the look in Frank's eyes and shuddered. "Besides, I'm not so sure we can handle them again."

Josh looked up at the fires and shrugged. "Okay. Let's do it."

We started north along the ridge. The smoke made a tunnel with walls of brown clouds that spread out and met overhead. Birds flew away from the smoke, towards us, then found themselves in the same alleyway we were. Deer and coyotes joined the migration as hunters and hunted ignored each other ahead of the larger threat. We were in a hurry, but the trails were narrow and rocky, and pushing too hard might mean losing a horse. I kept looking behind us, thinking Frank and Murray might be following us. There was so much commotion in the area it was hard to tell. One time when I looked behind, I thought I caught a glint of sunlight off something shiny, but I couldn't see what it was.

Most of the smoke rose into the sky, but some of it curled downward and settled around us, turning the air dirty brown and making it hard to breathe. We got tee-shirts out of our packs and tied them over our mouths and noses, just like we had back at the cave. Once again, it hit me how much we had been through in the last 48 hours. We didn't have much water, but wetting the tee shirts seemed to help keep the smoke away.

Late in the morning, as we rode carefully down a steep, rocky trail, I felt like I was underwater, rising toward the surface where the gap between the fires was visible in the distance to the north. My lungs wanted relief from the pressure of the smoke and of not knowing if we would make it through the gap before it closed on us. I had to fight to breathe evenly. Tension weighed on my head and shoulders. I wanted to run. I kept leaning forward to encourage the horses to speed up, then leaning back and reminding myself to keep to a pace that would get us all through. The horses didn't like the smoke or the flames on the hillsides. They were jumpy and hard to control.

When we reached the valley floor, the horses wanted to run, and we wanted to let them. Behind us, on the trail we had just zigzagged down, I saw two horsemen. "Josh, do you see them?" He nodded. "They can't be more than fifteen minutes behind us."

"Looks like Frank and Murray." Josh's voice was tight. They were coming after us. And we would be slower than them because we had the pack horses. "Damn. Here we go again." Then, I really wanted to run—and so did the horses. "It's gonna be hard to hold the horses back." Josh said. Exactly what I was thinking. But we held them to a slow canter. We had to. The smoke swirled and changed direction in the valley with the heat on both sides creating its own winds. Flames raged on the hills around us, moving north to meet at the low pass up ahead. The lightning strike fires were rushing along the hills toward the same pass that we had to go through to reach safety.

The fire felt alive. I could sense its anger and its desire. It had a will and a hunger for the trees and grasses. Both fires wanted to join into one. They leaned toward each other like great muscular arms of flame reaching out for their brother across the narrowing gap.

As we neared the low pass to the north, flames rose impossibly high above us. Like a lava river, the base of the fire flowed down the hillsides toward the pass, rushing through the brush as fast as we could travel on horseback. Frank and Murray were off the steep trail behind us and had reached the flat we were on. They were galloping their horses in the smoke. We would deal with them when they got to us. The fire was our problem now, not them. The flames were closing in from both sides.

"It's going to be close," I yelled over the roar of the fire.

"We're not going to make it," Josh yelled back. My son. I couldn't lose him here. But there was nowhere else to go. If we didn't make it through the gap, we wouldn't make it at all.

We urged the horses to go faster, and they did. The heat kept increasing as we galloped toward the gap. We were in an oven, baking between the flames. The opening that had seemed so huge this morning when we had left Russ had narrowed to an alleyway. Flames climbed pine trees on both sides of us and exploded in bursts of heat and light, punctuating the already frenzied growl of the fire in its fury. Hot fire-generated winds swirled around us trying to tear off the dry skin on my face.

The horses ran as fast as they ever had. Josh was in front as we raced toward the narrowing gap. "Let us through! Please!" I screamed at the fire "Have mercy! Haven't we been through enough?" But nobody could hear over the sound of the fire, not even Josh.

Then I got mad. "Screw you! You take pleasure in my pain! You're nothing but a cruel torturer!"

I changed tacks again. "At least save Josh! If you're out there, let him get through."

I was crying, but no tears came in the heat and dryness. "You're not even there. You never were. There's nobody listening." I felt myself giving up. I was getting weak and wanted to lie down. "Oh please, at least let him get through." My jaws were aching. I gritted my teeth as if I could will us through.

Cinders dropped from the sky and started small fires in the grass around us. We dodged the islands of fire that came alive in our path. We ran between rocks and trees among the flames until we had to ride on narrow paths between dangers. The paths were being taken away the further we rode. The heat was intense and came at us from all sides. The metal of my wedding ring was hot on my finger. It was too hot to sweat. I thought I might burst into flames at any moment.

After what seemed like an eternity, the horses plunged through a thick ribbon of smoke and emerged into openness. I felt a release of pressure from my lungs. My face suddenly felt cool, and I could see all the way across a meadow. In an instant, the fire was behind us, and in front of us was unburned grass and brush. I breathed the cool air and patted my clothes. I touched my face. We had made it through.

Did we make it because of the words I had screamed moments earlier—or despite them? I looked at Josh. He seemed okay too. I desperately wanted to jump off of my horse and hug him. But I couldn't do that yet; there were still cinders flying around us and starting small fires when they hit the ground. So, we kept riding forward until the deafening roar of the fire decreased and we could hear the crunch of the horse's hooves in the dry grass.

I kept looking back, expecting two horses and two riders to run out of the gap through the flames that had closed behind us. Nobody appeared.

When it finally felt like the fire wasn't about to catch us, I turned to Josh. "Let's stop here and give water to the horses. I need some too."

Josh tried to talk, but he coughed and had to drink more water. "That was crazy close." He tried to slow his breath but struggled with it. "Do we have a death wish on this trip?"

I walked over to him and grabbed him in a hug and held him as we stood among the rocks beside the trail. I wasn't sure about the death wish, but I knew I was happy to be standing in that unburned meadow. Josh squirmed after a second, but still I held on, savoring being alive and having a son who was alive with me. When I finally let go, he said, "Frank and Murray didn't get through, did they?"

I grimaced. "I can't see how they could have. They were gaining on us, but they must have been five or ten minutes behind us, and we almost didn't get through."

He coughed, then took a big breath. "Wow." He looked back toward the fires. "Those were some bad guys, and they tried to rob us. But still. That must have been awful. What a way to go." He shivered in the heat of the afternoon.

I put my hand on his neck. "Yeah. That's a bad end for anyone." I looked downhill, towards the rest of our route. "Let's go. If we push, we can get home after dark tonight."

We retightened all the cinches and checked the pack saddles. The horses were in good condition, despite all we had put them through. Turning North, we could see the top of Morgan Peak through the haze. Past that was home.

As I rode, the contentment that had settled on me when we found the gold and again when we got through the fires fell into the background. Replacing it was the old familiar sense of fear that it was all going to be taken away from me. I saw behind me a life of hiding my good luck from fate. Ahead, I saw a life of fighting against fate. I wasn't sure that was any better. I imagined me and fate tearing at the same bloody haunch of satisfaction, both wanting the spoils, both growling and showing teeth, hackles up, and the happiness tearing apart as we fought over it. I was so tired, and the thought of the fear and the struggle made me weary in my whole body. I hadn't achieved anything at all.

How could the money make our lives easier going forward? All I could think was how stupid it had been to take all those chances. How would I have carried on if Josh had been on the far side of that cave-in? I'm pretty sure that I would have killed myself inside the mine. I thought about the pain that would have brought to my family. Or the pain they'd have felt if Josh and I hadn't made it through the fires earlier in the day, or if Frank had shot Josh instead of just holding a gun on him. In my mind, I saw Jenny and Nate huddled together at the dining room table, crying for us. Our deaths would have stained their lives as the deaths of my parents had stained mine. But after I thought about it, I decided that they would survive. They're strong. Not like me. Loss like that didn't have to reverberate through their lives. But it always did in mine. Why was that? Why did I feel the losses in my life so much? And why did I fear them so much?

We traveled the ridgelines and the valleys for the rest of the day in heavy, yellow semi-darkness as the smoke blocked out the sun. The air smelled like an ashtray, dull and sickening. As the sun lowered in the sky, the daylight that made it through changed from sallow yellow brown to orange like the flames far behind us. I kept feeling like the fire was gaining on us, taunting us with the orange color suffusing the clouds.

After a while, Josh's voice broke my reverie. "What about Russ?"

I looked over at him. "Yeah, what about Russ? I like him, but I'm a little scared of him."

He clicked to his horse to move up beside me. "He saved us from Frank, so he's on our side, right? And he was fun to hang around the campfire with." He scrunched up his face. "But he put diesel fuel in the airplane, and the pilot died. That was murder."

I scanned the hills in front of us. "He didn't mean it, I don't think, but that's what it was. Manslaughter at least." Russ was going to have to carry the weight of that with him. I didn't envy him that. "And I'm still wondering about Stevie."

"Yeah. It's all strange. Even shooting the gun out of Frank's hand was crazy. We were standing within range of a ricochet. We could have been hurt. And he could have missed. There could have been a gunfight!" He flashed me a smile. "But we have the treasure, and Frank and Murray don't."

I wiped my forehead, and said, "He's on our side, as far as we know. But, yeah, he's dangerous, and he knows about the gold." One more thing I need to fight. Just when I had stopped dwelling on what I had lost, I found a new way to try to control the future: worrying about what was coming and fighting with fate for it. I slouched in my saddle.

At least we were safe for the moment, and we were headed home.

Chapter Twenty-Nine

BREATHE

We had come so far since the plane crashed in the upper meadow. I had been fighting fate, and fate had been working with me. We had found gold and rescued Kim and Julie. We had been saved from Frank and Murray by Russ, and we had survived the fire. I felt good. Tired to the bone, but good.

A gust of wind hit my right cheek, and adrenaline rose in my chest. Josh said, "Wrong way wind."

I raised my head and squinted to the east. "Diablo wind."

Another rush of air blew dust into our eyes. The smoke that had been following us all afternoon disappeared almost in an instant, and we could see westward again toward the ocean. The plume had shifted, and its smoke and embers drifted toward the sea. Ahead of us, the outline of Morgan Peak sharpened as the air cleared.

"Diablo winds brought good for once." I took a deep breath. "I had forgotten what clean air tasted like." It would be good to sleep in my own bed after the craziness of the past week. "We'll get there late, but we'll be home tonight."

The horses plodded along with their heads down, and Josh and I both dozed in our saddles in the late afternoon heat. We rode into the evening on the Bear Ridge Trail. The hot wind from the east gusted and slowed, not strengthening until after dark as we climbed the back side of the ridge above our valley. At the high point where the White Rock Trail that we had taken down toward the ocean only a few days earlier split from the trail we were on, we stopped to rest and to look down toward home. Gusts of wind came up the slope toward us, carrying bits of leaves and twigs that blew upward into the air and swirled around us.

"It seems like we're different people from when we started out," I said.

Josh started to answer, then stopped and pointed to the east. "Is that a fire over there?"

A red glow rose behind the hills to the east of our house. Over the smokiness of my clothes and the lingering stench inside my nose, I caught a fresh whiff of smoke. As we watched, the glow flickered and grew. "That is a fire. Oh, God." My stomach suddenly felt empty and cold. "It's going to move fast on these winds. It's in Zaca Canyon, upwind of our place. Jenny and Nate are probably asleep. They won't know it's coming. We came close to dying so many times on this trip, and now them. And I can't do anything about it." I wanted to cry, but knew I had to hold it together. We had to find a way to save the other part of our family—the part we had thought was safe.

Josh started to move his horse toward the edge of the flat area. "Dad let's go! We have to go wake them now!"

"Hang on. The trail's too steep to go loaded like we are. The gold doesn't matter. Leave it. Just dump it by the trail. Everything I care about in this world is you and those two down there."

Josh jumped off his horse and started moving rocks to make a hole. I stared down at the growing red-orange light of the fire, moving west in the valley upwind of my house where my wife and son were already in bed. I glanced over at Josh burying the gold. A great weariness came over me, and I felt my eyes well up with tears. I searched the blackness of the heavens and shouted, "I give up. I can't fight like this anymore." I turned around to where Josh was moving rocks. I gazed back up at the sky. "I see what you're doing here. You're taking everything I love away from me."

I was never hidden. I had been fooling myself. All my life of worrying and trying to keep my happiness small so fate wouldn't notice and take it away was a waste. I was never winning. A fire was racing down the canyon from the east toward my family, and I was powerless to stop it.

Then like a puppy nudging its snout into my hand for a scratch, I felt fate asking me to be thankful. The sky and the wind and the stars gently leaned against me, wanting me to be thankful for all of it. Everything. I was so afraid. But there was no other choice.

I looked around at the world of the mountains and the fires, and all that was beyond them. I was aware of every breath, and each inhalation fizzed like sparklers in my chest. In that moment, I knew what I had to do. I had to accept whatever came my way and keep living afterward. I had to know that whatever had been and whatever was to come was going to be as it was, and I couldn't change it. I could just live it.

I felt so small and so powerless, but not diminished. Simply knowing the grandeur and feeling the benevolence and the rightness of it. I threw out my hands to either side of me, flung my head back and turned my eyes up to the sky. All that immensity was asking me to be thankful, so I said it. "Thank you for my dad dying. Thank you for my mom dying and for my baby dying. And thank you in advance for whatever happens to us here tonight. I surrender."

When I said those last words, my breath left me, and I was empty. I looked up at the stars and the space between the stars. I drew my breath back in with a great whooshing sound, like all the world came through me in one grand inspiration. And then there was silence. There were no thoughts inside my head. All the fears and regrets and anger had flown out along with that breath. The wind blew leaves and dust up into the surrounding air, making silent whirlwinds above me. I gazed around at the silhouettes of the hills against the darkened sky and the menacing glow to the east. As I did, peace descended on me like a warm, heavy blanket, and I noticed a low musical humming coming from everything around me. The rocks and the sagebrush and the horses all vibrated with sound, their voices merging into one.

I heard Josh through the humming as he walked up behind me. "Dad, we can't give up. We have to go rescue our family. You can't surrender."

I turned to him, surprised that I could hear his words. On some level, I was surprised that he was still beside me. I held him by the shoulders and said, "I'm not giving up. I just stopped hating what already is and decided to stop being afraid of what's coming. Let's go wake them up."

Chapter Thirty

RUN

The fire behind us had been a slow flood that spread in many directions. The one ahead was a torrent, a firehose pointed straight down the valley, moving with force and speed and intent. This was a small fire that would run with the Diablo winds, raging forward as quickly. We got back on our horses and rode as quickly as the steep trail would let us. Once again, we wanted to run the horses, but to go too fast would risk losing a horse or one of us off the steep trail. It was frustrating to be racing the fire but not be able to run.

The next half-hour was excruciating. The hooves of the horses were slipping on the steep loose dirt and rocks. But when the trail reached the upper meadow, it flattened out, and we could run the horses. I half expected the plane to still be there against the tree with its tail in the air and gas leaking out of it. That morning seemed so long ago. Red flickering light played on the smoke above the hills to the east. The flames seemed to be just over the top of the hills, but I couldn't tell. We ran on the wide track around the meadow by the creek and slowed down as the road dipped into the darkness of the overhanging trees.

We thundered across the wooden bridge onto our property, the sound of our horses' hooves on the planks echoing off the barn. Our other horses were out of their paddocks, the whites of their eyes showing in the darkness. As we crossed the arena between the far stalls and the house, we saw that the yard wasn't deserted and quiet as we had expected. Instead, three cars were in the driveway, and all the floodlights were on. As we pulled up, Jenny was dropping a laundry basket into the bed of the truck. I got off my horse and we hugged. "Good timing." She kissed me on the lips, then grimaced at the scratches she got from my week-old beard. "I almost have everything out of the house. We need to leave. I think we can grab one more load." She motioned to Nate to follow her and ran up the steps again.

A man was standing on the driveway below the outlet from the water tank. He was holding a fire hose and directing the spray onto the roof of the house and the surrounding trees. He shut it off as we came into the yard and strode over to us. "Josh! Van! You made it!" I couldn't see who it was until he came closer. Then Russ's face became clear out of the darkness. "Where's the treasure?" he yelled as he approached.

I reached up, pulled my rifle from the saddle, and cradled it in my arm. "We had to leave it at the top of the ridge. It was too heavy to run down that trail with." The rifle felt comforting, but I wasn't sure why. "What are you doing here?"

"I was waiting below for you to come back. I looked you up in the phone book. I wanted to get some of the gold from you, but I saw the fire and woke up the family." He was talking fast, like he was late for something. "I let all the animals out while they've been pulling stuff from the house."

"Thank you." I patted his shoulder. I was grateful for Russ and wary of Russ in equal parts. Once again, he had helped us in a time of need. But he had been waiting to get part of the gold. The gold wasn't that important anymore. I would give him some of it.

Russ reached over and took the reins from me. He was taking short rapid breaths, and his movements were jerky. "I'm going back up the ridge. I'm going to get the gold."

I held up my hand. "Russ, no. It's too dangerous." I looked down at the rifle in my hand. I would give him some of the gold. Would I let him go take it all? Yes. Yes, I would. It really didn't matter anymore. All that mattered was the people who were going to be driving with me down the canyon. I reached over and put the rifle in the back of the new truck and turned back toward Russ. I needed to yell now over the wind and the roaring of the fire. "It's not worth it. You can't get on the trail to the ridge before the fire gets here. Wait for us. We'll go get it together after the fire is over and split it up."

Russ climbed on the horse. He was lit from the side with red light and seemed larger than he was—heroic almost, like a Revolutionary War statue come to life. "I'm going." Once he got on the horse, the frenetic energy settled into a firm resolve. His jaw was set. "I earned this. Stevie earned this." He turned toward the mountains.

"Russ!" I shouted. He turned back toward me. "Take one of the other horses too. The gold's under a pile of rocks where the White Rock Trail turns off toward the ocean. Josh left his red handkerchief sticking out of the pile." We had to leave. I looked toward the house. Nate and Jenny were coming out with their last loads. I turned back to watch Russ and the horses going across the yard toward the ridge trail. I didn't know if I would see him again.

Jenny came around the front of the truck with another laundry basket full of clothes. As she was about to put it in the car, she slapped at it to put out a smoldering ember. Then she slammed the door and came over to hug me again. "I was really worried about you two with the fires out there. We have to go. I think I got what we can't replace. The horses will have to find their own way. The dogs are inside the cars."

Wind-blown embers had been flying at us since we arrived. Now chunks of burning wood that had been lifted skyward by the heat were starting to land in the yard, and the flames were running through the oaks on the hill behind the house. Nate jumped into Russ's car. Josh followed in the new truck, and Jenny and I took off in the car after one last look at our house. I knew we might never see it again. "The fire will go down the valley between the ridges toward the reservoir," I said to Jenny. "The wind is taking it straight down the canyon. But I think we can outrun it."

She smiled and pointed forward. "We got this. Let's go."

Fire crews in red trucks passed us going up the road into the fire, sirens blaring, lights bright red in the night. More cars joined us from driveways and side streets until a line of us were snaking downhill. Deer and horses ran close to the road. I glimpsed a bobcat crossing in front of us, and a coyote appeared in our headlights on a curve.

"There was a lightning fire east of us yesterday, but they put it out right away," Jenny said. "It must have restarted in the wind. It's good that guy woke us up. Who was he? He banged on the door, then took off to let the horses out and spray water on everything. He was everywhere. Where was he going on your horse?"

I put my hand on her leg. "There's so much to catch up on—not just the fires. It's going to be a really long story." I looked over at her. Her hair was matted, and her face was sweaty and red, but she had never looked more beautiful to me. "Let me drive us out of here, then I'll tell you the whole thing."

An hour later, after crawling down the canyon with all the other fleeing traffic, we checked into a tourist hotel in Monterey that would let us stay there with our dogs. Jenny and Nate went to get food and drinks at the grocery store across the street while Josh and I showered and changed our clothes. Josh drank glass after glass of water from the tap. "I think I could drink that swimming pool out there," he told me.

When Jenny and Nate got back, they laid out fruit and sandwiches out on the bed. We hadn't had fresh food all week. Josh and I attacked the spread, growling when Nate tried to reach for an orange. Nate looked at us with wide eyes. "What happened? You haven't told us a thing. Give it up. Tell me." He lowered his voice and leaned in across the bed. "Did you guys find the treasure?"

Josh and I smiled at each other.

Jenny slapped her hand on the bed. "Yeah, come on! Tell us everything. Eat and talk, but talk. What happened?"

Josh took a deep breath. "We found gold." He paused to take in Nate and Jenny's wide eyes. "A lot. But we almost died a couple of times. I got a gun pointed at me, and I got trapped in a cave-in, and we almost burned to death in the fires, then I thought Dad was going to shoot Russ down there in the yard—just like I thought Russ's cousin was going to shoot me." He exhaled. "But the gold's up on White Rock Ridge, and I guess now Russ is going to get it all."

I burst out laughing. "That's it. That's the whole story from beginning to end in a nutshell. Now we can all go to sleep."

"Not a chance," Jenny said sternly, but she was smiling. "Start from the beginning."

I finished chewing my bite of sandwich and took a deep breath. "So, Russ is the guy who woke you up and let the horses out and was watering the roof. He was the stepson of the guy who died in the airplane. I also know him from when we were kids, but I'll get back to that later. The stepdad tried to go into the mountains in the plane to find the mine that we found. But Russ didn't know that he had gone down, or that he had died, so he was out there looking for the pilot—and the gold—when we ran into him."

I kept going and told the story as completely as I could, with Josh interrupting to tell his version where he thought I was missing an important point. Then we both backtracked to tell some more. Neither Josh nor I told them how close we were to dying in the mine or in the fire. When Josh was talking about Frank and Murray and the gun, I looked over at Jenny. She had tears in her eyes. I reached over and took her hand. "What is it?"

She wiped her eyes with the back of her hand and sniffed. "We almost lost you both out there. I'm just crying because you're here and we're safe."

In the motel bed that night, I told Jenny about my experience on top of the mountain. "Despite all the fury and the winds and the fire, it was strangely peaceful. I don't remember when I stopped hearing the humming, but it's gone now. I'm still peaceful, though, and I'd like to keep this feeling. Something shifted for me."

She put her hand under her head, pushing the pillow into a bunch so she could see me better. "What changed, do you think?"

"When I was on top of that mountain and the fire below was rushing toward you guys, I felt the weight of all that I had risked in the past week and all I had done to make up for my past mistakes. I felt all the years of believing that if I kept going back over the losses I had experienced, it would somehow protect me and us from more being taken away." I looked away into the corner of the room as I gathered my thoughts. "The capper was thinking about you and Nate asleep in our house, unaware. The prospect of the fire coming down the valley taking you two was too much. It broke me. It ground me into dust under its weight. Then I gave in. I decided to listen to the smartest person I know." I kissed her on the forehead. "I listened to you—to what you had said the night before the plane crash, about the beautiful things that grow out of tragedies. Then I stopped fighting what I couldn't control. Instead, I became thankful for it. And I said that up on that mountain, out loud. I said thank you for everything in my life, and all the weight came off me at once. It's a lightness I'm feeling now." I ran my hand through her hair. "I love you so much. You know that, don't you?" Tears were rolling down my cheeks.

Jenny was crying too. "I've known all along that you love me." She smiled at both of us blubbering. "But it's different now. It feels like it's flowing from you instead of seeping out around all the bricks you put up to support yourself in your sadness. Your love for me is mixed up with your love for you, and it's stronger somehow that way."

I fell asleep with her in my arms and didn't move all night.

We woke up to brown-gray skies the next morning. The atmosphere was gloomy, like a slow-moving storm was blowing in, raining ash and worry.

We left the motel in hopes of driving back up the canyon towards our house. In the breakfast room, we'd heard from some of the other guests that the Diablo winds coming down the canyon had slowed overnight and that the fire had been stopped at the reservoir. We didn't know if they were able to save our house, but we weren't optimistic. We'd also been told by the desk clerk that people were bringing stray animals they found to a corral below town. When we stopped there, we found most of our horses.

But we couldn't go up the canyon. The remains of the fire were still smoldering, and all the roads above the reservoir were blocked off. The wind had shifted back to a steady, slow wind from the south, and smoke from the main fires was everywhere. The two fires in the rough country to the south that we had ridden between the day before had grown together and were moving north like a lava flow, unconcerned with anything in their way. Fire crews were out in the wilderness trying to stop the wall of flames that was the width of the rugged mountain range, almost from the ocean to the inland valley.

We spent the early part of the day caring for the animals in the corrals, then we returned to the motel to wait. On the news, we saw tanker airplanes dropping fire retardant through the smoke in advance of the flames. We watched footage of bulldozers and fire crews trying to clear the brush, but the fire was too big and the terrain too steep for them to be very effective. They couldn't contain it, and it was moving toward the populated areas to the north.

The next day, news came to us that the people in charge of the firefighting had made a momentous decision. They'd decided to pull all of their men and machinery out of the fire zone to the south and were setting them up on the ridges above the Carmel Valley watershed in a desperate attempt to save that river valley and the homes and businesses there. Our house and the others around it were already lost to the smaller fire. Now they were trying to save thousands of houses. They were afraid that if they didn't stop the fire before it reached the valley, it would burn through the communities there—and maybe even all the way to Monterey.

While we were taking care of the animals that morning, convoys of men and equipment passed us heading up the valley. They were like an army mobilizing for battle, but in red vehicles and yellow tractors instead of camouflage paint. Over the next couple of days, the troops cleared brush and trees off the hilltops above the valley and set backfires down the slopes toward the south where the fire was advancing. It was an all-or-nothing strategy, putting all the resources on one ridgeline to protect one watershed. They were leaving the wild mountains and valleys of Big Sur to burn unchallenged, but the attempts to stop the fire early had failed.

The line held. By morning—our third morning in the motel—the news came that the northern front of the fire had been contained, and if the winds held, would be stopped that day. Small fires broke out north of the line, but fire crews rushed to put them out. Shortly after that, we were allowed to go look at our property.

As we drove up from the paved road, the extent of the damage unfolded slowly. The wood fence by the road was burned. Stumps of posts remained two feet above ground. The water tank on the hill was charred but still there. The house was not. Only the chimney stood, solemnly looming above the foundation. As we got closer, I could see that the water heater remained as well—rusted, but still upright.

As we climbed up the front steps into the rubble, glimpses of our lives peeked through the ashes. A frame of a bicycle. A vase, broken. The kitchen faucet. Each of these objects we had handled daily without thinking; now they took on special significance because we would never use them again. Jenny walked around to the back of the house where the dining room had been. She reached into a pile of broken dishes that had fallen when the cabinet burned around them. She came back to me holding a single teacup. "Grandma's China. The teacup survived, but nothing else." I hugged her, then she went back to the car.

I stood where the front porch had been and looked at the yard. A blackened branch remained in the center of the orchard marking where a peach tree had been. The pine trees beside the corral stood—lonely, charred, without needles or branches.

Within moments, I was ready to leave too. Our lives had been here, and they weren't anymore. Nate was the last to come to the car, but he hadn't spent more than fifteen minutes in the wreckage. I looked at him after he climbed into the back seat. His head was down, and his voice was small. "When I thought about coming back, I kept imagining how it might be. I couldn't picture this until I was here. There was no way to know until I saw it. It's all gone."

"We have insurance." I reached back and grabbed his knee. "We'll start over. It won't be easy, but we all got out alive. We have each other."

And I believed that. I was strangely thankful, despite everything. Fate wasn't coming after me. It never had been. Fate was as it always was: capricious and indiscriminate. It was me who was different.

Chapter Thirty-One

INSPIRATION

When I picture that sixth plane crash now, I should see the vivid image of Russ's stepdad with blood on his face and the wrecked plane behind him. I should feel the fear that coursed through me because of what the accident might mean for my future. It should remind me of the mine dust that I tasted for days or call up the musky vegetable odor of the rattlesnakes. I should hear the pine trees exploding near us as the fire enveloped them and relive the destruction of my home.

But, instead, the sixth plane crash brings me back once more to the top of the mountain, knowing the fire was headed toward my house and family. I think about being overwhelmed with the weight of all that I had risked and almost lost. I return to the sorrow I felt for everything that had been taken from me and the fear of what was about to be taken. I feel the emptying of all that was inside me and the inhalation—the inspiration—of what felt like the entire world, of everything flowing through me. And I come to rest in the moment when the anxiety and longing were gone. I find myself back in a place of gratitude for all that was and all that was to come.

All my life, I worried about what fate would take from me next. I tried to hide, and that didn't work. I tried to fight, and that was worse. With both strategies, I was trying to force everything to go my way. It took risking everything for me to find thankfulness. The words I said on the mountaintop brought me peace but not complacency. Surrendering didn't keep me from riding down the mountain to wake the family. Thankfulness won't stop me from working for what I want. Accepting what already is and what is coming opens me up to the wonder of the present moment, and I am filled with awe.

On the mountain, I knew that whatever happened that night was right. It was like a prayer—like the grandest prayer that I could make to the unimaginable vastness and beauty that is all there is. All I said was thank you, thank you, thank you.

And I keep saying those words now, every day.

Chapter Thirty-Two

FIRE BREAK

O ver the next week, we kept thinking we would
see or hear from Russ. We kept our eyes out for
the horse he had been riding, but we didn't see it.
His car stayed parked by the corral with the keys stashed
above the visor.

After the fire was out and the fire crews had left, Josh,
Nate, Jenny, and I saddled our horses with borrowed gear
and rode the trail from town up to the ridge. We rode first
through the ashes and blackened wood of the windblown
fire that burned down our house. We climbed up a steep
trail through untouched maples in the creeks and poison
oak reaching for the sun, red and shiny and beautiful in
its way. The trail looked unaffected until we reached the
ridge. There, the devastation was laid out before us. The
ridgeline trail, once three or four feet wide, was twenty
feet wide or more, cleared by tractors. The prints of metal
bulldozer tracks were visible in the scraped soil. Below and
to the south, all was burned, either by backfires or by the

advancing flames of the wildfire from the south. Behind us, piles of brush had been cut and pulled back away from the ridge. We rode in mute shock toward where the White Rock Trail split from the Wildcat Ridge Trail. "It's all churned up." Josh's disappointment saturated his words. "If Russ didn't get it, it's been buried by the tractors."

We rode through stretches of brick-colored fire retardant—the liquid slurry that had been dropped from airplanes and helicopters onto the advancing flames. When we got to the fork in the trail where we had buried the gold, it looked the same as what we had been riding on. Tractors had scraped whatever had been there and pushed it aside, widening the firebreak at the point they had made their stand on the ridge. The four of us turned our horses toward the ocean at the top of the hill, as if we had agreed upon the action ahead of time. We gazed into the blue distance, standing still like four sentinels. The only movement was the horses nodding their heads or swiping at a fly with their tails. Josh got off his horse and started searching on the ground, walking in circles with his head down. "Russ could have found it," he muttered. "Maybe he got through that night and is off somewhere with all the treasure."

I got down and started wandering too, leading my horse as I did. "We may never know. If he didn't make it through, he might have burned up. If he did, he might disappear with the gold and never tell us. What's more important to me than any gold is you guys." I looked out at the horizon and then back at my family. "But I have to admit, I would have liked to be rich too. That gold would have been enough to make us rich." I sighed. "Remember all those fantasies we had when we were sitting around the dining room table with the metal box in front of us before we opened it? Those fantasies would have been realities, plus some." No one said anything. "And I'm sad the redwood table is gone. That's one possession we can't replace." I turned to Jenny. "You knew it too. I'm surprised you didn't run out of the house that night dragging it behind you, all three hundred pounds of it." She smiled at me, but it was only a half-smile. I kicked a rock. "We'll never be able to get a slab of redwood like that again. And I wouldn't want to because it would mean cutting down a tree that big."

She was still gazing out toward the ocean. "If we had a bigger truck, I might have carried it out with me on my shoulders."

"You saved your drawings, though. Those are worth more than the table."

She nodded. "They're a part of me that I want to find again. Having them to study and touch might help me find it."

While Jenny and I talked, Nate was walking beside Josh, hands behind his back. "What are we looking for?"

"Anything that's not rocks." Josh pointed at the ground. "We cleared out a hole right about here and put the saddlebags into it. Then we covered it back up with flat rocks until there was a bit of a pile. It would have been easy for Russ to find if he got up here."

"How would he have carried it?" Nate kicked the ground. "There were a couple hundred pounds of gold, weren't there?"

Josh shrugged. "He could have loaded it on the horses and walked out. He's a determined guy."

After a half-hour of wandering around the area, picking up rocks, and tossing them aside, Josh sat down on at the edge of the cleared area and stared out at the sea. "We found the gold, and we fought for it, then we lost it." He hung his head for a moment, then he looked back up at me. "I'm not sure I'm going to college right away, in any case. I want to go, and I think it'll be different from high school." A slow smile moved across his face. "We met Julie and Kim and I'm happy about that. I think I need to get some more experience. Julie was talking about taking a year and working for the Peace Corps. I want to do something like that. When I get back, college may be more valuable to me." He idly picked up a rock and tossed it down the hill.

Nate shrugged. "I don't mind living at home when the time comes. I could keep in touch with my friends and help you guys out. I mean, junior college is probably easier than going to a UC or a state school, so I can do both."

Jenny had strolled toward the ocean and turned back toward where Josh was sitting. I watched Josh as he kept tossing rocks, staring out to the west. Then I saw him look down where his hand was and tense up. "Dad!" his head whipped around toward me. "Leather!" He rolled over onto his knees and started moving rocks, quickly throwing them to the side. I could see a leather strap appearing as he dug. Nate and I crowded in too, tossing rocks behind us. The strap was attached to a saddlebag. We kept going, and Jenny joined us. After a few minutes, we found another saddlebag.

"I can't believe it!" Josh shouted. "It's here! It's really here!

He was right. It was all there. All the gold. The saddlebags were heavy with it. Our hands were raw by the time we were able to lift them.

Nate reached for the first one and undid the brass buckle. When he peered inside, he said, "What? Rocks? Just more rocks?"

Josh and I started laughing.

"Is this all a joke?" Nate turned to us with a red face. "Did you guys bring home rocks instead of gold? Why are you laughing? It's not funny."

Josh pulled the fossils out of the bag, reached into the rags, and brought out a strap of gold that shined dully in the sun. He handed it to Nate. "Cookies and sodas, brother. Cookies and sodas and ski trips and vacations in Hawaii. That's what you're holding in your hand."

Jenny held out her hand, and Josh gave a strap to her. She inspected it, then looked at me. "You told me you found gold, but I didn't really believe it until now. It's so heavy." She pointed at Josh with the strap of gold, then at me, and frowned. "You still took too many chances. You're both still in trouble. You may even be grounded."

Everyone laughed. Nate danced around the outside of our group with a gold bar in his hand, then came back and put his arms around all of us. "This is great, but next time you two go find gold and fight bad guys, can I come?" I put my arms over his, and Josh and Jenny grabbed our waists. We stood in the sun for a moment, laughing with our heads together.

We led the loaded horses down the trail to the upper meadow. It was still golden brown and green, untouched by the fire that had charred the canyon below. The trees by the creek were burned on the bottom but green on top where the fire didn't reach. The truck sat in the driveway where we had left it the day before in case we found the gold. We loaded the packs behind its seat, then Josh and Nate led Jenny's and my horses back down the hill toward the town corral. I slid into the driver's seat and started the engine, then turned the key back off. There was something under the windshield wiper. I looked over at Jenny, opened the door, and stood up to retrieve the piece of yellow lined paper. With the door open and my foot on the doorframe, I read it aloud:

I couldn't make it up the hill that night. The fire was too hot, so I rode on down the valley and away. Your horses are in the town corral now. The bear isn't following me anymore, so I'm heading to northern California to figure out what I want next. Send me a note to my post office box 6503 in Monterey to let me know how it all came out. They'll forward it to me. You remember how you told me you would share the fossils with me? I'd like it if you would put some aside for when I come back.

Ah, Russ. I found myself looking forward to seeing him again. His bear wasn't following him anymore, and neither was mine. I knew now that whatever fate brought me, I would be thankful for it.

End

I hope you enjoyed reading *Darker Than the Sky*.

You may not know it, but reviews are the most important selling tool any author has.

If you would take a moment and post a review on Goodreads and on the website of the retailer where you bought this book it would mean a lot.

If you don't feel like writing anything, that's okay. Even just voting on the number of stars you think the book deserves helps so much.

Thank you in advance,
Matt Tracy

Also, please visit my website to see my other books and to sign up for my newsletter.

https://www.matttracyauthor.com/

Made in the USA
Columbia, SC
08 October 2024

43322813R00176